UNIVERSITY SECRETS

Also by Jack Sheffield

The Teacher Series
Teacher, Teacher!
Mister Teacher
Dear Teacher
Village Teacher
Please Sir!
Educating Jack
School's Out!
Silent Night
Star Teacher
Happiest Days
Starting Over
Changing Times
Back to School
School Days
Last Day of School

The University Series
University Tales
University Challenges
University Secrets

Short Story
An Angel Called Harold

UNIVERSITY
SECRETS

1990/91

Jack Sheffield

bantam

TRANSWORLD PUBLISHERS

UK | USA | Canada | Ireland | Australia
India | New Zealand | South Africa

Transworld is part of the Penguin Random House group of companies
whose addresses can be found at global.penguinrandomhouse.com.

Penguin Random House UK, One Embassy Gardens,
8 Viaduct Gardens, London SW11 7BW

penguin.co.uk

Penguin
Random House
UK

First published in Great Britain in 2025 by Bantam
an imprint of Transworld Publishers

001

Typeset in 11/15 pt Palatino by Six Red Marbles UK, Thetford, Norfolk
Printed and bound in Great Britain by Clays Ltd, Elcograf S.p.A.

The authorized representative in the EEA is Penguin Random House Ireland,
Morrison Chambers, 32 Nassau Street, Dublin D02 YH68.

A CIP catalogue record for this book is available from the British Library

ISBN: 9780857505255

Penguin Random House is committed to a sustainable future
for our business, our readers and our planet. This book is
made from Forest Stewardship Council® certified paper.

MIX
Paper | Supporting
responsible forestry
FSC
www.fsc.org   FSC® C018179

For Phil Patterson, agent and friend

Contents

Acknowledgements

In the late eighties I moved from my headship into higher education. It gave me the opportunity to teach again and encourage the next generation of teachers. I remember this time in my life well and have recounted it in this, the third novel in the University series, through the eyes of my hero character, Tom Frith.

It was a wrench to leave behind my Teacher series of fifteen novels but refreshing to have this new impetus to my writing. The University series became the new project and for that I have to thank my hardworking editor at Penguin Random House, the ever-patient Imogen Nelson.

I have been fortunate over the years to have had the support of the excellent team at Transworld. Special thanks must go to Viv Thompson, who puts up with the fact I am a frustrated copy-editor at heart. Her cheerful and understanding correspondence keeps me grounded and, along with copy-editor Richenda Todd and proof-reader Debs Warner, she continues to improve my novels.

There is a terrific literary agent out there who usually phones me when he is walking his dog. I refer to Phil Patterson of Marjacq Scripts. It was a partnership that began with a chicken and lettuce sandwich at the Winchester Writers' Conference in 2006. Bribery was never this cheap! In return he promised to read my first novel, *Teacher, Teacher*, and we've never looked back since. If you're ever interested in Airfix Modelling Kits circa 1980, he's the man for you.

My main supporter is, of course, my wife Elisabeth. Her patience is remarkable. The discussions we have about developing plots while enjoying her latest culinary creation are always eventful. Writing novels is a way of life for me now. With the support I have around me, may it long continue.

There are a host of wonderful booksellers and events managers out there. Particular thanks must go to Steph at Waterstones Milton Keynes, Nick at Waterstones York, Fiona at Waterstones Alton and Sam at Waterstones Basingstoke.

Finally, if you've borrowed this book from your local library, keep in mind they are the cornerstone of a cultural society. The eight-year-old Jack who visited Compton Road Library in Leeds began a journey that is now well travelled.

Prologue

Conversations . . . countless words. They fill our waking days, yet most are soon forgotten. Everyday chatter can drift away like ripples in a pond, but there are times when words are spoken – and secrets shared – that are remembered and may change lives forever. Where dreams are either fulfilled or cast aside and shattered.

Such a day was dawning for Tom Frith, a thirty-four-year-old lecturer at the University of Eboracum in the City of York. It was Monday, 10 September 1990, and an eventful academic year stretched out before him.

On this sunlit autumn morning he strode confidently into the reception hall, an old leather satchel over his shoulder. He walked hand-in-hand with his new fiancée, Inger Larson. Back in July, at the end of term after the staff dinner dance, the Norwegian music lecturer had happily accepted Tom's proposal of marriage and he was content with his good fortune. Since then it had been a whirlwind summer, with a visit to Oslo to meet up with

Inger's family, a holiday in France and the selection of an engagement ring.

Peter Perkins, the cheerful head porter, immaculate as always in his blazer and regimental tie, looked up from behind his desk. 'Congratulations, Dr Frith, Dr Larson. Everyone is thrilled at the news.'

'Thanks, Perkins,' said Tom. 'I'm a lucky man.' He looked into Inger's blue eyes. 'I still can't believe she said yes.'

Perkins smiled at the tall, broad-shouldered lecturer. 'You make a fine couple.' Then he glanced up again at this imposing yet gentle woman. She looked tanned and healthy after their holiday in the Dordogne. 'Dr Larson is a special lady.'

'Oh, Perkins,' said Inger with a twinkle in her eyes, 'you say the nicest things.'

'I'm just so pleased for you both,' he said.

'Anyway, I must rush,' said Inger. 'I've arranged to meet up in the music room with some of my first years who arrived over the weekend.' She smiled at Tom as she hurried away. 'See you at the staff meeting.'

The music room was empty when Inger walked in, and as she began to unpack her shoulder bag, she reflected on the words of the friendly head porter. Yes, she and Tom made a fine couple. It had taken time but she had realized that not only was he a good man whom she had grown to love, but he would keep her *safe*.

For too long she had lain awake at nights recalling the terror of that terrible time in Norway. Four years had passed since Kai Pedersen had come briefly into her life.

The suave engineer had impressed her with his work on Norway's Atlanterhavsveien, the Atlantic Ocean Road, built on several small islands and connected with viaducts and eight bridges. She and Kai had been enjoying a drive out to the largest of them, the Storseisundet Bridge, when it happened. At first he had kissed her gently but then had lost control. *'Jeg vil ha deg nå,'* he had muttered. 'I want you now.' She had ripped his cheek with her nails in the struggle, but it was to no avail. What had followed had been brutal.

She had told no one, not her parents and definitely not her younger brother, Andreas. He would have sought retribution. Applying for the teaching post in York had been an opportunity to move on and dedicate her life to music. It was only when she had finally come to trust Tom that she shared her story and made him promise never to reveal it. Since then, it was rare for her to relive those moments in the still of the night. The memory that had seared her soul was distant now and she had found a kind of peace with the man she loved.

Back in reception, Perkins put a large carrier bag on the counter. 'This is your mail. Lots of cards from your colleagues in the faculty. Your pigeonhole would have been overflowing if I'd stuffed all these in.'

'Thanks,' said Tom. 'I'll take them to my study and open them there.'

'So when's the big day?' asked Perkins.

'Undecided. Probably sometime next year.' He pushed his long brown wavy hair from his eyes and smiled. 'There's a lot to do before then.'

The telephone on the counter rang and Perkins answered it. 'Yes, Professor. Dr Frith is here now,' and he passed the receiver over to Tom. 'Professor Grammaticus, for you.'

'Good morning,' said Tom, slightly surprised to receive a call at the reception desk.

'Tom . . . glad I've caught you. Spotted you both coming in from my window. Can you call in for a chat?'

'Of course,' said Tom. 'Shall I collect the teaching-practice file from my study? I've completed the work we discussed.'

'No, just bring yourself.' There was a pause.

'What is it, Victor?'

'Tom . . . the police are here.'

Chapter One

A Day of Letters

Perkins grinned and stared after the young lecturer in his baggy oatmeal cord suit. 'Young love,' he murmured to himself. 'I remember it well.'

Tom wondered why the police were in Victor's study and hoped there hadn't been an accident or a problem with one of the new students. He strode quickly through a dramatic Victorian archway and down a flight of Yorkshire stone steps. Before him was the familiar sight of the ancient quadrangle, which seemed frozen in time. A verdant lawn was bordered by a path of worn cobblestones and surrounded by walls of weathered brick. There were high sash windows beneath the steep rooftops of grey slate tiles. This was where the original teacher-training college had opened its doors over one hundred and fifty years ago.

Beyond the quadrangle was another archway that led to the buildings of the latter part of the twentieth century. There were impressive lecture halls alongside tall, pebble-dashed blocks for student accommodation, but

Tom's attention was elsewhere. He walked around the quad, opened the door marked 'Alcuin' and climbed the metal stairs to the top floor. There was an imposing study door on which a brass plate read:

Professor Victor Grammaticus
Head of Faculty of Education

He knocked twice and walked in.

'Morning Tom,' said Victor with a welcoming smile. 'Thanks for calling in.'

The professor was beginning his second year as the Faculty Head. He cut a distinctive figure: stick-thin with long grey hair tied back in an incongruous ponytail. Over his crisp white shirt and blue bow tie he wore a black waistcoat. He gestured to a balding, heavy-set man in a well-worn suit standing beside him. 'Tom, this is Detective Chief Inspector Greybourne from York Police. He has some news for us.'

The chief inspector looked impassive and stared at Tom for a moment. 'You're Dr Thomas Frith.'

'Yes, I am. How can I help?'

'That's to be decided,' he murmured. There was a pause while the inspector took out a notebook and riffled through the pages.

Victor broke what was becoming an awkward silence. 'Tom, the chief inspector had a meeting this morning with the Vice Chancellor. It concerns a letter that was delivered to York Police Station.'

'Really, what about?' asked Tom.

'Dr Wallop,' said Victor.

The chief inspector studied his notebook. 'Dr Frith . . . you will recall that on Friday, the ninth of June 1989, Dr Edna Wallop' – he glanced at Victor – 'your predecessor as Head of Faculty, suffered fatal injuries following a fall.'

'That's correct,' said Victor. 'The verdict was accidental death. We were informed that Dr Wallop had tripped at the top of the stairs.'

'A dreadful day,' said Tom.

The chief inspector studied Tom carefully. 'We've received a letter indicating it may not have been an accident.'

'Really!' exclaimed Tom. 'Who sent it?'

Chief Inspector Greybourne remained impassive. 'It was anonymous. So we're obliged to look into it once again. It's the way we work.'

'I see,' said Tom.

The chief inspector closed his notebook. 'One of my colleagues will be back this week to talk to you and other interested parties. I'll make the arrangements with the Vice Chancellor's PA. Thank you for your time. That's all for now.' He departed quickly, leaving both Victor and Tom looking bemused.

'Strange,' murmured Victor.

'Exactly,' said Tom. 'Who on earth would want to reopen the case?'

'I guess they're just doing their job,' mused Victor. He glanced at his wristwatch. 'Well, not quite the start to the new academic year I imagined.' He smiled at Tom. 'Faculty meeting at ten. We'll catch up later with your teaching-practice file.'

'Fine,' said Tom.

'And congratulations,' said Victor. 'You and Inger will make a great team.'

Tom grinned and set off for his study.

On the winding tree-lined path out of the university the detective paused. Before him was Lord Mayor's Walk with its busy morning traffic and, beyond that, the ancient city walls, mellow in the morning sunlight. He took a folded photocopied sheet of paper from his pocket, opened it and stared at the typed letter.

It read:

The death of Dr Edna Wallop at Eboracum University on the evening of Friday, 9 June 1989 needs reinvestigating.

It was no accident.

In particular, Professor Victor Grammaticus and Dr Thomas Frith both benefitted from her demise.

Greybourne replaced it in his pocket and looked up suddenly as a parliament of rooks in the high elms screamed a warning. As he drove back to York Police Station he wondered about the sheltered world of academia.

Tom walked along Cloisters corridor to Room 7. The label on the door read 'O. Llewellyn/T. Frith'.

When he walked in, a stocky, suntanned Welshman looked up from his desk. 'Welcome back, boyo,' said Owen. 'Thought we could celebrate tonight with a pint.'

Tom had shared a study with Owen for the past two years and they had become firm friends. The superbly fit son of the valleys taught physical education and coached the university's rugby team. 'Good idea,' said Tom, but his mind was elsewhere.

Owen picked up on Tom's subdued mood. 'What's wrong? You look like one o'clock half struck.'

Tom shook his head in dismay and dumped the carrier bag of greetings cards on the coffee table and his satchel on one of the armchairs. Two wooden desks butted up against each other in front of the latticed dormer window and he sat down at the empty one. 'I've just been in Victor's study. A policeman was there. He said they're reopening the investigation into Edna's death.'

'Whatever for?' Owen stroked his unshaven chin and shook his head. 'The evil cow fell down the friggin' stairs. End of story.' Edna Wallop had been deeply unpopular and the fiery Welshman had no problem speaking ill of the dead.

'Apparently someone has sent an anonymous letter to the police,' said Tom, 'and they're obliged to follow it up.'

'Waste of bloody time,' muttered Owen. 'Have you told Miss Norway?'

'No, she's in the music room meeting up with some of her first years.'

Owen stood up, muscles rippling under his T-shirt. 'In that case, forget it. There's always a screwball out there stirring things up.' He patted Tom on the shoulder. 'Come on, you sad Englishman, let's get downstairs for the meeting.'

*

In the staff common room, Dr Elizabeth Peacock had arranged chairs into an approximate semi-circle facing a large table covered in folders and photocopied lists. The flame-haired Dance and Drama tutor, known as Zeb, was the Deputy Head of Faculty. A lively, popular and outspoken thirty-something, she was the perfect foil for the studious, academic Victor Grammaticus. When all appeared ready she walked outside into the quad, lit up a cigarette and sat down on one of the benches. In a blue leotard, *Fame* leg warmers and a baggy off-the-shoulder sweatshirt she cut a striking figure. There was a call from the other side of the quad and she looked up.

'Hi, Zeb, how are you?'

Zeb smiled and waved at the tall, elegant woman who had suddenly appeared. 'Rosie, come and join me. You look great.'

Rosie Tremaine had arrived at Eboracum from Cornwall a year ago and taught English Literature alongside Tom. Suntanned and smiling, Rosie had auburn hair in a short-cropped boyish hairstyle and her stylish green linen trouser suit matched the colour of her eyes. She sat down next to Zeb.

'So how was your summer?' asked Zeb.

Rosie smiled. 'Great. I spent most of August in the Lake District with Sam. Fresh air and fun.'

'Perfect,' said Zeb. 'He's a good man and obviously crazy about you.'

Sam Greenwood had also arrived a year ago and taught in the science department. A ruddy-faced, sandy-haired Mancunian, it had taken him almost a year to pluck up the courage to ask Rosie to join him on a walking holiday.

'So, how was New York?' asked Rosie with a mischievous grin. 'And more to the point, how did you get on with the dishy Indian doctor?'

Zeb grinned. 'Vijay was the perfect partner. When he wasn't attending his conventions we explored the city and enjoyed the best restaurants.' Zeb looked guiltily at her cigarette and stubbed it out. 'He wants me to cut down on smoking and I'm trying hard.'

Vijay Kapoor was a neighbour of Zeb's in Crayke village on the outskirts of York. An eminent consultant surgeon at York Hospital, he had become captivated by the dynamic dance teacher and a whirlwind romance had ensued.

'I haven't caught up with Inger yet,' said Rosie. 'How about you?'

'Only briefly. She's getting to know some of her first years this morning. I've seen her engagement ring. It's lovely. A solitaire from Barbara Cattle's jeweller's in Stonegate. She looks really happy. Sounded like she and Tom had a busy summer.'

'It's great news. I'm really pleased for her,' said Rosie. Then she paused and the hint of a frown crossed her face. 'She was so good to me last term . . . helped me through a difficult time.'

Zeb nodded knowingly. 'That's all in the past now and time for a fresh start.' She waved her hand dismissively. 'You just picked the wrong man. It happens. He was a manipulative bastard. You're well rid of him.' Rosie's affair earlier in the year with a local solicitor had ended badly: it had turned out he was married. 'And . . . speaking of odd couples . . . look who's here, the man of the moment and his little friend, the two amigos, Starsky and Hutch. They stick together like glue, those two.'

Tom and Owen had appeared outside Cloisters doorway deep in conversation. At six feet two, Tom was six inches taller than Owen.

'Over here,' called Rosie.

The two men grinned and hurried round the cobbled path where Zeb and Rosie both leapt up and gave Tom a hug and a kiss on the cheek. 'Congratulations,' said Rosie.

'Great news, handsome,' said Zeb. 'You're a lucky man to capture the Norwegian goddess.'

'What about me?' pleaded Owen with affected disappointment.

Zeb rubbed Owen's black curly hair playfully and stood back to assess him. 'You're just a scruffy Welsh degenerate. How about tidying yourself up a bit? Maybe having a shave now and then? Even a new T-shirt would help.'

'It's my rugged look,' said Owen and flexed his muscles. 'Women love it.'

'It's a good job Sue does,' said Zeb with a grin. 'I don't know how she puts up with you.'

Sue was Owen's wife, a physical education teacher at a local school. Their son, Gareth, was now sixteen months old.

Tom smiled at the friendly banter. Their mutual respect was obvious and it was good to be back among friends and colleagues.

'Anyway, come on, you lot,' said Zeb. 'Meeting time.'

The staff common room was a hive of activity and full of chatter as over forty members of the Faculty of

Education gathered together, shared holiday news and found a seat. Inger was one of the last to appear. She waved at Tom and hurried to join him on the back row. 'Busy morning,' she said. 'I've got a terrific bunch of first years . . . some real talent.'

Tom smiled and squeezed her hand just as Victor got to his feet and surveyed the rows of faces. 'Welcome back, everyone, to another year of opportunities, and many challenges ahead with the National Curriculum gathering momentum. I hope you've all had a restful holiday and are ready for the new academic year. Almost all the first years have registered over the weekend and the rest of our students will be arriving towards the end of this week.' He gestured to the noticeboard behind him. It was covered in squared paper, divided into colour-coded sections. 'As you can see, the timetable is complete so please do a careful check to ensure all is as it should be.' He held up a sheaf of papers. 'Term commences next Monday and copies of student lists have been prepared for each department.'

Victor scanned the room. 'We have one new member of staff to introduce. Following the departure of Royce Channing, our new Head of Art is Ben Laverick and I know you will make him welcome.' Victor smiled towards a tall man with shoulder-length hair and a camera bag over his shoulder. In his blue jeans, Doc Marten boots and psychedelic shirt he looked as though he had just stepped out of the Glastonbury Festival. He gave Victor a nod of acknowledgement. Sam Greenwood, sitting behind him, noticed the handsome newcomer give Rosie Tremaine a direct look and a gentle wave.

'Also,' continued Victor, 'I should like to thank Tom for all his work regarding school placements. With our increasing numbers we are now having to go far and wide to ensure all our students have the opportunity to work in suitable schools. The list is now complete and displayed on the new noticeboard next to your mail in the pigeonholes. So, once again, be mindful of all these dates when planning off-campus experiences, particularly when next year's field week comes around.' Victor glanced to his left, where Zeb looked relaxed. 'That's enough from me for now but, before I pass over to Zeb, I need to see representatives of all departments this afternoon for a brief meeting in the science block at two o'clock. Thank you for your time, everybody.' He sat down calmly, although still troubled by the unexpected police visit. *Life is never simple*, he thought.

Zeb rose to her feet. 'Good morning, everyone, and welcome back. You've only got to see how busy the car park was over the weekend and early this morning to realize a new group of young people, most of them fresh from sixth form, have arrived with anxious parents. I've arranged for some of our second-, third- and fourth-year students to return early and give them guided tours tomorrow after they've settled into their accommodation and found the refectory. It's hard to imagine but think ahead for a moment. This cohort of students may well be approaching senior management positions in their schools at the end of this decade when the new millennium comes round. So remember ... we're faced with launching futures and this is their special time. Let's do our very best for them.'

She paused and nodded. She could see the message had struck home. 'With that in mind, I'm hoping many of you will be around this week to support the various social activities we've organized for Freshers' Week. In particular, I expect you all to come along to the Friday-evening disco in the student common room.' She smiled knowingly. 'I'm happy to introduce you to some of the new dance steps.' There was laughter and the sound of the clatter of crockery at the far end of the room. 'Meanwhile, good luck, everybody, and see me if you have any queries. Coffee and cake is now being served.'

Inger was checking a list on her spiral notepad. 'How did it go?' asked Tom.

'Better than I could have hoped,' she said. 'Some great voices and an especially talented violinist, Adam Kite. One to look out for. What about you?'

Tom stared out of the window and shook his head. 'Actually, something unexpected cropped up on my way in while you headed off to your music room.'

Inger could see that Tom was troubled. 'Come on. Let's get a coffee and you can tell me about it.'

Owen, Rosie and Zeb were sitting by the far window that looked out on the quad and waved them over. Zeb glanced up at Tom. 'Victor told me about your meeting this morning. Don't give it another thought.'

'Meeting?' queried Inger.

'That's what I wanted to tell you,' said Tom. 'A policeman was here. He said they're reopening the case about Edna.'

15

'Whatever for?' said Inger in surprise. 'She fell down the stairs. It was an accident.'

'Some vindictive bastard has sent an anonymous letter to the police,' muttered Owen.

Zeb nodded. 'Victor said they're obliged to check it out again.'

Rosie looked around the room at the throng of lecturers. 'Well, no one here would have written a letter like that. It's got to be an outsider with a grudge.'

'I'd like to have five minutes with him,' growled Owen.

'Or *her*,' added Zeb.

They all sipped their coffee in silence, each with their own thoughts.

In York Police Station, Chief Inspector Greybourne tossed a manila folder across the desk to his colleague, DI Montgomery. 'It's that woman who fell down the stairs at the university just over a year ago. Verdict, accidental death.' He reached in his pocket. 'This is a copy of the letter that arrived at the front desk last week. Have a read . . . see what you think. We've no choice but to follow it up.'

DI Montgomery was a tough-looking man brought up in County Durham and known as an 'old-school copper'. He didn't suffer fools gladly. After scanning the letter quickly he placed it back on the desk. 'Precise, well written, grammatically correct.' He smiled. 'An academic?'

DCI Greybourne nodded. 'That's what I thought . . . plus a rather distinctive typeface. Give this to your mate, Sergeant Porterfield, to check out. There might be something in it. There won't be any forensic evidence left at the scene. There were no blood stains on the carpet at the top of the stairs, so nothing to indicate an attack with a blunt instrument. But it's possible someone gave her a gentle push. To begin with, tell Porterfield to hone in on the two mentioned in the letter. They both came out smelling of roses.'

DI Montgomery picked up the folder and paused by the door. 'It's DS Porterfield's birthday today. He won't be thrilled to get this job.'

The chief inspector gave a sinister smile. 'In that case buy the ginger sod a pint before you tell him to get his arse in gear. We need this sorted.'

Later on that morning Tom, accompanied by Inger, returned to Room 7 to open the bag of mail and congratulations cards that Perkins had passed on to him.

Owen was sitting at his desk, reading a letter. He looked a little sad.

'What is it?' asked Tom.

'It's a letter from Chris Scully.'

'What's the latest with him?'

Owen sighed and shook his head. 'He could have played rugby for England one day. By far my best prospect.'

The room went quiet as they all recalled that fateful day last summer. The daredevil nineteen-year-old, after a night of drinking with his rugby friends, had dived off the Ouse Bridge and broken his spine on the stone buttress below. Now he was destined to spend the rest of his life in a wheelchair.

Owen folded the letter and replaced it in the envelope. 'He's not coming back. His parents have decided he's staying down in Hampshire and receiving specialist help.

I've kept in touch with them and we've got him interested in wheelchair rugby.'

'That's good,' said Tom. 'He could excel at that.'

Owen placed the envelope carefully in his top drawer. 'I hope he does,' he said quietly and glanced at his watch. 'I'm meeting up with some of my first years in the refectory so I'll catch you later.' He got up and closed the door behind him.

'It broke his heart,' said Tom.

'I know,' said Inger. 'It shows.' She emptied the bag of cards and letters on to the coffee table. 'Come on, let's open these.'

A few minutes and a dozen cards later Tom picked up an envelope and stared at handwriting he knew so well.

'What is it?' asked Inger.

He opened it. 'As I thought. It's from Ellie MacBride.'

For a moment Inger frowned. The enigmatic Yorkshirewoman had been the topic of many discussions over the past two years. Attractive and dynamic, Ellie had been in her late twenties, a mature student, when she had started her teacher-training course at Eboracum. Her main academic subject was English and she had quickly been identified by Tom as an outstanding student. The concern for Inger was that Tom appeared oblivious to the fact that Ellie clearly wanted more than a tutor–student relationship.

'Oh no!' exclaimed Tom.

'What's wrong?' said Inger.

'She says she's not returning to complete her course.'

'Whatever for?'

'Her parents need her to take over their market stall in Barnsley.'

'But surely that's an insubstantial reason,' said Inger. 'There must be something else.'

Tom looked dismayed. 'I guess so . . . but what? She had the potential to be a great teacher. Rosie will be sad. She was due to supervise Ellie's special study on Victorian literature this year.' Inger gave Tom that special look he had come to know so well. 'Go on,' he said.

'Tom, think about it. We got engaged at the end of last term and she goes home knowing she's lost any chance with you. That could be the reason.'

'I hope that's not the case,' said Tom. 'I thought I had made it clear to her I didn't want a relationship.'

Inger had her own thoughts. Tom's occasional naivety was both endearing and frustrating. 'Either way,' she said, 'it's sad and I agree: she was a great student. There was even talk about her being elected President of the Students' Union in a year's time.'

They continued to open the various cards, including a few with Norwegian postmarks. There was a cheerful one from her brother Andreas and his girlfriend Annika. 'Display them in your study,' said Tom. 'Owen's stuff is all over the place in here.'

Then the telephone rang. It was the Vice Chancellor's personal assistant, Miss Hermione Frensham. 'Hello, Dr Frith. The Vice Chancellor wondered if you were free to call in. There's something he wishes to discuss.'

'Of course. What time?'

'Now, if convenient.'

'Of course. I'm on my way.' He replaced the receiver

and looked at Inger. 'The VC wants a word. We can catch up over lunch if you're free.'

Inger stood up and kissed him on the cheek. 'Cheer up. It will be fine.'

Tom went down to the quad and out past reception, where Perkins gave him a friendly wave. He walked along the winding tree-lined path that led to the Vice Chancellor's residence, known as the Lodge. It was a distinctive building with churchlike rooftop finials and a pair of octagonal towers. Miss Frensham could be seen at her desk beyond one of the canted bay windows. He rang the bell and she ushered him through a world of mahogany bookshelves and watercolour paintings towards the Vice Chancellor's study.

When he walked in, he found the cherubic figure of the Vice Chancellor, Canon Edward Chartridge, talking to a pensive Victor Grammaticus.

'Good morning, Thomas,' said Edward. 'Do take a seat and thank you for your prompt attendance.'

Tom sat down in one of the comfortable armchairs. 'Good morning, Vice Chancellor.'

Edward made a steeple of his hands and stared thoughtfully at Victor and Tom. 'I'm aware you have met Chief Inspector Greybourne. His concerns could well be routine but, as I explained to him, the reputation of Eboracum is of the utmost importance. With this in mind, it was important to share with you the fact that both your names were included in the anonymous letter.'

'Whatever for?' asked Tom, shocked.

Both Edward and Victor smiled and shared a knowing glance.

'Thomas,' said the Vice Chancellor gently. 'It's a fact that you both benefitted from her departure.'

'Surely that is very tenuous,' said Tom.

'Quite so,' said Edward.

'Were there any clues as to who might have sent the letter?' asked Victor.

Edward shook his head. 'None were shared with me. I'm told initial police inquiries will begin shortly and, Victor, I shall need to know what transpires. So please keep me up to date.'

'Of course,' said Victor. 'So what next?'

Edward leaned forward in his chair and looked thoughtful: '*Virtus et labor.*'

'Virtue and hard work,' said Tom.

'Well done,' said the Vice Chancellor. 'I recall you, too, are a Latin scholar.' He stood up. 'That will be all for now, Thomas. Miss Frensham will show you out. Perhaps you could stay a little longer, Victor.'

Tom smiled at the efficient Miss Frensham as he left. It was well known that she was the eyes and ears of the Vice Chancellor.

As he walked back towards reception he was unaware he was being watched.

Chapter Two

The Thief of Time

'Does it always have to be this loud?' shouted Tom.

'That's how they like it!' replied Inger with a smile.

It was Friday evening, the Freshers' Ball was in full swing, and Tom and Inger were taking their turn behind the bar. Bombalurina's 'Itsy Bitsy Teeny Weeny Yellow Polka Dot Bikini' was blaring out on full volume in the student common room and eighteen- and nineteen-year-olds were bouncing up and down and singing along to the music.

It had been a busy week for them, as they settled into their hostels, made new friends, collected timetables and discovered the city of York. The ball was the final event before lectures began next week and the second-, third- and final-year students would arrive. Tonight, however, was a chance to dress up, drink alcohol and dance till they dropped.

Among the tutors, it was only Zeb who had managed to match the energy levels of the students on the dance floor.

Owen was propping up the bar drinking a pint when she appeared beside him. 'A gin and tonic please, Inger . . . and go easy on the tonic.'

'Impressive moves, Dancing Queen,' said Owen. 'You've still got it.'

'Cheeky bugger!' said Zeb. 'I can still show these teenagers a thing or two.'

Owen pointed towards Ben Laverick, the new Head of Art, who was photographing groups of students. 'He's busy,' he said.

'Never seems to go anywhere without his camera,' said Tom.

Zeb sipped her drink and looked thoughtful as Rosie walked towards them. 'He's got his eye on Rosie. Sam had better watch out.'

Rosie ordered an orange juice and gave Inger a meaningful look. 'Can we have a word? I've got an idea.'

'Sure,' said Inger. She looked at Tom. 'Just taking a break with Rosie.'

Tom nodded and Owen walked behind the bar to take her place. Inger picked up her glass of wine and followed Rosie out into the last of the evening sunshine. They walked towards the quad, found an empty bench and sat down.

'This is mysterious,' said Inger with a smile.

'It might seem a strange request,' said Rosie, 'but are you free tomorrow? Sam and Tom are going with Owen on their rugby trip.'

'Yes, I've nothing planned. What's on your mind?'

'I'm driving to Barnsley market,' said Rosie. 'We can be there in an hour.'

Inger was curious. 'Barnsley?'

'Yes . . . and I think you know why.'

Inger looked thoughtful. 'Ellie MacBride,' she said quietly.

'Exactly,' said Rosie. 'She's halfway through her degree and one of our best students. Tom told me about her letter. It makes no sense. Why would she give it all up to run a market stall?'

Inger looked down at her drink. 'There is the possibility she realized she and Tom wouldn't get together.'

'We need to put that to one side,' said Rosie. 'I should just like to talk to her about her studies. So, will you join me?'

Inger nodded. 'Why not? Let's do it.'

'Fine.' They clinked glasses. 'I'll pick you up at ten.'

Early on Saturday morning the eastern sky was amber gold with backlit clouds like rose petals. Morning light caressed the distant land with its mantle of mist while Gideon Chalk, the university bursar, parked his Audi 100 outside the Lodge. The Vice Chancellor had requested a meeting, and Gideon was soon settled in an armchair and wondering why he had been summoned on a Saturday morning.

'Thank you for calling in, Gideon. I thought this would provide a quiet moment before term begins on Monday.'

'Of course, Edward. Happy to meet up whenever you wish.'

Gideon was a diminutive man in a dark three-piece suit who had arrived at Eboracum a year ago with an excellent reputation for his accountancy skills. Columns of figures dominated his world. As always, his cadaverous face was grey and his balding patch sported an ineffective comb-over.

'I'll come straight to the point,' said Edward. 'It concerns the incident at the end of last term. I thought it best we address this issue once and for all.'

'Ah, yes . . . I see,' said Gideon, suddenly tense.

At the dinner dance last July the inhebriated bursar had been escorted out of the Assembly Rooms by the police. It followed an accusation that he had behaved inappropriately towards one of the barmaids. No charges ensued and, over the summer months, Gideon presumed the fracas had been largely forgotten.

Edward leaned forward. 'I felt it was important to begin the new academic year with a clean slate.'

'I agree,' said Gideon, trying hard to remain composed.

'So I must stress that we want no repetition of the unfortunate scene at the end of last term. It does the university no good at all. The reputation of Eboracum is paramount.'

'I do understand. An abberation on my part. I assure you it was out of character. I confess to having imbibed a little too much champagne as it was a time of celebration.' As always, Gideon was obsequiously respectful, mixed with an inner confidence.

'Celebration?'

'But of course.' Gideon produced one of his superficial smiles. 'The university finances have never been healthier. We are solvent again, having tightened our belts last year.'

'I see,' said Edward and he sat back in his chair. 'Yes,

there is that.' He recalled the vote of confidence from the university's governing body following the publication of the most recent balance sheet.

Gideon began to relax. 'You will also be aware that the increase in student numbers swells the coffers, particularly following the acquisition of a selection of properties outside the city walls suitable for accommodation. I've been kept busy during the summer vacation.'

Edward nodded in appreciation. 'Encouraging news, Gideon. May it long continue.'

There was a pause. 'In that case, will that be all, Vice Chancellor?' said Gideon. A formal end to the proceedings seemed appropriate. 'I know you are a busy man.'

'Yes, that's all I wished to discuss,' said Edward. 'I'll let you get on.'

Gideon smiled and stood up. 'I'll be at my desk first thing on Monday,' he said and walked towards the door.

'As will Miss Frensham of course,' added Edward.

Naturally, thought Gideon. He didn't care for the Vice Chancellor's highly efficient and perceptive personal assistant. Likewise, she did not trust the evasive bursar who strutted past her desk each morning on his way to his office. In particular, she hated the smell of Turkish cigarettes that surrounded him like a malodorous cloak.

Owen Llewellyn was riding his racing bike along Lord Mayor's Walk. Beside him the city walls were honey gold in the morning light and a busy Saturday lay ahead. It was the first game of the rugby season and he had arranged for his 1st XV to return early from vacation for a match in Hull. A coach had been booked for ten o'clock, and both

Sam Greenwood and Tom had agreed to come along and support.

At the university gates he leapt off his bicycle and wheeled it towards reception. Suddenly, through the trees to his left, he spotted Gideon Chalk walking out of the Lodge. He jumped back on, sped down the empty winding path and dismounted next to Gideon's shiny car. 'A word if I may, please, Mr Chalk,' he said.

'I'm busy,' muttered Gideon.

There was no love lost between the adversaries, the Welshman and the bursar, fire and ice.

'It's important,' said Owen, and positioned his bicycle between Gideon and his car door. 'As you know, I visited one of your properties up the Hull Road, a three-bedroom semi. There are eight members of my rugby team still living there. I've since heard that nothing has been done to improve the dreadful conditions.'

'It's Saturday. See me on Monday,' said Gideon curtly.

Owen didn't move. 'So are you going to help these students or not?'

'They signed the contract,' said Gideon with a scowl. 'There's nothing I can do. They're lucky to have a roof over their heads. Accommodation is at a premium in York.' His fingertips covered his lips as he spoke and Owen sensed, as he often had before, that the bursar had something to hide.

The Welshman was furious but somehow kept his temper. This problem had been going on too long. 'Can't you see that this is *their time . . . a special time*. You're taking it away from them. They won't survive another winter in that house and they can't find anywhere else.'

'That's not my concern,' said Gideon bluntly. Once again there was a hint of truculence in his voice. 'Now please move.'

Owen reluctantly wheeled his bicycle back up the path while shaking his head. 'This won't go away,' he called out. 'I'll see you on Monday.'

Shortly after ten o'clock, Rosie and Inger were heading south. They chatted as the miles flew by. 'So what do you think about Ben Laverick?' asked Inger.

'Very arty. Good-looking in a rakish sort of way.'

'I saw he made a beeline for you last night.'

'It's nothing,' said Rosie. 'I helped him find an apartment at the end of last term.'

'Sam might see him as a rival,' said Inger.

Rosie smiled. 'You're fishing now. Sam is fine. Good company. I'm helping him improve his chess.' Rosie was a south of England chess champion with a fiercesome determination to succeed.

'Is that all?' added Inger, her tone whimsical. 'What about your walking holiday?'

'Behave,' said Rosie. 'Anyway, what about you and Tom? When do I have to buy a new hat?'

'Probably next year. I need to get my parents on side. They want a church wedding in Norway, but that's not my scene. Something a bit more low key in York would suit us both.'

It was shortly after eleven o'clock when they drove into Barnsley, the market town with its long tradition of glass-making and mining. Thirty years ago there had been seventy collieries within a fifteen-mile radius of the town centre. Now, few were left. Even so, the Saturday market was always busy. Rosie parked nearby and they joined the hundreds of shoppers looking for bargains. It was lively and noisy, with stallholders shouting their wares. Inger and Rosie walked past the huge number of stalls selling meat, fresh fish, prize-winning pork pies, crusty bread, bags of sweets and even second-hand chairs and woodworking tools. Then they saw what they were looking for. Right in the centre of the market was a line of trestle tables filled with displays of colourful fruit and vegetables.

'There she is,' said Rosie.

They both stopped for a moment and stared. There were three women serving on the stall. Ellie MacBride, dressed in a T-shirt and denim dungarees, was giving an elderly lady a punnet of strawberries. Slim and rosy-cheeked, thirty-year-old Ellie looked a picture of health. Her black wavy hair was tied back with a red ribbon. Alongside her stood a woman with the same high cheek-bones and cheerful smile, who was clearly her mother. A teenage girl, presumably a Saturday helper, was weighing carrots at the far end of the stall and then putting them in a brown paper bag.

Rosie and Inger approached the stall and Ellie looked up in surprise. 'This is unexpected,' she said with an enigmatic smile.

'Lovely to see you again, Ellie,' said Rosie. 'How are you?'

'I'm fine, thanks, and I'm guessing you're not just here for your weekly shop . . . or to talk about Victorian literature.'

'No,' said Inger. 'We're here to find out why we are losing one of our best students.'

'So,' said Rosie. 'Can you spare some time?'

Ellie looked at her mother. 'I'm taking a break, Mam. These are some of my tutors from York.'

Her mother gave them a curious look, almost defensive. 'Fine,' she said. 'Me and Kathy can manage.'

Ellie removed her apron. 'I only live round the corner. Let's go there for a cup of tea. My dad will be in. He fell off a ladder in the summer, so we got young Kathy to help out.'

A few minutes later they were walking towards the middle of a row of terraced council houses and in through the front door.

'Hi, Dad,' called out Ellie. 'I'm back.'

'Tha's early,' came the reply in a broad South Yorkshire accent.

'I've brought some visitors.'

''As thee now?'

Mr MacBride was sitting at the kitchen table in a collarless shirt and braces, peeling potatoes. His left foot was bandaged.

'This is Dr Tremaine, my English tutor, and Dr Larson, who teaches music. They wanted to speak to me . . . *about my decision*.'

'Ah see,' he said and rubbed his stubbly chin thoughtfully. 'You'll 'ave t'excuse me f'not gettin' up. Ah fell an' m'foot's badly.'

'Sorry to hear that,' said Rosie.

'I hope you're recovering,' added Inger.

'Thanks, luv, ah'll be fine.'

'I'll make a pot of tea,' said Ellie hurriedly.

'Go in t'front room if tha wants t'talk,' said Mr MacBride. He gave Inger and Rosie a calm, thoughtful look. 'Ah'm reckoning like us tha's a bit sad she's not going back t'that university.'

'We certainly are, Mr MacBride,' said Rosie in a determined voice. 'We just want to know why.'

'Reason's obvious, ah reckon . . . it 'appens.' He tapped Ellie on the arm. 'There's some chocolate digestives in t'cupboard.'

The front room was cosy with a black lead fireplace and, on the mantelpiece, a family photograph next to an old clock. There were two easy chairs, each with an antimacassar draped over the back, and a battered leather sofa. An old mahogany G Plan coffee table stood in front of them on the hearth rug. A cheap television set perched in the corner on a chipped sideboard.

Inger and Rosie sat down side by side on the sofa. Soon Ellie walked in with a tray.

'Is tea OK?' she asked. 'We've got instant coffee, if you prefer.'

'That's fine,' said Rosie.

'Thanks,' said Inger.

Minutes later they were sipping strong tea. Ellie closed the door that led to the kitchen and sat down expectantly in one of the armchairs. Rosie put down her cup and saucer. 'I was looking forward to working with you this year,' she said.

'Likewise,' said Ellie, 'but it wasn't to be.'

'So what was it?' asked Inger. 'You're halfway through your course and the market stall seems to be up and running, even with your father incapacitated. Surely your parents would want you to continue with this opportunity.'

'That's true, but once they had read the letter, that finished it. I had no choice.'

'Letter?' said Rosie. 'What letter?'

Ellie looked surprised. 'The one to my parents from Professor Grammaticus.'

Rosie glanced at Inger. 'Did you know Victor had written a letter?'

Inger shook her head. 'No one has mentioned it.' She turned to Ellie. 'Have you still got it? Could we see it?'

'Of course,' said Ellie. She stood up. In the far corner of the room was a battered bureau with a drop-down lid. She opened it and pulled out a beige envelope and handed it to Inger. Inside was a letter with an Eboracum crest addressed to Mr & Mrs MacBride. Inger scanned it quickly and passed it to Rosie. The message was clear and hinted at a possible affair between Ellie and one of her tutors. It emphasized this behaviour would not be tolerated and could cause great harm to the university. Typed at the bottom was the name Victor Grammaticus.

Ellie leaned forward and clasped her hands. 'I told my parents the truth: there was no affair and I didn't want to cause trouble for Tom.'

'We know that,' said Rosie.

'They were really concerned,' said Ellie. 'My dad said I had brought shame on the family. Mam was distraught.

Then, when my dad fell off a ladder and sprained his ankle, I was needed on the stall. It just seemed the simple solution.'

Silence fell while Inger studied the young woman before her. 'I know you had feelings for Tom,' she said.

Ellie sighed and answered with blunt honesty. 'He was great to me, gave me confidence.' She gestured around the room. 'Coming from this to a university was a big step. No one in my family had ever done it before.' She looked at Inger, her eyes soft with sorrow. 'Tom was always going to be yours, Inger.' She glanced down at the engagement ring and gave a wistful smile. 'It's you he wanted, not me. I understand that now.' For a while there was only the ticking of the clock while Ellie dabbed tears from her eyes.

Rosie passed the letter back to Inger. 'It's not signed,' she said quietly.

Inger nodded and leaned forward. 'Ellie, I don't know who wrote this letter but it certainly wasn't Victor. If it had been, he would have signed it. Someone is creating mischief here.'

Ellie frowned. 'Who would do that?'

'I don't know,' said Inger, 'but we can try to find out.' She put the letter back in the envelope. 'Can we keep this for now?'

Ellie nodded, clearly perplexed at how this conversation had developed.

Rosie took Ellie's hand in hers. 'Think hard, Ellie. You're only a couple of years away from achieving a degree and joining a profession that you clearly love. You could be a great teacher and have a different life.'

Ellie nodded. 'I know. I need to consider and talk to my parents.'

Inger and Rosie stood up. 'I'm pleased we've spoken,' said Inger.

'Thanks for the tea,' said Rosie.

'You're welcome,' said Ellie.

Mr MacBride waved as they walked out of the front door.

'Goodbye, Mr MacBride,' said Inger.

'Goodbye, luv,' said Mr MacBride.

'You have a fine daughter,' said Rosie.

'Ah knaws,' he said and continued to peel the potatoes.

As they walked back to the market, Inger and Rosie could see Ellie was deep in thought. Her mother looked curiously at them.

Inger smiled. 'While we're here, please can I have a few of those delicious Victoria plums?'

Ellie nodded. 'Pound of plums for the lady, Kathy,' and the young girl moved swiftly to weigh a bag of juicy fruit.

'And two red apples, please,' said Rosie.

'Help yourself,' said Ellie with a grin, 'and thanks for coming. I've a lot to think about.'

'As have we,' said Rosie.

Ellie leaned over the stall to shake hands. 'And congratulations, Inger,' she said quietly. A knowing look passed between the two women.

Rosie took out her purse. 'No,' said Ellie. 'On the house.'

Inger and Rosie picked up their bags of fruit and walked away.

When they looked back Ellie was deep in conversation with her mother.

The rugby game was won comfortably by Owen's 1st XV and the return journey from Hull was accompanied by a few raucous songs. 'Good to be back,' said Owen as the coach drove into the university car park.

'A great day out,' said Sam Greenwood.

'Come whenever you're free,' said Owen. 'We need the support. Unless you're hanging on to your Cornish chess champion's coat tails on Saturdays.'

'No chance,' said Sam. 'She and Inger are thick as thieves. Shopping today. Don't know where. She didn't say.'

Tom shrugged his shoulders. He'd had a similar conversation with Inger before leaving her apartment that morning. Meanwhile, a pint and a pie beckoned at the Keystones pub at Monk Bar. The young men on the back seat were collecting their sports bags and looking forward to their own Saturday evening in York city centre. Monday morning lectures seemed far away.

In the car park everyone climbed off the bus as the tall, fair-haired Jonny Halliday cycled past. He pulled up next to Owen. Jonny, a student in the science department, was the new President of the Students' Union. 'How did it go?' he asked.

'Won by twenty points,' said Owen. 'An encouraging start to the season.'

'Good news,' said Jonny. 'We could do with a write-up for the *Echo*.' The *Eboracum Echo* was the students' monthly newspaper.

Owen looked at Tom and patted him on the back. 'We have a qualified wordsmith here.'

Tom smiled. 'OK, just this once, but you need the club secretary to do it in future.'

Owen looked up at the gangling final-year student. 'Jonny, just a thought. I spoke with the bursar this morning. Some of our off-campus student accommodation is in a poor state.' He pointed to a group of the players who were setting off down Lord Mayor's Walk. 'This should be a great time for them here in York. Friendships, sport, a wonderful city. A special time. But it's being ruined for them because their living conditions are so bad.'

'I agree,' said Jonny.

'Do what you can in some of your meetings,' said Owen. 'I know you have a big say on the Students' Council. The Vice Chancellor could be supportive if you present a decent case.'

'We need Ellie MacBride to write one of her articles in the *Echo*,' said Jonny.

Owen glanced up at Tom. 'We're not sure she's coming back to complete her course. Family commitments down in South Yorkshire by all accounts.'

'That's disappointing,' said Jonny. 'Let's hope it gets resolved. She's great. OK, see you later.'

He cycled away, leaving Owen, Tom and Sam staring after him.

'A good lad,' said Sam. 'Excellent choice for president.'

'But can he stand up to bastards like the bursar?' murmured Owen.

*

Late that evening, the three men were watching *Match of the Day* in the pub. Arsenal had beaten Chelsea 4–1 and the barman was calling last orders. Owen had locked up his bicycle in the university cycle shed, so Sam gave him a lift home. Tom drove back to Inger's apartment by the Knavesmire and tiptoed into the bedroom. He undressed quickly and climbed into bed beside her. 'Had a good day?' he asked sleepily.

'Just shopping,' she said simply.

The following Tuesday morning at nine o'clock Tom walked into the English block for his first lecture of the term with English Three. 'Good morning, everybody. Welcome back.' He scanned the room. 'Good to see a full turnout. This semester we're looking at Victorian literature, beginning with Charles Dickens and *David Copperfield*.' On the whiteboard he wrote: 'Procrastination is the thief of time.' 'So . . . what do you think he meant?'

Ellie MacBride raised her hand and smiled.

Chapter Three

Reasons to Be Cheerful

It was just after eight o'clock on Monday, 1 October, and Tom and Inger were driving into work. The season had moved on and dappled sunlight filtered through the trees alongside the Knavesmire. It was a mellow autumn morning and in the hedgerows leaves were tinged with gold amidst the hammocks of spiders' webs. On the car radio, Elton John was singing 'Sacrifice' while Inger was deep in thought.

'You're quiet,' said Tom as they approached the city centre.

'Just thinking.'

'About what?'

'Where we should live.'

'Well ... your apartment is bigger than mine,' said Tom, 'and it's more central. On fine days we could walk into the university.'

'That's what I thought, but I know you like your own space in Haxby.'

'If I didn't pay rent there, it would save a lot of money, so maybe I should move sooner rather than later.'

'Then there's all your belongings.'

Tom smiled. 'You mean my two suits, one jacket, four shirts, a pair of jeans and not much else.'

'Yes, I've noticed,' said Inger, checking out the frayed cuffs of Tom's ageing cord suit.

'Point taken,' said Tom. 'So let's do it. Everything I own would fit on the back seat of my car. It's mainly clothes, books and a guitar with a broken string.' He stopped at the traffic lights before Micklegate Bar. 'I think I have to give four weeks' notice. I'll read the contract again. I could be in well before Christmas.'

'Sounds a good plan,' said Inger.

At present, Tom stayed in his rented cottage north of York in Haxby village during the week, and moved in with Inger each weekend. They drove past the railway station as Derek Jameson on BBC Radio 2 introduced Roxette singing 'It Must Have Been Love'.

'Have you a busy day ahead?' asked Tom.

Inger sounded preoccupied. 'Yes – voice, orchestra, theory, the usual.'

'And how's the concert?'

'Rehearsals have gone well. It's only a couple of weeks away now.' Inger's annual concert featured her choir and orchestra. It was one of the cultural highlights of the academic year. 'What about you?' she asked.

'School-practice visits. My first years are out in schools, so I'm on the road this morning. Then, this afternoon, it's lectures with Primary Three and English Four. So maybe catch up with you later.'

They drove past the art gallery, along Gillygate and turned into Lord Mayor's Walk. A police car was driving through the gates of the university.

'Not again,' muttered Tom. 'I've been grilled twice already.'

'But you were watching the drama production that night. So what's the problem?'

'I keep being asked where Victor was, but he only left his seat for ten minutes during the interval. They've also homed in on Edna's bitter dispute with Kimberly Stratton, a fourth-year student during that year.'

'A brilliant scientist, I recall,' said Inger, 'and editor of the student newspaper.'

'Richard was furious at the way Edna treated Kimberly.' Professor Richard Head was in charge of the science department, working alongside Sam Greenwood. 'The police have interviewed Richard already. They're spreading their net far and wide.'

'But surely Edna fell,' said Inger. 'She wasn't pushed.'

'That's what they're investigating and they're very determined.'

'Never mind,' said Inger as they parked and set off for reception. 'They'll soon move on to something else.'

Perkins was behind his counter writing in his leatherbound day book when they walked in.

'Good morning, Dr Larson, Dr Frith,' he said cheerily.

'Good morning, Perkins,' said Inger. 'I've got those two concert tickets you wanted for yourself and your wife.'

'Wonderful,' he said. 'Thank you so much. She loves a bit of classical, does my Pauline.'

Inger opened her shoulder bag, took out her purse and handed over the tickets.

Perkins nodded towards the quad. 'That policeman is in again, the grumpy one with the ginger moustache.'

Tom shook his head in dismay. 'It's puzzling. He's trying to find out if there was foul play in Edna Wallop's fall down the stairs. I was nowhere near it at the time.'

Perkins nodded. 'He's off to see Professor Grammaticus again. He must be fed up as well.'

'I'm sure he is.'

'Anyway,' said Perkins. 'At least the *Echo* might lift the spirits.' He patted the pile of newspapers on the counter. Each month the *Eboracum Echo* dealt with topical issues and was popular among the students.

'First issue of the term out today,' he said. 'Good headline.'

It read: 'REASONS TO BE CHEERFUL' above a photograph of Jonny Halliday and the Vice Chancellor. They were shaking hands and looking content with life. The headline reminded Tom of the popular hit record of over ten years ago by Ian Dury and the Blockheads. In fact he still remembered all the words. It was the follow-up to 'Hit Me With Your Rhythm Stick' and had captured the public imagination.

Tom was soon on the road again and heading north. Before he reached Thirsk he turned off down a country lane towards a pretty North Yorkshire village with a Norman church, a pub and a high street full of shops and a post office. Appleby Bank Primary School was a Victorian building of red brick next to the village green. Adam Kite, a music student training to be a primary school teacher, was the first on his list. Tom parked under the shade of an avenue of horse chestnut trees.

An elderly lady was sitting on a wooden bench outside the school reading her *Daily Mail*. She looked up as Tom walked past, then pointed furiously at the headline that read '50 per cent of children are below average'. 'Schools today aren't what they used to be,' she called out. 'Not like in my day.' Tom wondered if it was worth pointing out that, depending on which mathematical formula you employed, 50 per cent of children always would be *below average*. However, he guessed he would be fighting a losing battle and strode towards the school gate.

In the entrance hall he was met by the headteacher, Miss Victoria Howson, a petite woman wearing spectacles and a tweed suit.

'Hello again, Miss Howson,' said Tom. 'Thank you for taking one of our students.'

'You're very welcome and it's a particular pleasure this time. Everyone is very excited. Assembly will begin shortly and Mr Kite has brought his violin.'

Tom followed Miss Howson into the school hall and sat down. Eighty children were sitting cross-legged in rows on the wood-block floor. Three female teachers were at the other side of the hall, one of them at the piano. Adam Kite was standing at the front of the hall, holding his violin and looking out at the eager faces before him. The five-year-olds on the front row were close enough to touch his shoelaces. Many of the six-year-olds on the row behind were missing two front teeth and gave gap-toothed grins. The older children looked intently at the newcomer and wondered what would happen next.

Miss Howson stood up and waited for absolute silence. 'Good morning, boys and girls,' she said with a warm smile.

'Good morning, Miss Howson. Good morning, everyone,' chanted the children in perfect unison.

'Today is a special day. We have a student teacher, Mr Kite, with us for the next two weeks. So I want you all to make him welcome and show him that Appleby Bank is a happy school where we take care of each other.' Then she gestured towards Tom. 'We also welcome back Dr Frith from Eboracum University in York. He is visiting us again to see how hard you all work, so please be polite if he speaks to you.' She turned towards Adam. 'Now, we have a special treat before our morning assembly because Mr Kite has brought his violin with him. Can anyone tell me anything about a violin?'

Hands went up. 'Deborah,' said Miss Howson, pointing to a nine-year-old with rosy cheeks and pigtails.

'It's a musical instrument, miss. My big sister's got one and it's very squeaky.'

'Good answer,' said Miss Howson. She turned to Adam and peered playfully over her spectacles. 'And I imagine it can be.'

He grinned and nodded and played a single high-pitched note. There was laughter and Tom thought, *A good start.*

'Now, Mr Kite is going to play for us.' She sat down next to Tom and all eyes turned towards the young man at the front of the hall. He was wearing his old school blazer and tie.

'This is my violin,' he said, 'and I was your age

when I began to have lessons. I play the strings using my bow.' He demonstrated by playing a quick scale. It was obvious immediately he was very accomplished. 'I should like to play a famous violin solo called "The Lark Ascending".'

Tom smiled. The Ralph Vaughan Williams solo was one of Inger's favourites.

Adam looked out at the curious faces. 'Does anyone know what a lark is?'

A hand went up immediately on the back row. 'It's a bird, sir,' said ten-year-old Tommy Booth. 'A songbird.'

'That's right, well done.'

The girl next to him raised her hand. 'When I get up early, my mum says I'm up with the larks.'

'That's right,' said Adam. 'It means you're an early bird.'

A bristle-haired boy waved his hand vigorously. 'And our dinner lady says stop larking about when we're naughty in the dinner queue.'

Adam grinned. 'That's right. It can mean that as well, having fun or being lively.' He propped the violin under his chin. 'So sit very quietly and listen, and imagine a beautiful songbird flying high in the sky.'

He began to play and everyone looked in wonder at this talented young man. He closed his eyes as his long nimble fingers danced over the strings and he swayed with the music. It was moments like this that Tom treasured in his professional life. He looked at this confident student, at ease with himself, on the first day of his teaching practice. Then he turned to Miss Howson, who had created this opportunity, and nodded. She gave a gentle smile, knowing this was the perfect way to provide this talented youngster with the confidence to become an effective teacher. When Adam finished, the hall was filled with thunderous applause. He gave a small bow and walked to sit next to the young deputy head, Miss Precious. He would be working in her class and supporting her cross-curricular project about 'The Weather'.

The assembly concluded with the hymn 'Morning Has Broken', followed by the Lord's Prayer and a few notices about the forthcoming Harvest Festival. As the children filed back to their classrooms, Tom approached Adam. 'Well done. That was really special for those children.'

Adam looked up shyly at Tom. 'Strange, isn't it?' he said. 'I was nervous when I walked in here this morning. I'm lucky having my violin.' He held it up. 'I can hide behind my music.'

'No need to hide, Adam. Enjoy this opportunity. You've just held a hall full of children and teachers in the palm of your hand. Congratulations. I'll be back next week to see one of your lessons.'

'Thanks for being here,' said Adam. 'I appreciate the support, and Miss Precious is really encouraging. She plays the piano beautifully. I might suggest a duet later,' he added with a smile.

Tom wrote a few positive comments in his carbon-copy notebook, tore out a page and left it in Adam's school-practice folder on the teacher's desk. There was a group of six-year-olds next to him and he crouched down. The children were arranging model farm animals in various enclosures. One little girl was holding a model of a unicorn. Tom smiled at her. 'Is your unicorn going some-where in your farm?'

She looked up at him and shook her head sympathet-ically, 'No, of course not,' she replied defiantly.

'Oh, why not?' asked Tom, a little surprised.

The girl gave him a condescending look. 'Animals live on a farm . . . unicorns live in fairy tales.'

'I see,' said Tom. 'I should have known.' He turned to Adam. 'Never underestimate children.'

'Quite right,' added a smiling Miss Precious.

Tom said goodbye and thanked Miss Howson on his way out. Soon he was on the road again.

Five miles away in the next village was Healey Grange Primary School. Two of his English One students, Becky Salter and Jane Granger, were there. An intriguing duo, they were two inseparable friends from Whitley Bay. They had known each other from their time in pri-mary school and were interviewed on the same day at Eboracum.

Tom had visited this school once before and, as always, he was impressed with the headteacher, Mrs Blos-som, whose enthusiasm for her work had sustained her throughout a long career. She was clearly thrilled to have these young women in her school. 'A breath of fresh air,' she said. 'They will both go far. They may look different but both throw themselves wholeheartedly into the job.'

'I know what you mean,' said Tom. The two eighteen-year-old women were both confident and eager but had sharply contrasting sartorial styles. Becky sported a Suzi Quatro hairstyle, a frilly shirt and leather jeans, while

Jane wore a white blouse, an M&S two-piece suit and black lace-up shoes.

It was another successful visit. Both students had made a good start alongside experienced teachers. Tom saw Becky in a mathematics lesson measuring and weighing with a group of mixed-ability eight-year-olds. Jane was in the reception class supporting an early phonics activity using flash cards. They were both completely engrossed in their work. Once again, Tom left supportive carbon-copy notes in their folders and thanked the teachers.

Mrs Blossom looked a little sad when Tom left. 'I'll be retiring at the end of this year after almost forty years in the profession. It's good to see your students, Dr Frith. They're the future. I hope they will love it as I have done.' She gave Tom a wry look. 'I've found adjusting to the new National Curriculum something of a challenge, so maybe it's time for someone else to take over.' She shook hands with him. 'Thank you for calling in. You are always welcome, regardless of teaching practice.'

After that heartfelt farewell Tom drove back to York, reflecting on a morning of phonics, maths and music. He was hungry and, shortly after midday, he walked into the refectory, a huge building of glass, concrete and stainless-steel counters. Tutors tended to gather in the far corner away from the hurly-burly of student chatter that filled the hall.

He collected a quiche salad and a soft drink before spotting Professor Richard Head sitting alone. The nerdy scientist was studying a copy of the *Echo* while dividing a jacket potato into two identical hemispheres. Richard was particular in all aspects of his life. He was a brilliant academic who always walked in straight lines, arranged place mats so they were parallel with the table edge and washed his hands after every contact with a doorknob. He was an interesting colleague.

'Hi, Richard,' said Tom as he sat down. 'How's things?'

'Hello, Tom.' He put down his knife and fork. 'Mixed, I suppose. Just had another dreadful half-hour with a policeman who, quite frankly, lacked competent powers of analysis.'

'About Edna, I presume?'

'Yes. He said I was apparently in the clear as I was busy doing the sound and lights for Zeb's production that evening.'

'We both were,' said Tom.

'Then it got a bit confrontational. He was like a dog with a bone and wanted to know where Kimberly Stratton was that night. He had heard Edna was causing her trouble and that her study was on the top floor close to the stairs. I told him she was an outstanding student, one of the finest in my science department.'

'Quite right,' said Tom. 'She was.'

'Then he asked about her boyfriend, Gio.'

'I remember Gio. Terrific student.'

'Correct. Giovanni Carmichael, English father, Italian mother. He got a first in Mathematics and was head-hunted by Unilever. He and Kimberly now live in Port Sunlight. The police are going there next to interview them both.'

'I suppose there are plenty of people with a motive,' said Tom, 'but it still remains an accident.'

'Anyway,' said Richard, holding up his copy of the *Echo*. 'Good to see the student newspaper branching out a bit. One of my final-year students, Oliver Brakespeare, has written a round-up of world news on page two. Bit of everything . . . the war against Iraq, the reunification of Germany and even Margaret Thatcher's idea for a new Magna Carta to guarantee the rights of all European citizens.'

'Good to hear,' said Tom. 'Meanwhile . . . how's Felicity?'

'The same,' said Richard simply.

Felicity Capstick was a science lecturer in Sheffield and, like Richard, a lover of astronomy. It was this passion for the stars that had brought them together and they were now engaged. However, it was Felicity who was the driving force behind all their decision-making.

'Any wedding news?'

Richard peered myopically through his thick spectacles. 'No, I leave all that to her.'

Likewise, thought Tom. 'So . . . how's astronomy these days?'

Richard's eyes lit up. 'Ah, glad you asked. Saturn's largest moon, Titan, is creating some interest, plus a forty-four-kilogram meteoroid passed above Czechoslovakia and Poland.'

'Oh dear,' said Tom. 'Anyone hurt?'

'Fortunately no.' He stared out of the window, deep in thought. 'Also, Felicity is wondering whether we should be called *astronomers* or *astrophysicists*. We spend hours discussing it.'

'I'm sure you do,' said Tom, who had finished his

quiche in quick time. 'Anyway, things to do. Enjoy your lunch.' He left Richard carefully separating the sliced carrots and the chopped celery so they didn't overlap.

On a nearby table Rosie Tremaine sat down next to Ellie MacBride. 'Would you like to call in after lectures?' she asked. 'We can decide a way forward for this year's dissertation.'

'Yes, fine,' said Ellie. 'It's Primary Three next with Tom. After that I'm free.'

'That's good. Call into my study at afternoon break.' She looked thoughtful. 'I'm afraid there's no joy regarding that strange letter. I asked Perkins but he had no recollection of a letter addressed to your parents. Also, headed notepaper is readily available. All the clubs and societies use it, so it could have been anybody.'

'Thanks anyway,' said Ellie. 'Somebody out there clearly doesn't want me here.'

'Is there a disgruntled ex-boyfriend hidden away somewhere?'

'Don't think so,' said Ellie with a grin. 'There're a few of those but we always parted on good terms.'

'By the way,' said Rosie, 'loved your article about student accommodation. The bursar doesn't come out of it well, does he, even though you've not mentioned him by name?'

'I'm just hoping he sees sense, and I know the Vice Chancellor reads the *Echo*. He's even endorsed it with his photo on the front page. Someone needs to stand up for those poor students.'

*

When Tom returned to their study, Owen was eating a sandwich and reading the rugby reports in the *Echo*. 'Thanks, Tom. Great summary of that first game, apart from the fact I didn't get a mention as a master tactician.'

'Goes without saying,' said Tom as he looked in the filing cabinet for his notes on 'Classroom Management Strategies with Mixed-Ability Children'.

Owen grinned. 'Anyway, thanks. It's a good report and Jonny Halliday gave us plenty of reasons to be cheerful. He praised all the sports teams and waxed lyrical about the great food in the refectory, particularly the pork pie salad. He also said there was a pub for every day of the year within York's city walls. If that doesn't cheer you up nothing will.'

Tom smiled, picked up his notes for Primary Three and hurried downstairs to his lecture. Ellie caught up with him in the quad.

'Hi, Tom,' she said with a smile.

'Hi, Ellie. How's life?'

'Fine. Glad to be back. I was a bit confused for a while. That letter upset my parents.'

Tom nodded, a concerned expression on his face. 'So Rosie said. I know she and Inger are doing their best to discover who sent it.'

'I'm so grateful to them. But for their visit, I wouldn't be here.'

'That would be sad,' said Tom. 'You have a great future ahead of you.'

'Hope so,' said Ellie with feeling. 'I'm sorry if I caused you some conflict. You've been a terrific mentor for me.'

'I just want you to fulfil your dreams.'

Ellie didn't answer as they approached the English block and caught up with the rest of the group.

It was the end of the day, lectures had finished and Zeb had called in to see Victor. He prepared a cafetière of coffee and put out a plate of delicious homemade biscuits on the art deco coffee table.

'Ooh, what a treat,' said Zeb. 'I presume Pat made these.'

'Yes, he's into baking again.'

Victor's partner, the wonderfully creative and exuberant Patrick St John-Stevens, was a professional artist and a keen supporter of York's amateur dramatics. They lived in a beautifully furnished house in Easingwold, a little over ten miles to the north of York.

'So, a busy day?' said Zeb.

'Yes, made worse by another interview with the police.'

'Oh dear,' said Zeb. 'The problem is that Edna attempted to destroy the careers of so many in our department; that makes it easy for the police to be suspicious.'

Victor looked thoughtful. 'Sadly, yes.'

Zeb studied her friend. 'Come on, what is it? You're clearly troubled.'

Victor sighed. 'I'm concerned for Tom. This police investigation simply won't go away. We've discussed it many times. To be frank . . . it's threatening our careers. I know Edward is deeply concerned.'

'But you're both obviously innocent,' said Zeb.

'I'm not sure the police think that way. They're pressing hard.' Victor clasped his hands and stared out of the window. 'There's a harbourer of dangerous secrets out there.'

'A warped evil bastard,' said Zeb with feeling. 'Not to mention the letter sent out in your name to Ellie MacBride's parents.'

'Very true,' said Victor pensively.

'We nearly lost a brilliant student.'

Victor sat back and sipped his coffee. 'Shall we move on to something more cheerful? How's Vijay?'

Zeb gave a wide-eyed smile. 'Simply wonderful. He took me to the Dean Court Hotel on Saturday evening and we had a lovely meal.' Then she frowned and put down her cup and saucer.

'What is it?'

'There's a problem. He wants me to meet his parents.'

'That's good, isn't it?'

Zeb sighed deeply. 'I'm not sure they would see me as a perfect fit for Vijay.'

'Why's that?'

'Because of what's gone on in the past. He's forty now, a Hindu and completely westernized, but his parents still want him to marry a young Indian woman. Apparently they've tried often enough.'

'In what way?'

'Well, for a start, they've always preferred an arranged marriage.'

'I see,' said Victor. 'Old traditions.'

'Vijay said that, over the years, they have introduced him to many eligible young Indian women. It always followed the same pattern. They would meet in one of their houses, settle down in the sitting room with tea and some food, then the parents would leave them to get acquainted. After Vijay and the woman had discussed their future aspirations for an hour, his parents would return. Later they would ask, "What do you think?" and he would always say, "No." '

'Which went on for years,' said Victor.

'Quite right. Vijay said it never changed. They would insist the young woman had a good background, was a good cook and well educated. Also, she would be of the same caste with a similar upbringing. The last young woman was called Rina and his parents were furious when he rejected her.'

Victor looked at his trusted colleague. Zeb was a dynamic and positive woman but he could see how, beneath the surface, she was deeply concerned.

Zeb selected a biscuit and sat back in her chair. 'So, Victor, my friend . . . any advice?'

'Plenty,' he said with a smile. 'First of all we need to buy you an elegant sari.'

Their conversation continued into the early evening.

Tom and Inger were driving home and pulled up on the driveway outside Inger's apartment. They were both tired after a busy day.

'How did your school visits go?' asked Inger.

'I saw your protégé, Adam Kite. He played his violin in school assembly and captivated the children and staff. It was simply wonderful. You would have loved it.'

'I'm so pleased. Yes, he's really special.'

Inger unlocked the front door and they walked in.

Tom put his copy of the *Eboracum Echo* on the hall table.

'I guess we need to talk again about me leaving my cottage,' he said.

'Yes, let's do that.' She took off her coat and hung it up in the hallway.

'So, decision time,' said Tom. 'Am I staying? It's not the weekend.'

Inger stretched up and kissed him on the cheek. 'I'll look in the fridge.'

Tom glanced down at the headline – 'REASONS TO BE CHEERFUL' – and smiled.

Chapter Four

A Leap of Faith

It was eight o'clock on Tuesday, 16 October, and, in her converted barn in Crayke village, Zeb was eating a bowl of cereal. The radio was playing and she was swaying her hips to Maria McKee's 'Show Me Heaven' after a night of passion with Vijay. He came up behind her and put his arms around her waist. 'I've booked a meal for us.'

'Where?' said Zeb.

'It's an Indian restaurant in Leeds owned by a dear friend of mine.'

Zeb put down her bowl on the worktop and turned to face him. 'Is this part of my training?'

He smiled and kissed her softly. 'You might say that. I thought we could drive over this evening. You'll like Deepak. He's a Punjabi Hindu and his parents moved to Leeds after partition and the exodus from Pakistan. He and his wife serve great food.'

'Sounds good,' said Zeb. 'I'm enjoying my introduction to Indian culture. It's just the prospect of meeting your parents that makes me nervous.'

'Don't worry,' said Vijay. 'They will love you and nothing is arranged yet. We have plenty of time.'

Zeb glanced at the clock. 'Actually, at this moment we haven't. I have a lecture at nine.'

Vijay picked up his jacket from the back of the chair. 'I'll drop you off on my way to the hospital.'

'Fine. I'll be finished tonight by four thirty.' Then she hurried back to the bedroom. 'I'll need a dress to change into.'

'I'll start the car,' shouted Vijay. As he switched on the ignition he thought about his parents, both in their mid-sixties now. His father, Atul, was a cautious but reasonable man, whereas his traditional mother, Prem, would be hard to win over. However, they were nothing of a challenge compared with his two fiercesome aunties, Usha and Krisma. *All in good time*, he thought as Zeb grabbed her shoulder bag, locked the front door and jumped into his Jaguar XJ.

As they drove towards York, the world was burnished in amber and gold sunlight. Each day the temperature had dropped, and beyond the hedgerows an autumn mist covered the distant countryside with a mantle of silence. As they approached the city centre and drove past the chocolate factory, Vijay thought fondly of his mother's cooking. Images of saag paneer, aloo gobi curry, rajma and jeera rice flickered through his mind. Then he glanced at the remarkable woman sitting beside him and smiled.

She had changed his life and a new journey lay before them, one that would require him to take a leap of faith.

Perkins smiled when Zeb walked into reception. 'Good morning, Dr Peacock. Wonderful concert last night. My Pauline said it was the best ever.'

'Morning, Perkins,' said Zeb. 'I agree. We have so much talent among the students these days.'

'And among the staff,' added Perkins, and she blew him a kiss as she skipped towards the quad.

Inger's concert had proved to be a triumph. A full house of concert-goers in the music room had enjoyed a mix of classical and contemporary music. The highlights included the choir singing Handel's *Messiah* and Adam Kite's violin solo, J. S. Bach's Chaconne. This was followed by an effortless change of mood when Inger played Gershwin's 'Rhapsody in Blue'. The finale featured the remarkable Arabella Esposito. By huge demand, the gifted second-year soprano gave a reprise of 'Pie Jesu', made popular by Andrew Lloyd Webber in his 1985 Requiem. She had received a standing ovation.

As the lights went up, Inger had walked to the centre of the stage and praised her choir and orchestra. In a classic black dress and a diaphanous blue silk scarf, she looked stunning. It was at moments like this that Tom realized how lucky he was that this beautiful woman had agreed to be his wife. Then there was a surprise as the Vice Chancellor joined Inger on the stage. He thanked everyone for their attendance and congratulated Inger and her students for a wonderful evening. He held up an elegant, embossed invitation card. 'I am happy to announce,' he said in his best toastmaster voice, 'that the university choir has been invited to represent Eboracum at a distinguished music festival in Vienna next year.' He passed the card to Inger amidst whoops of delight from the students.

Next the longest-serving member of the choir, twenty-two-year-old music student Alexandra Midwinter, had presented Inger with a bunch of red roses. The slim mezzo-soprano approached the microphone and offered a few well-chosen words of thanks on behalf of her fellow students. She spoke as if there was a song in her heart and a camera flashed as Ben Laverick, beyond the apron of the stage, recorded the moment. Inger received the bouquet and kissed Alexandra on both cheeks as the rest of the choir gathered around her.

Suddenly Alexandra had become a point of stillness in the moving throng. Her hair was the colour of autumn acorns and she moved with the grace of a deer. She paused and looked down, directly at Ben. Her eyes were the colour of moss on limestone and, in that moment, the new Head of Art was captivated. He raised his camera once more, adjusted the focal length and recorded a perfect head and shoulders image as she looked down the lens. It was a photograph that would have lasting impact.

Just after Zeb had hurried into reception, Hermione Frensham walked along the winding path towards the Lodge. The branches above her head shifted with a sibilant whisper and patterns of soft sunlight danced at her feet. Edward Chartridge, Canon Emeritus of York Minster, was standing by the front door in a dark suit and clerical collar, reflecting on life. He was watching a solitary robin as its feathers ruffled in the breeze.

'Good morning, Vice Chancellor,' said Hermione cheerily. She believed it was important to be formal with her employer. There were standards of professional decorum that must be maintained. Suddenly the rooks in the high elms cawed raucously and shattered the silence.

'Good morning, Hermione,' said Edward with a startled smile. He glanced up. 'Noisy this morning.'

'Probably warning of predators,' said Hermione.

'Ah yes,' said Edward and tapped the side of his nose with a forefinger. 'There are always a few of those around.'

Hermione nodded in agreement but kept her thoughts to herself. Gideon Chalk had just pulled up in the car park. She followed Edward into the warmth of the hallway. 'I thought last night was quite remarkable,' he said.

'I agree,' said Hermione. 'It was one of Dr Larson's finest concerts and your announcement about Vienna was a wonderful surprise. We must get it in the diary.'

'It's the second weekend in March,' said Edward. 'Have you ever been?'

'No, I haven't, but I've heard it's a wonderful city.'

'Perhaps you ought to join the party. I'm sure Dr Larson would appreciate the company.'

'Oh, thank you,' said Hermione in surprise. 'I should love to go.'

'And you can keep your eye on Mr Laverick.'

'Really?'

'Yes. Immediately after the concert he asked if he could make a photographic record of the event and I agreed.'

Hermione merely nodded in agreement. The new head of the art department was a little over-familiar for her liking. 'Would you like your coffee a little earlier this morning?' she asked. 'I've bought some of your favourite biscuits from Bettys Tea Rooms.'

'Perfect,' said Edward.

Life was far from perfect in York Police Station. Chief Inspector Greybourne was looking at the anonymous letter once again and shaking his head. DI Montgomery and DS Porterfield were sitting on the other side of his desk and wishing they were somewhere else.

'So, we've drawn a blank, have we?' said the chief inspector.

Inspector Montgomery nodded disconsolately and stubbed out his cigarette. Sergeant Porterfield was holding a Mars bar but decided this wasn't the best moment to be chewing on something that the adverts declared would help him 'work, rest and play'. They had both returned from Birkenhead the previous evening and gone straight to the pub.

'Waste o' time,' said DI Montgomery. 'I interviewed the two clever dicks at Port Sunlight but they had witnesses that put them in the clear, plus everyone at the uni has a cast-iron alibi.'

Sergeant Porterfield shook his head in despair. 'Boss, none of 'em are *normal*. There's a professor with a brain the size of a football, a drop-dead-gorgeous woman who's a friggin' chess champion and a nutty scientist who won't touch doorknobs.'

Chief Inspector Greybourne held up the letter. 'I wish I

knew who wrote this. I'd kick him from here to kingdom come and then stick this where the sun don't shine.' He sighed. 'Police work isn't what it used to be. Catch a villain and bang 'em up.'

'Yer right there, boss,' said DI Montgomery. 'Everything's gone soft.'

Sergeant Porterfield shoved the Mars bar back in his pocket. The ginger-haired enforcer had clearly had enough. 'I even heard today, from Bernie on the desk,' he muttered, 'that we're offering victim support to a woman whose lawnmower got nicked.'

The chief inspector put the letter back in the manila folder and pushed it away. 'OK, I'll ring the Vice Chancellor and tell him we're done.'

At morning break Inger was sitting with Owen in the staff common room. Above the murmur of a hundred conversations, colleagues kept congratulating Inger as they passed by with their hot drinks.

'Well done, Inger,' said Owen. 'I'm no connoisseur of classical music but last night was superb. I'm so glad we got a babysitter. Sue loved it.'

'Thanks, Owen,' said Inger, looking around. 'I thought Tom might be here.'

'Victor wanted a word,' said Owen. 'Something about the police giving up on the witch hunt.'

'Thank goodness,' she said. 'It's gone on long enough.'

The television in the corner was burbling away and a few members of staff had gathered round and were watching intently. Owen caught sight of Margaret Thatcher giving an interview and shook his head in disgust. 'At least Kinnock's got it right. At the Labour Party Conference in Blackpool he said the way forward is for the UK to invest in education and training. Now Maggie's closed the pits we need a fresh start.'

'Perhaps we do,' said Inger cautiously. She kept her political views to herself and, after all, the socialist Welshman was a dear friend.

He got up to leave. 'See you later. I've got Primary Two in the gym,' and he hurried out.

A few minutes later Tom walked in and sat down next to Inger.

'I've just heard from Owen,' she said. 'The police investigation has ended.'

'Yes, Victor confirmed it. The news has spread like wildfire. Also, I finally managed to speak to my landlord this morning and I've given him notice. I move out at the end of next month.'

Inger smiled. 'That's great. So, our first Christmas together . . .'

'Special times,' said Tom. 'Looking forward to it.'

Inger sighed. 'My parents have been asking me about the wedding again. I've made it clear they can come here to York. This is my home. I don't want to get married in Oslo.'

'Suits me,' said Tom. 'My mother was on the phone last night. She assumed we would be getting married in a church in Norway. I told her that's not what we wanted and it would probably be a register office. She sounded disappointed.'

'Just like my parents,' said Inger. 'They're a different generation. But' – she looked determined – 'it will be *our* day and *our* decision.'

At lunchtime Rosie and Inger were in the refectory, enjoying some time together. It had been a busy morning and it was good to find a little private space.

'Have your feet touched the ground since last night?' asked Rosie.

Inger smiled. 'Just about. The Vice Chancellor asked me to call in to confirm a few arrangements for Vienna. His PA is doing all the travel and hotel bookings. So Hermione is coming as well and she's as thrilled as I am.'

'It's exciting news,' said Rosie.

'Apparently, Ben Laverick has asked if he can be involved and the VC said yes. He's going to photograph the event.'

'Interesting,' said Rosie with an inquisitive grin. 'I wonder how Tom will feel about the handsome Lothario spending a weekend in Austria with his fiancée?'

Inger sighed and shook her head. 'I doubt it would cross his mind to worry about it. There was a time I thought Ben had got his eye on you.'

'No, thanks. I'm happy with Sam,' said Rosie. 'Safe and reliable.'

'Very wise, although you have to admit our Head of Art is really quite dishy. Changing the subject, what happened to your book on Oscar Wilde?'

Rosie suddenly appeared animated. 'I finished it over the summer and sent the first three chapters to a few agents. One of them has got back to me showing interest. She's asked to see the full manuscript. So, I'm hopeful.'

'Good luck with that,' said Inger. 'I'll look forward to reading it.'

'I might share it with Ellie MacBride,' said Rosie. 'Her special study this year is Victorian literature.'

There was a pause and Inger looked pensive. 'How is she?'

'Apparently seeing a lot of Jonny Halliday, if that's what you're hinting at.'

'I didn't know.'

Rosie smiled. 'You sound relieved.'

Inger shook her head. 'That's all in the past now.' She held up her engagement ring. 'We've moved on.'

'You still haven't shared any wedding plans.'

'Nothing to say yet. Our parents aren't pleased. They want a traditional wedding. You know the scene ... churches, bridesmaids and confetti. But my brother agrees that we should have what we want, and he said that, wherever it is, he's happy to play for us.' Andreas Larson, Inger's talented brother, was first violin in the Oslo Philharmonic Orchestra.

'And what *do* you and Tom want?'

'Something simple would suit us.'

'There's a register office in Bootham. Check it out.'

Inger nodded. 'Will do.'

It was almost one o'clock when they walked out together. 'Speak of the devil,' said Rosie. 'It's your Austrian companion.'

Ben Laverick was holding a handful of posters. He

pinned one on to the staff noticeboard and set off for the quad.

'Let's see what it is,' said Rosie. On a stylish A3 sheet it read:

A photographic exhibition by Ben Laverick
The Silence of Dreams
An evocative view of Eboracum life
Friday 16th November, 7.30 p.m. onwards
in the Art Studio

'Interesting,' said Rosie. 'We must attend. I know he was photographing you last night at the concert.'

'Awkward,' said Inger. 'Do you think he invades people's personal space?'

Rosie raised her eyebrows. 'I think he would like to.'

They both smiled before heading their separate ways.

At afternoon break, Zeb called into Victor's study for a catch-up. They sat drinking herbal tea and munching on a selection of Pat's shortbread.

'So, any news?' asked Zeb.

'Edward confirmed the police have called off their investigation into Edna's accident.'

'About time too,' said Zeb. 'We need to find the mischief-maker who sent in the letter.'

'I agree.' Victor leaned over and took a brightly coloured poster from the satchel next to his chair. 'Ben Laverick gave me one of these. He's putting them up to adver-tise an exhibition of his work. It's next month. We need to get it in the diary and make an appearance.'

'Yes, we must,' said Zeb. 'I've noticed the art department seems very lively at the moment. Some of my drama students have volunteered to be models for their life-drawing classes.'

'Interesting,' said Victor. 'I presume they get paid.'

'Yes, but I don't know where the budget comes from.'

'I'll ask him,' said Victor. 'And what about you? How's Vijay?'

Zeb smiled. 'He's taking me to an Indian restaurant tonight. All part of my cultural development before I meet his parents.'

'It must be serious then,' said Victor with a knowing look.

'Too bloody true . . . but it's clearly important to him.'

'Good to hear. He's an impressive man.'

'I'm thinking of finding out a bit more about the Hindi language.'

Victor smiled. 'In that case, when you get to meet the owner of the restaurant say "Namaste".'

'Namaste?'

Victor grinned. 'It's just a greeting.'

'Fair enough,' said Zeb. 'Namaste it is.'

Victor sat back and looked at this woman whom he knew so well, a gifted drama teacher who had lived life to the full. Lately it had been a helter-skelter journey for her, full of changes and challenges. 'I've an idea,' he said. 'Let's fix up an afternoon tea at my place. Pat makes the most delicious Indian tea that includes spices. He brews water in a pan over the stove, adds fresh ginger and milk. It could be fun.'

'And informative,' said Zeb. 'Thanks, a great idea.'

They parted when the bell rang for lectures.

*

At five o'clock, Ellie MacBride climbed the stairs to Cloisters corridor. She tapped on Rosie's door and walked in. Rosie was at her desk, marking work.

'Hi, Ellie. Won't be long. Help yourself to a hot drink and there're some biscuits in the tin.'

Ellie boiled the kettle, selected two matching mugs featuring views of the Cornish coastline and spooned in some Nescafé Gold. She put a few biscuits on a small plate and unpacked her shoulder bag. She liked Rosie's study. It reflected her tidy, meticulous tutor. On a table by the window was a beautiful chess set, the curtains were azure blue and there were photographs on the mantelpiece. A bright vase of sunflowers stood on the windowsill and the books on the shelves were neatly arranged. She took out her notepad as Rosie sat down on one of the armchairs.

'Let's make a start,' said Rosie. 'This year it's a dissertation on Victorian literature. What have you done so far?'

Ellie opened her ring binder of notes. 'I've prepared some background on Charles Dickens, Charlotte Brontë, Thomas Hardy, Alfred Tennyson, Elizabeth Barrett Browning and Matthew Arnold.'

'That's fine,' said Rosie. 'Then, as we progress through the year, we'll include such luminaries as Elizabeth Gaskell, Anthony Trollope, George Eliot and, my personal favourite, Oscar Wilde.'

Ellie was scribbling notes quickly.

Rosie sipped her coffee and sat back in her chair. The woman opposite had always been a conundrum. 'You look pleased to be back. How are you now?'

Ellie appeared thoughtful for a moment. 'Mostly fine. Two steps forward, one step back is the pattern of my life.'

'I understand,' said Rosie. 'We all experience that. How's the market stall? I guess your father is fully recovered.'

'He's fine and pleased I'm back here. My mother took some convincing that all was well, but she has come round. The letter caused them grief.'

'I'm sure it did. That was a bad business but, rest assured, we shall find out who sent such a malicious letter and they will be dealt with.'

'Thank you,' said Ellie. 'I really appreciate that.'

'So, we can move on now,' said Rosie and both women shared a look that spoke volumes.

Twenty miles away, Vijay turned off the northern Leeds ring road and pulled into a large car park in front of an imposing building with the sign 'The Cardamom Restaurant' lit up above the entrance porch. When he and Zeb walked in they were welcomed by the owner, Deepak, a short, stocky Indian with a flashing smile. 'Welcome to my humble restaurant,' he said and bowed. 'Vijay, my friend, please introduce me to this beautiful woman.'

'This is Elizabeth,' said Vijay.

'Like our queen,' said Deepak. He bowed to Zeb and smiled. 'Good evening.'

Zeb bowed in return. 'Namaste,' she said with confidence.

'Ah, our Hindu greeting,' said Deepak. 'I congratulate you, Elizabeth.'

Zeb smiled. 'Thank you. Actually everyone calls me Zeb.'

'Then Zeb it will be,' said Deepak. 'Vijay has told me a lot about you.'

'All good, I hope.'

He shook his head. 'No, not good . . . but rather *excellent*, perfect, the woman of his dreams.'

Vijay tapped Deepak on the shoulder. 'You flatter to deceive, my friend. Now, we have both had a long day and we're hungry, so what can you recommend?'

'I'll ask Padma to come and speak to you. She is in the kitchen but has a lot of help this evening. I shall tell her that her second favourite man has arrived.' There was laughter as they walked in and Deepak ushered them to a private candlelit table in the far corner of the dining room. Soft sitar music played in the background.

Padma was a slim, elegant woman with beautiful smooth skin and high cheekbones. She bowed briefly in welcome but then Vijay gave her a big hug. 'Padma,' he said, 'you look younger every time we meet.'

Padma gave Zeb a shrewd look. 'Does he use this flattery on you?'

'Only when necessary,' said Zeb. 'It's lovely to meet you, Padma. I'm Zeb.'

'You are welcome, Zeb, and I'm so pleased to meet you at last. You must be a remarkable woman to have stolen the heart of this stubborn man.'

'Perhaps,' said Zeb, 'but this evening I am more interested in your cuisine. I need a few tips before I'm introduced to his parents. So what do you recommend?'

Padma thought for a moment. 'We're preparing some delicious murgh makhani. It's butter chicken, a traditional Indian dish that originated in Delhi. I can make it mild or spicy, whichever you prefer. It's simply a curry made from chicken with spiced tomato and butter sauce and served with basmati rice and naan bread.'

'Sounds perfect,' said Vijay. He looked at Zeb. 'Shall we go for the mild option to begin with?'

'Yes, why not?'

Padma looked at Zeb. 'And perhaps a glass of wine while you are waiting?

'Thank you,' said Zeb. 'Maybe a Shiraz or a Sauvignon Blanc. Whatever you recommend.'

Padma looked at Vijay. 'And of course water for our dedicated teetotal surgeon.'

She hurried away and Zeb looked across the table. 'Lovely people. Clearly good friends.'

'We go back a long way. I'm pleased you've met them.'

An hour later and after a delicious meal, Vijay and Zeb were still deep in gentle conversation. 'So tell me more about your family,' said Zeb.

Vijay spoke quietly. 'Both my parents came from an educated background. I'm their only child and they are very proud and protective.'

'I can understand that,' said Zeb.

'My father and his two brothers were in business together in India. They designed and built canals for the British government in Baramati near Pune. Eventually the three brothers divided their wealth equally and came to live in England, where they opened a shop in Leeds. They live there still.'

'And they'd prefer you to have an arranged marriage?' asked Zeb.

'Yes. They've made many introductions over the last twenty years, all to no avail. None of them were right. At first I felt very guilty about it – I thought I had let my parents down.'

'And how do you feel now?' asked Zeb softly.

Vijay looked across at her above the flickering candlelight. 'I believe I have made the right decision. Everything comes to he who waits.'

Chapter Five

The Silence of Dreams

It was a bitterly cold evening as Tom and Inger walked towards reception. The first harsh frost heralded the changing season and the trees, like sentinel shadows, were stark in the moonlight. Winter was coming.

'Cold night,' said Tom as he put his arm around Inger's shoulders.

'Important to show support,' said Inger as she pulled her scarf a little tighter.

When they reached the quad, they found the cobbled pathways had been salted and the grass sparkled with frost. Before them, the art studio was a beacon of light and they hurried towards its welcome warmth. It was Friday, 16 November, the evening of Ben Laverick's photography exhibition. On the entrance door, beneath a banner that read 'The Silence of Dreams', a large poster featured the photograph of Alexandra Midwinter that Ben had taken at the concert. She was looking directly towards the lens of the camera while soft lighting from the stage lit up her face. It was a remarkable portrait of a beautiful woman.

When Tom and Inger walked in, Ben gave them a friendly wave. He was wearing a white T-shirt, tight black jeans and a black jacket with padded shoulders and turned-up cuffs. With his long hair hanging over his shoulders, he looked like a charismatic drug dealer from *Miami Vice*. He was in conversation with the Vice Chancellor, standing next to a table where two of Ben's art students were serving wine and soft drinks.

'Big crowd,' said Tom as he collected two glasses of Merlot.

'Impressive,' said Inger as she took in the exhibition before her. The walls and hessian display boards were filled with black-and-white A3 photographs mounted on stiff manila card. It was a striking collection reflecting hours of work.

Edward Chartridge, in a black woollen Crombie coat over his clerical collar, was full of bonhomie. 'Congratulations, Benjamin,' he said effusively. 'This is a first for Eboracum.' He stretched out an arm in an elaborate gesture. 'So many magnificent images.'

'Thank you, Vice Chancellor. I'm grateful to you for supporting this modest event.'

Edward smiled at the self-deprecating comment and scanned the room. 'So who are your influences in the world of photography? I'm familiar with Tim Graham, the royal family photographer – in fact I have his recent book of photographs in the Lodge.'

'Yes, his work is exceptional and he captures the Queen

so well, both at work and play. For my part, I'm a fan of Vanley Burke, who depicts the lives of the West Indian community so beautifully. Then, of course, there's Anna Fox, with her extraordinary use of flash and colour.'

'But I see you prefer black and white,' said Edward.

'Yes, it's the tonal quality that appeals to me.'

The Vice Chancellor nodded. 'Well, thank you once again, Benjamin, for the invitation and I'll let you circulate.' Edward shook his hand and returned promptly to the cosy warmth of the Lodge, a good book and a sweet sherry.

Inger spotted Rosie staring at a collection of photographs and she wandered over to join her, while Sam Greenwood gave Tom a wave from the far side of the room. He was with Owen, looking at some photographs that had been taken in the gymnasium.

'Hi, Rosie,' said Inger.

'These are brilliant,' said Rosie. 'There's a lovely one of you conducting.'

Before them was a series of images depicting last month's classical concert. In particular, Ben had captured members of the orchestra during moments of concentration. Suddenly he was standing beside them. 'Thanks for coming,' he said.

'There's a huge amount of work here, Ben,' said Inger. 'You've clearly been very busy.'

'Thanks. I'm trying to develop this medium within our courses.'

'So what cameras have you used for this exhibition?' asked Rosie. 'Everything is so sharp.'

'A couple of my favourites, a Pentax LX and a Nikon F3. It's the long lens that makes a difference. I can really zoom in on my subjects.'

Rosie looked up at the huge poster and gave a wry smile. 'Like Alexandra Midwinter.'

There was a pause as Ben leaned forward and looked into her green eyes. 'Yes,' he said. 'Exactly like that.'

'So, what's next?' asked Rosie.

Ben pondered for a moment and glanced around the room. 'I'd like to think there are lots of images here that can be used in the next prospectus and maybe when the individual departments have their open days.'

'I would definitely like these of the choir and orchestra,' said Inger. 'My students would love it if they were displayed in the music room.'

'Of course,' said Ben. 'Let me know when.'

'I've seen adverts in York for digital cameras,' said Rosie. 'What do you think about them?'

'Mixed at the moment,' said Ben thoughtfully. 'It's a fascinating time in photography. I've been brought up with film, relying on chemically developed, light-sensitive emulsions. Now we're moving on to digital technology. In fact, I've just bought one but it will take me some time to get used to it.' He looked around at the milling crowd. 'Anyway, I'll leave you to it. Thanks again for your support,' and he walked over to talk to Zeb, who had just picked up two glasses of wine.

'He's a charmer,' said Inger. 'Did you see the look he gave you?'

'Penetrating,' said Rosie with a whimsical smile. 'I felt as though I had been undressed.'

'Is that wishful thinking?' whispered Inger.

'I know what's on your mind,' said Rosie with a grin.

Zeb looked up at Ben as he approached. 'This is brilliant,' she said with a smile. 'You must be pleased.'

'Thanks, Zeb.'

'I love the natural uninhibited look of all the subjects,' she said. 'It's uni life in the raw.'

Ben grinned. 'I've tried to move away from the traditional notions of beauty. I prefer the authentic, gritty power look.' He stared down appreciatively at Zeb and then stepped back to consider her slim figure. 'In fact, Zeb, you would make the perfect model for our life-drawing classes.'

'I'm guessing I should take that as a compliment.'

'If you wish.'

'So I'm raw and gritty, am I?'

'Much more than that. You have fire in your soul.'

'Thanks, Ben, I'm sure my partner would agree.' She smiled, held up the two glasses of wine and returned to Victor on the other side of the room.

'I didn't know he'd taken these,' said Owen. 'I remember him calling in the gym for a few minutes but I was busy.'

'These ones with the trampoline are good,' said Sam. There was a series of shots of a young gymnast doing a somersault.

'You look intense,' said Tom.

'I was shitting bricks in case the poor sod got it wrong,' said Owen. 'It's a long way down from there.'

'So, what do you think?' asked Sam. 'They're all high-quality photographs.'

'Too arty-farty for me,' said Owen, shaking his head. 'And if that big picture of Alexandra Midwinter doesn't tell you something, then you Mancunians are definitely missing something.'

'Are you saying they're more than friends?' asked Tom.

'Give us a break, Englishman. Look at the bloody photo. It's saying, *Come to bed, your place or mine?*'

'Well, good luck to him, I say,' said Sam. 'As long as he doesn't make a move on Rosie it's fine.'

'I wouldn't put it past him,' said Tom.

Sam shook his head and flexed his shoulders. 'It won't happen. He knows where I would stick his long lens.'

'Painful,' said Tom.

'Too bloody right,' added Owen with a grin.

An eager Richard Head approached Ben. He wiped his spectacles on his Aran jumper and looked up excitedly at the Head of Art. 'One of my students mentioned you had a new digital camera.'

'Yes, a Dycam Model 1. I'm just getting used to it. It can connect directly to my PC for downloads.'

'So what personal computer have you got?'

'An Apple Macintosh portable.'

'I know it. Felicity has got one. She loves it.'

'Felicity?'

'My fiancée. She's a science lecturer in Sheffield.'

'Must be good to have a partner with shared interests.'

'Yes,' said Richard. 'Science dominates our lives.' Ben smiled; he could see why Richard was animated. 'We're both particularly excited about Tim Berners Lee and his World Wide Web. Felicity said it's one of the most important technologies of all time.' His eyes were bright with excitement. 'It means we can use hypertext for automated information-sharing between scientists across the world.'

Ben nodded. 'And between ordinary mortals like me. Eventful times, Richard.'

'Quite right, Ben. A decade of digital determination is ahead of us. Anyway, well done.' He shook hands and wandered off to stare myopically at the vast array of images.

Ben homed in on Victor and Zeb. They were sipping wine and staring at a selection of photographs depicting students trudging to lectures and leaning against walls while smoking cigarettes.

'So what's your verdict?' asked Ben.

'It seems a long way from the posed Hollywood glamour shots when I was a student,' said Victor. 'You've definitely captured real life.'

'I agree,' said Zeb. 'So what do you call this approach?'

Ben smiled. 'It's generally known as "grunge aesthetic".'

'Interesting,' said Zeb. 'What's that?'

'It simply challenges the traditional notions of beauty,' said Ben. 'I try to capture what is really around us in the streets, on the campus, in those intimate moments that are not often shared.'

Victor was always challenging. 'Tell me, Ben ... My partner is a huge fan of Sunil Gupta. What's your view of his work?'

Ben was aware of Victor's partner and had met him at various functions. 'Tell Pat he's one of my icons.' He glanced at Zeb. 'He uses photography to respond to the injustices suffered by gay men.'

'Quite so,' said Victor.

'Then he is to be congratulated,' said Zeb. 'I'll check out his work.'

'Thanks for your support this evening,' said Ben. 'I know how busy you are,' and he continued to circulate.

'Well, Victor, we've done our bit,' said Zeb, 'and, sadly, I'm knackered. How about you?'

'Likewise. The weekend beckons.'

'And I've got Vijay's parents calling in tomorrow.'

'Good luck with that. I'm sure it will be fine. Vijay will be a sensitive host.'

Zeb smiled through gritted teeth. 'And thank goodness Ben won't be there to record it.'

They walked out into the darkness.

Early on Saturday morning, Tom was in his cottage in Haxby and packing his books into boxes. These were his most precious possessions. For him a life without books was unthinkable. They were friends that marked the passing of the years. He picked up J. R. R. Tolkien's *The Fellowship of the Ring*. It had been an unexpected gift from Henry Oakenshott, the former Head of the Faculty of Education. Sadly, Henry had passed away and the formidable Edna Wallop had taken his place. He opened the novel and stared fondly at the dedication written in neat, cursive handwriting. It read:

To Frodo from Gandalf.
Enjoy your journey, Tom.
With best wishes,
Henry Oakenshott, September 1988

He sighed and ran his fingers over the page. Henry had been a kind and caring man and Tom wished he could have known him for longer. In the meantime, he would remember his words and enjoy the journey. It was the beginning of a new adventure and by the end of the month he would be living with Inger. His portable radio was on the worktop and Phil Collins was singing 'One More Night', which seemed appropriate.

Three miles away in Easingwold the mood was calm. Victor was enjoying listening to Radio 3. There had been a brief discussion concerning the former Prime Minister, Edward Heath, and his recent visit to Baghdad. He had returned with thirty-three freed hostages with a promise from Saddam Hussein to release a further thirty. However, it was when Delius's *Song of the High Hills* was introduced that Victor truly relaxed. He sat back with a sigh. He found the music as soothing as his cup of camomile tea.

Pat came in from the kitchen to serve some French toast along with a bacon, cheese and onion omlette. As he was dividing it in half he noted, 'You look thoughtful.'

'Yes. Owen Llewellyn has been to see me on a couple of occasions about off-site student accommodation. For some of his students it sounded to be very poor. There was also a broad hint in the recent *Echo* that Gideon Chalk may well be lining his pockets as well as balancing the university's books.'

'So what are you going to do about it?'

'I need to adumbrate the finer points.'

'Oh, Victor,' said Pat with a smile. 'I do love your use of language even when I've no idea what you mean.'

'It's from the Latin "ad" meaning "to" and "umbrare" meaning "cast a shadow".'

'So now I know,' said Pat with a gentle hint of sarcasm. 'On the other hand you could have said you were intending to make sure that dreadful man got his just desserts.'

Victor smiled and picked up his knife and fork. 'I untie a knot with slow teasing, Patrick. More haste, less speed.'

Pat smiled. Victor only called him Patrick when he was deadly serious.

In Crayke village Zeb was dashing around her kitchen while, on Radio 1, Bruce Springsteen was belting out 'Dancing In The Dark'. Vijay came in and turned down the volume. 'Good news,' he said. 'I've just spoken to Padma and she's coming to give you a hand with lunch. She's going to say you've asked for training in Indian cuisine.'

Zeb leaned against the worktop and gave a great sigh. 'Thank God,' she muttered.

'Which one?' said Vijay with a smile. 'Brahma, the Creator, Vishnu, the Preserver, or Shiva, the Destroyer?'

'I don't care but Vishnu sounds promising to help preserve my sanity.'

He wrapped his arms around her. 'Go out the back and have a cigarette. I know you want one. Then leave the rest to me. My parents won't be here for three hours and by then Padma will have provided us with a delicious lunch.'

Zeb reached up and gave him a kiss. 'You're just perfect,' she said.

'And that's what I shall be telling my mother about you,' he called after her as she grabbed her handbag and hurried out.

At ten o'clock, Tom locked up his cottage and walked out to his car with the whisper of leaves whirling around his feet. On this iron-grey morning the trees were spectres against a gun-metal sky and a cloak of mist covered the frozen land. It was the time of the dying of the light and the smell of woodsmoke hung in the air. Tom scraped ice from his windscreen and blew on his key before unlocking the driver's door.

When he arrived outside Inger's she was in the hallway ready for him. She was wearing her best winter coat with a warm scarf, furry boots and a woollen hat.

'You look great,' he said. 'Perfect for a cold day.'

'Thanks,' said Inger. 'I was hoping to call in at the market. It's always fun browsing the stalls on a Saturday morning.'

After parking in the university car park they walked up Gillygate, past the Minster and into York city centre. They strolled across King's Square and the entrance to the Shambles, with its queues of sightseers, and wandered into the busy market. Next to a stall labelled 'Arnie Wainwright's Pork Pies' was Vinyl Pete's Records, where shoppers were browsing the huge selection of records. On a stepladder was a loudspeaker playing Belinda Carlisle's '(We Want) The Same Thing' and Tom and Inger shared a smile.

The shoppers were singing along while Vinyl Pete was doing a roaring trade. With his long hair hanging over the collar of his sheepskin coat and a roll-up cigarette hanging from his lips, he cut a distinctive figure.

'Come on,' shouted Vinyl Pete, 'let's be 'avin' you. Ah've got 'em all. Whitney 'Ouston, Berlin, 'Appy Mondays, Status Quo an', o' course, Kylie. No fancy London prices 'ere.'

Suddenly there was a cheerful call from the far side of the stall. 'Hi, Tom, hi, Inger,' and Tom spotted his English One students Becky Salter and Jane Granger and waved back. This had become the two inseparable friends' favourite shopping trip each week. After much deliberation Becky had just bought A-Ha's 'Crying In The Rain' and Jane had finally decided upon 'Close To Me' by the Cure.

Meanwhile, Inger rummaged through a box and held up the best-selling classical album *In Concert*, featuring José Carreras, Plácido Domingo and Luciano Pavarotti.

'Bit o' classical for the beautiful blonde lady,' announced Vinyl Pete in a loud voice as he slipped the record into a brown paper bag and Inger paid. 'An' is there anything else y'fancy, darlin'?'

Inger smiled, took Tom by the hand and walked on.

Becky Salter and Jane Granger headed for the mobile coffee shop opposite Vinyl Pete's stall.

'Hi, girls,' said a nineteen-year-old man with a fierce crew cut and rampant teenage acne. 'Fancy a coffee?'

'Maybe,' said Becky.

Jane tugged her sleeve and gave a slight shake of the head.

'Come on,' he said eagerly. 'It's cold out here.'

Becky looked at Jane, who shrugged her shoulders. 'Nothing ventured, nothing gained,' she said quietly.

Minutes later they were sharing a plastic table and drinking frothy coffee while the young man was trying desperately to impress.

'Ah'm Raymond Brightside, a trainee copper.'

'I'm Becky and this is my friend, Jane.'

Raymond quickly worked out he had the better chance with Becky. 'D'you fancy going to the Odeon Cinema to watch *Back to the Future Part III*?'

Becky shook her head. 'Already seen it,' she said.

'And so have I,' added Jane.

Raymond moved his chair closer to Becky. He had no interest in Jane. 'Ah've jus' passed an exam,' he said proudly.

'Really?' said Jane, who had equally quickly worked out Raymond had no 'bright side'.

'What's that?' asked Becky.

'It's summat called a GENKA.'

'Genka?' said Becky and Jane simultaneously.

Raymond nodded eagerly. 'Gender Neutrality an' Knowledge Awareness,' he announced proudly.

'And what's it about?' asked Becky.

Raymond thought for a moment. He needed to answer this carefully. Unfortunately, his blinkered life had been fashioned by his parents in Chapeltown, Leeds. They were both racist bigots and he had accepted their teachings without question. When the course was over and he had brought back his GENKA certificate, he realized that would have to change.

'It means ah'm now a politically correct copper an' ah've got a certificate t'prove it.'

'Well done,' said Becky.

'It sounds as if it has changed your life,' said Jane, seeking to offer to encouragement.

'So mebbe in future we could go out for a curry?' he asked hopefully.

Becky looked at her watch. 'What time are we meeting our boyfriends?'

'About now,' said Jane quickly and they left in haste.

'Boyfriends?' said Becky.

'We can live in hope, I suppose,' said Jane with a grin. 'It's still early days.'

Lunchtime in Zeb's converted barn was going well. Zeb and Padma were in the kitchen making hot rotis. As each one puffed up, Zeb, in an elegant sari, carried them to the dining area and served Vijay and his father. Thanks to Padma the lunch went smoothly.

Vijay's mother, Prem, was interested in Zeb's kitchen. 'Beautifully clean,' she said while admiring the sparkling surfaces that Zeb had polished the previous day, taking care to remove every ashtray. 'My son is very particular about hygiene, with him being an eminent surgeon.'

'But of course,' responded Zeb with a smile.

'Zeb is a wonderful student of Indian cooking,' said Padma.

'But still a beginner,' said Zeb.

Prem smiled but seemed unconvinced.

In the dining room, Vijay was talking to his father: Atul was a perceptive man. 'So, I can see this woman is special to you,' he said.

'Very,' said Vijay.

'It's your mother you have to convince that she is suitable.'

'I know that,' said Vijay.

'You've refused so many,' said Atul.

'This is different, Father,' he said. 'I want your blessing, of course. Please take your time. I know this is very sudden for you. Before the end of the year I should like you to come back and visit again – and bring my aunties, Usha and Krisma.'

'I see,' said Atul. 'A wise decision . . . and a brave one.'

'Talk to my mother. Tell her how I feel. The way forward is clear. You either lose your son or you keep your son and gain a daughter. This is the woman I love.'

Atul sat back in his chair. He knew when to make his feelings known and when to be silent. Eventually the three women brought in the food. There was mixed vegetable paratha and bowls of aloo gobi and aloo palak that looked appetizing. Zeb had played safe for the sweet course with a tiramisu from the supermarket. The conversation was convivial, polite and free-flowing. Vijay was the perfect host while his parents remained thoughtful.

*

Back in the centre of York, in a riverside apartment, Ben Laverick was in his kitchen and spooning coffee into his cafetière. He had been awake most of the night and by early afternoon the woman in his bed had dozed off once again.

In the silence of his bedroom, Alexandra Midwinter was dreaming.

Chapter Six

The Eighth Commandment

His name was Theodore Drinkwater and he was almost
a thief.

It was a coincidence that Inger happened to be in the
same antique bookshop in the city centre. She had seen an
ancient copy of *Little Dorrit*, the Charles Dickens classic,
in the window of Walter Popple's Book Emporium. The
book had an indigo cover with gold block lettering and
she knew it would make the perfect Christmas gift for
Tom. It was Saturday, 1 December, a bitterly cold morning, and Inger was taking advantage of some free time
while Tom was busy packing the last of his books before
finally moving into her apartment that afternoon. The bell
above the door rang as she walked in and a grey-haired,
bespectacled man behind the counter looked up from his
mug of tea and gave her a gentle smile. 'Good afternoon
and welcome,' he said.

'I'm interested in the copy of *Little Dorrit* in the

window,' said Inger, 'but would like to have a look around first if I may.'

'Of course,' he said. 'It's a bit of a maze but let me know if you require any assistance.'

Inger decided to seek out the music section and was greeted by a warren of tall bookshelves. After meandering through the narrow walkways she came across a veritable treasure trove of music manuscripts. She picked up William Stickles *TriChord Popular Music Selection* along with Johnny Mercer and Henry Mancini's 'Moon River'. Everything was quiet and motes of dust hovered in the soft light. Inger assumed she was the only customer until she heard a sound of shuffling footsteps. Almost out of sight was a crouching figure holding a book. She saw him slip it into his zip-up bomber jacket and stand up. There was surprise on his face when he caught sight of Inger and he hurried to leave the shop.

Once again, the bell rang and Inger followed him to the door. 'Back in a moment,' she said, and the grey-haired owner gave a beatific smile.

Outside on the pavement Inger called out, 'Wait there, please. It's Theo, isn't it?'

The young man stopped, eyes wide and clearly alarmed. Tall and slim with a ruddy complexion, he had black hair with a severe fringe.

'You're one of Richard's students,' she said. 'Year One science . . . and I've seen you in the chapel choir.'

'Yes,' he replied hesitantly.

Inger stared at him almost in disbelief. 'I saw you take a book and hide it under your jacket. I want you to pay for it or replace it on the shelf.'

'Sorry,' he said quietly. He took a deep breath and walked back into the shop.

Inger followed him to a bookshelf labelled 'Classic Fiction'.

Theo unzipped his jacket, took out a 1950s hardback copy of *Little Women* and replaced it on the shelf.

'I want you to wait for me by the counter,' said Inger firmly.

'Please don't tell him,' said Theo desperately.

Inger frowned and gave an imperceptible shake of her head. 'Not yet.'

They both stood by the counter as Inger smiled at the owner. 'I'll take the copy of *Little Dorrit*, please.'

'An excellent choice,' said Mr Popple. 'Let me wrap it for you.'

When they left the shop Inger looked at the forlorn figure before her. 'We need to talk,' she said. 'There's a coffee shop near St William's College. We'll go there.'

Back in Haxby village Tom was in his kitchen, staring at an empty fridge. With a sigh he pulled on his scarf and duffel coat and walked outside. He shivered as he hurried across the road to the supermarket. The village was gripped in an iron fist and a severe frost covered the streets and pavements.

Minutes later he was standing at the checkout with a few basic provisions. Behind him in the queue was a young woman and he stared at the contents of her trolley. The oracle that was Owen Llewellyn had once told him you could tell a lot about a person by assessing the contents of their trolley. He saw green, yellow and red peppers, tomatoes, carrots, potatoes and onions, along with various tins of soup. Tom stared down at his trolley and the two bottles of Merlot, block of cheese, carton of milk and packet of Scott's Porage Oats. He smiled and reflected that, in the past, he had always hidden a packet of Liquorice Allsorts under an iceberg lettuce, or a packet of chocolate digestives beneath a thick-sliced loaf. *After all*, he thought, *you never know who you might bump into*. Today, however, shopping was different. Later that day he would finally be moving into Inger's apartment with the last of his possessions. He smiled as he thought of sitting by Inger's fireside with a glass of wine. When he walked back into his cottage he picked up a broom and wondered where to start.

Inger put two cups of coffee on the table and sat down opposite a forlorn Theo. 'So, what on earth made you do that?' she said. 'It's stealing!'

He sipped his coffee. 'I needed the money,' he said quietly.

'Why?'

He shook his head. 'It's difficult.'

'Tell me.'

'I'm not sure . . . It's complicated.'

'If you don't explain yourself,' said Inger, 'I'll have to take this further.'

Theo looked up from his coffee. 'There's this man in Leeds, Ricky Skinner,' he mumbled. 'Last time I visited my sister he was in the street outside with some of his mates. He told me he could keep Cora supplied if I joined his gang. They were stealing everything from cars to old ladies' purses. He told me to collect books and memorabilia . . . said York was perfect.'

'Collect? You mean *steal*.'

'Well . . . yes.'

Inger was surprised. 'So it's not just books you're intending to steal.'

He shook his head. 'He wants books, medals, snuff boxes, lockets, anything that fits in my jacket. York is full of shops that sell this sort of thing. Then I have to deliver the stuff to my sister in Leeds and he collects and takes it down to London and sells it there.'

'Who is this man?'

He shook his head. 'No idea. It's not for me. It's to help her. I don't see any of the money.'

'I still don't understand,' said Inger. 'How can stealing help your sister?'

'She has a medical condition. He can help her get what she needs.'

'And what does she need?'

There was a pause and he stared down at his coffee again, 'Cannabis,' he murmured quietly. 'It's cannabis.'

Tom was piling the last of his belongings on the kitchen floor of his cottage when he saw Sam's Citroën pulling up outside. Sam and Rosie had offered to help with his removal to Inger's and he welcomed them with a smile.

'Moving day,' said Rosie as she stepped inside and surveyed the scene. There was a pile of books, a cardboard filing box, a battered old guitar and what looked like a pillowcase of dirty washing. On the worktop were cleaning materials and a bag of shopping.

'So what shall we do?' asked Sam.

Tom looked at the chaos around him. 'It's just a final clean-up and then load what's left. I think I'm almost there.'

Rosie shook her head in dismay and grabbed a cloth and a bathroom spray. 'I'll start upstairs,' she said and looked at Sam. 'You load up all this stuff, then we can mop the floor.' The two men stared at each other, relieved that someone had taken charge.

Finally the property was clean and empty. The cars were loaded up and Tom locked the door and posted the keys through the letterbox. Then he took a final look at the cottage, climbed in his car and set off for York.

Later on, Tom, Inger, Sam and Rosie gathered around Inger's kitchen table. After unloading Tom's belongings, Inger had prepared sandwiches and hot drinks.

'Did you say cannabis?' asked Tom.

'Yes,' said Inger. She looked at Sam. 'It was Theo, one of your first years. He was full of remorse when I left him. It's how we handle this that's important.'

'His sister needs help,' said Rosie. 'Did he say why she needs it?'

'Yes,' said Inger. 'Apparently she's in chronic pain, with anxiety and depression. Both she and Theo have had a difficult upbringing. Apparently their early life was fine. They lived in Herefordshire in a village called Cusop Dingle. Then they moved to Leeds, where their father was a vicar. Sadly, he and his wife were killed in a road accident. As young children Theo and his sister finished up in the care system in a series of really bad places. They've had a tough time. His sister is called Cora. I've got her address.'

'A sad story,' said Sam.

'Cannabis is dangerous, isn't it?' asked Rosie. 'Aren't there lots of problems and side effects?

'It's powerful stuff,' said Sam.

'And illegal,' said Tom.

Sam looked thoughtful. 'I can understand the need. It activates receptors in the brain and there's a reaction in the nerves that regulate pain.'

'You can see why Theo is desperate,' said Inger. 'He needs to help his sister.'

'Surely it's a harmful drug,' said Rosie. 'I just don't know enough about it.'

'There's definitely harm attached,' said Sam. 'It can irritate the lungs and cause respiratory problems.' He had drifted into his science mode. 'Heart rate often elevates. Also, motor skills and coordination can be affected, leading to clumsiness. It varies from one individual to another.'

'We need to stop the supplier,' said Inger. 'It's a dealer called Skinner.'

'How?' said Rosie.

'Maybe we need to persuade him,' said Tom with feeling.

Inger looked alarmed and stared at Tom with concern. 'That sounds dangerous.'

Tom shook his head. 'I'll take Owen with me.'

'No, you won't,' said Inger. 'That's just foolhardy.'

'Hold on,' said Sam suddenly. 'Let's think this through. My sister is a nurse in Leeds. She's brilliant and I know she would help. Let me talk to her about it first. I'll ring her tonight.'

'Sounds sensible,' said Rosie.

'And Theo is in the chapel choir,' said Inger. 'I could call into the morning service tomorrow, then he would know we're keen to help.'

'I'll come with you,' said Rosie.

The conversation moved on and soon they relaxed with their refreshments. It was mid afternoon before Sam and Rosie got up to leave.

'So, we'll all meet up again tomorrow night at Victor's,' said Rosie. 'Zeb said it was just a soirée for a few staff.'

'Kicks off around seven,' said Sam.

Inger nodded. 'We could pick you up.'

'Yes, please,' said Sam.

Rosie smiled and gave Inger a hug.

'See you tomorrow morning in reception,' said Inger. 'Before the chapel service.'

'I'll be there,' said Rosie. She glanced around the apartment. 'And good luck.' She leaned forward and added quietly, 'I see he brought a bag of washing.'

Inger returned the knowing look. 'Yes, I noticed.'

Soon Tom and Inger were unpacking boxes of books. The main problem was finding space for them. There were so many. After filling the bookcases, Inger created a long line of books on the pine sideboard beneath her print of Edouard Manet's *Bar at the Folies-Bergère*. Finally, a couple of boxes were returned to Tom's car to be taken to Eboracum and added to the bookcases in his study.

By five o'clock, Tom's meagre collection of clothes had

found space in Inger's wardrobe and on the pegs in the hallway. Then they both settled down in the lounge with a bowl of soup and crusty bread and Inger switched on the television to watch the news. These were eventful times. Margaret Thatcher's reign was over. She had resigned a week ago with a tearful farewell to Downing Street. Having led the government for over eleven years she was the longest-serving prime minister of the twentieth century. She had been succeeded by John Major after he had defeated Douglas Hurd and Michael Heseltine. Then a map of the Channel Tunnel appeared on the screen. Workers from the UK and France had met forty metres beneath the English Channel, the first land connection between the UK and mainland Europe for thousands of years.

'I wonder how they did that and didn't miss each other,' mused Tom.

Then, on a very different note, the reporter announced that a verger at Exeter Cathedral had pocketed £50,000 from collections and public gifts over a seven-year period. He claimed he had felt undervalued with his £7,500 annual salary and this led him to purchase expensive cars and luxury cruises. At least there was still £11,000 in the cathedral safe when he was finally caught.

'That reminds me,' said Inger. 'I need some coins for the chapel collection tomorrow morning.'

Tom smiled. 'I don't think the Vice Chancellor will be going on luxury cruises.'

Then Inger switched over to BBC Two to watch a classical concert for AIDS relief while Tom took the soup bowls back to the kitchen and washed up. He settled down once again on the sofa as Inger flicked through the channels.

It was a choice of *Challenge Anneka* on BBC One, with Anneka Rice solving adventurous problems in the Scilly Isles, or tuning in to Channel 4 to watch an epic six-man dog-sled journey across Antartica. They agreed the husky dogs were a slight favourite, and Inger opened a bottle of wine.

It was late before they switched the television off and Inger flicked through her records and selected Lloyd Webber's *The Premier Collection*. Last Christmas she had bought a Sony Company Midi Hi-Fi System for £199.99. It had proved a good buy and they relaxed together while listening to the *Evita* classic 'Don't Cry For Me Argentina'. Finally they walked hand in hand into the bedroom.

'A new beginning,' said Tom softly and kissed her gently.

'That's right,' said Inger with a smile, 'and I'll show you how to work the washing machine in the morning.'

They awoke on Sunday morning to a frozen world of ice, with flakes of snow pattering against the windowpanes like winter confetti. Inger prepared two bowls of warming Scott's Porage Oats with a spoonful of honey. She left Tom to discover the mysteries of the washing machine before walking out to her Mini.

Snow had fallen overnight and the Knavesmire was covered in a white shroud that curved gracefully to the distant trees. Dank piles of leaf mould had formed beneath their gnarled trunks while small creatures of the woodland were sheltering beneath the brittle hedgerows. Inger parked in the university car park and headed carefully for reception: the winding pathway was a silver ribbon of ice. Rosie was there, hidden under a warm coat, scarf and woolly hat. Together they walked through the quad and round the back of the Lodge to the university chapel.

They followed a few students and members of staff under the Norman archway and into the sanctuary of this beautiful church. They were welcomed by John Wright, a final-year student, one of Victor's protégés and the photographer for the *Echo*. He gave them a hymn book and a service sheet and they sat down on one of the back pews.

'It really is a special place,' whispered Inger as they took in the scene. Tall candles flickered by the pulpit and gave a fiery glow to the altar rail of Victorian pine. Morning light illuminated the stained glass in the east window and created a kaleidoscope of flickering patterns on the stone floor.

Suddenly the Vice Chancellor was beside them. 'Good morning, Dr Larson, Dr Tremaine,' he said in a gentle voice, 'and welcome to our haven of peace in a busy world.'

'Good morning, Vice Chancellor,' said Rosie.

Inger smiled up at Edward in his clerical collar, white surplice and full-length cope. Around his neck there was a white stole beautifully stitched with intricate gold crosses. 'Good morning,' she said. 'I've heard you have a particularly good choir. Some of my students are involved and they tell me the music lifts the spirits.'

'And so it does,' he said. 'Enjoy the service.' He walked away towards the two semicircular arches on the north side of the nave to light the final candles. A sombre Theo Drinkwater approached them. He was wearing a magenta choir robe over his white Aran jumper and blue jeans. 'Hello,' he said and looked cautiously at Inger. 'Thanks for yesterday.'

Inger smiled up at him. 'You're not alone, Theo. We're here to support you.'

'And we've a few ideas that might help your sister,' said Rosie.

Theo's eyes widened in surprise.

'Let's talk after the service,' said Inger. 'Meet us in reception.'

Theo nodded and returned thoughtfully to the choir stalls.

Canon Edward mounted the steps to the pulpit and welcomed the congregation. He said they were moving towards the festival of Christmas and thanked the choir for their dedication. Then he glanced down at the *Book of Common Worship* and in sonorous tones recited, 'The grace of our Lord Jesus Christ, the love of God and the fellowship of the Holy Spirit be with you all.'

The congregation responded with 'And also with you' while Inger sat back to listen to the choir; there were many familiar faces. Soon everyone stood for the first hymn. As they sang the final verse, Canon Edward sat down while Theo moved silently towards the pulpit and Inger and Rosie realized he was about to read the first lesson. As he approached the lectern, only the ticking of the old church clock, installed in 1912 to commemorate the coronation of George V, could be heard. He stared down at the chapel

Bible and then looked up and spoke clearly: 'This morning's reading is from the Book of Ephesians, chapter four, beginning at verse twenty-eight.' Inger noticed Canon Edward lean forward to check his service sheet and then sit back, looking puzzled.

Theo glanced up at Inger and Rosie, gave an imperceptible nod and began to read out loud in a clear voice. 'He who steals must steal no longer; but rather he must labour, performing with his own hands what is good, so that he will have something to share with one who has need.'

Inger and Rosie shared a common understanding as he said these words.

At the end of the reading he said, 'This is the Word of the Lord,' and the congregation responded with 'Thanks be to God.' When he returned to the choir stalls he bowed his head in prayer.

After the service, Inger and Rosie waited in reception until Theo arrived, looking both sad and curious. 'Have you spoken to your sister?' asked Inger.

'Yes,' said Theo. 'She was furious. Told me I was risking my career. She didn't know the drugs guy had been in touch.'

'Your sister is right,' said Inger. 'Stealing will simply make the matter worse. We need to find another way to help her.'

'Dr Greenwood . . . Sam came up with an idea,' said Rosie. 'He has a sister in Leeds who is a nurse. He told me she's going to call in to speak to Cora.'

Theo looked desperate. 'But it's only the cannabis that takes away the pain.'

'There may be other ways,' said Inger. 'Don't lose hope. We'll talk again.'

'When is your next lecture with Sam?' asked Rosie.

'Tomorrow at eleven.'

'Then we'll see if there's any news,' said Inger. 'And, by the way, well read this morning, and the singing was excellent.'

'I love it,' said Theo. 'I was once a choirboy in my dad's church.' He sighed deeply. 'But that seems a lifetime ago now.'

'Stay strong,' said Rosie.

'I'll try,' he said quietly. 'And thanks.'

On Sunday evening staff gathered in Victor and Pat's spacious open-plan art deco kitchen in Easingwold. Victor knew these relaxing wine and nibbles events on occasional weekends helped to boost staff morale. It was also an opportunity for Pat to show off some of his latest culinary creations. Displayed on the worktop were potato wedges, parsnip and pear fritters, caramelized clementine possets, cranberry and pistachio filo cups, mincemeat flapjacks and a magnificent cheeseboard. It was a feast, while in the background Inger was playing a few mellow jazz classics on an old upright piano.

The room hummed with conversation. Zeb, Victor and Pat were discussing arrangements for a staff night out on the last day of term to Pat's Music Night at the Joseph Rowntree Theatre. Zeb, in her Jane Fonda leggings and a *Fame* sweatshirt, was enthusiastic. 'Let's make a group booking,' she said, 'and I'll spread the word tomorrow.'

By the patio doors that led out to Pat's art studio, Rosie was telling Richard Head that a literary agent had agreed to represent her after reading her Oscar Wilde biography. 'I'm so excited,' said Rosie. 'It would be wonderful to be published.'

'I agree,' said Richard, while twiddling his lanyard. 'Felicity and I have begun a manuscript entitled *Cosmic Capers*. She picked the title. Perhaps you could give me your agent's contact details.'

'I'm not sure that's the right genre for her,' said Rosie apologetically.

Meanwhile, Sam was sharing the news with Tom and Owen about Theo and Cora Drinkwater. 'My sister, Julie, has met up with her today and knows a way forward.'

'That's great,' said Tom.

'So what's next?' asked Owen.

'There are groups she can get involved with,' said Sam. 'Julie's used to this stuff. It's a long, slow road to recovery but she'll get there.'

'So is it just cannabis?' asked Owen. 'No cocaine or anything?'

Sam nodded. 'That's right.'

'I remember marijuana being available in my old school in Wales,' said Owen. 'You just had to know the right people.'

'A couple of years before I came here the issue of drug-taking was big on TV,' said Tom. 'Back in 1986 I remember the cast of the teen TV soap *Grange Hill* released a song titled "Just Say No". It reached number five in the charts.'

'Don't remember that,' said Owen.

'There was a character called Zammo McGuire,' said Tom. 'He'd become addicted to heroin.'

'I remember,' said Sam. 'It was all the rage. Kids in our street in Manchester were wearing Wham T-shirts with "Choose Life" on the front and going around singing George Michael songs.'

By mid-evening, Pat was serving up coffee in mugs featuring Van Gogh's *Starry Night* and Zeb was rounding up the troops, reminding everyone they had work tomorrow. It was a tired but happy group that finally ventured out into the freezing cold beneath a blizzard of stars.

On Monday morning the Vice Chancellor was standing in reception talking to Perkins when Rosie walked in. 'Good morning, Rosemary,' said Edward. 'It was good to see you and Dr Larson in chapel yesterday.'

'A wonderful experience,' said Rosie. 'I must attend more often.'

Edward beamed with delight. 'We're proud of our chapel services,' he said with enthusiasm. 'They go like clockwork.' Then he paused and looked thoughtful. 'Except, perhaps, for yesterday, of course.'

'What do you mean?' asked Rosie.

'Just thinking of young Drinkwater, a bright and willing young man with a lovely tenor voice. Strange he changed the first reading.'

'Really?' said Inger.

'Yes,' said Edward. 'It was supposed to be the first of our Christmas readings. I've no idea why at the last minute he chose the eighth commandment . . .'

Chapter Seven

Owls in the Moss

It was Friday, 14 December, and the last day of term had finally arrived. Inger had prepared Tom's favourite winter-warmer breakfast: namely Scott's Porage Oats with honey and chopped banana. She was in the hallway on the telephone talking to her brother in Norway. Andreas had called her before he left for a rehearsal with the Oslo Philharmonic Orchestra.

'*Hva er dine planer for julen?*' he asked.

'Plans for Christmas?' said Inger. 'Yes, we're coming to you next week but spending Christmas Day with Tom's parents.'

'That's good,' said Andreas, slipping neatly back into English. 'Then maybe you can confirm what you're doing about the wedding. Our dear parents talk of nothing else. It's becoming tiresome.'

'Don't worry. I'll contact them. We've only just confirmed the date. It's Saturday, the twenty-third of March, the beginning of our Easter holiday, in a register office here in York. There was a cancellation so the date was free.'

'Ah . . . so not in a church. Good luck telling them that.'

'It will be fine. I'll explain it to them.'

'I'm really pleased for you, little sister. I'll tell Annika. I'm meeting her for a coffee later. We'll get it in the diary. She will be so excited.'

Inger smiled. 'Give her my love.' She knew her brother was fortunate to have such a creative and dynamic partner.

'Will do,' said Andreas. 'And, yes, great news.'

Inger glanced at her wristwatch. 'Must go. Busy day ahead.'

'Same here. Rehearsals can't wait. So, bye for now.'

Inger replaced the receiver and walked back into the kitchen, where Tom was washing his cereal bowl. He looked up and smiled. 'I heard that you told him the date.'

'He's delighted . . . just not sure about my parents, but we can deal with that next week.' She checked the time again. 'We had better get going. I've got reports to complete for Victor, plus my choir is organizing a buffet lunch in the music room.'

'And it's Pat's Music Night this evening,' said Tom as he grabbed his coat and scarf. 'So, let's go.'

They stepped outside, where a white shroud of a billion snowflakes covered the land. The previous week the UK had ground to a halt after heavy snow. Electricity supplies had been cut and the army had been called out to restore power. Happily, life was returning to normal and an eventful day lay ahead.

*

Back in Easingwold, Victor and Pat had finished sharing a cafetière of coffee.

'Time to go,' said Victor. 'Is there anything you need for tonight?'

'I think we're fine,' said Pat as he collected his programme for the evening. 'It's a full house. All three hundred and sixty-five tickets have been sold and your staff party have got prime seats in the dress circle.'

'That's wonderful,' said Victor.

'Also, there's a fairly informal after-show party with wine and nibbles. It should be lively. There're a dozen singers in the ensemble, plus the orchestra, and it's up to you if you want some of your colleagues to stay on. Everyone is welcome.'

'Fine,' said Victor. 'I'll spread the word. Just let me know if you need anything. I'll be coming straight from work at around seven.'

'Thanks,' said Pat. 'Wish me luck.'

Victor smiled and gave him a hug. He knew how important this was for him as director of performance. 'It will be a triumph as always,' he said as he put on his warmest coat and walked out into the bitter cold.

Pat stood in the doorway and shivered as he watched Victor drive away while reflecting how fortunate he was to share his life with this generous and brilliant academic.

Zeb, who now – finally – owned a car of her own, was driving into the university car park. It was a second-hand two-door Austin Metro. Low slung and with a sporty stripe down each side, it had appealed to her immediately and the car salesman in York had given her a good deal, even after she refused his offer of a night out on the town. Vijay had left earlier for the hospital. He had finally organized a family party for a couple of days before Christmas. The guest list included his fiercesome aunties, who were destined to pass judgement on the love of his life. However, it no longer held any fears for Zeb. She was confident that her competence in Indian cuisine would pass the test.

As she approached reception, she found Perkins outside sprinkling salt on the frozen cobbles. He glanced up. 'Good morning, Dr Peacock. A bit parky this morning.'

'Morning, Perkins,' said Zeb, looking down at the bag of salt. 'That's very thoughtful. What would we do without you?'

He smiled and glanced back at the car park. 'Are you pleased with your new car?'

'It's perfect,' said Zeb.

Perkins grinned. 'It looks sleek and racy.'

'That's the problem with men,' she said. 'I always know what they're thinking.' Then, unexpectedly, she gave him a peck on the cheek and strode confidently towards the quad.

The astonished head porter walked back to his desk with a smile on his face. *That doctor is clearly having an effect,* he thought.

Tom and Inger had climbed the stairs to Cloisters corridor. 'See you later,' said Tom as Inger opened the door to her study.

'Essays to mark,' said Inger. 'Plus I'm going to spread the word about our wedding date, starting with Victor.'

'And I'll talk to Owen.'

Inger smiled. 'Good luck.'

Tom carried on down the corridor and opened the door to Room 7. Owen was at his desk and the Welshman was not in a good mood. 'Bloody reports,' he muttered. 'I'm using the same sentences again and again.' He looked up appealingly. 'I could do with you coming up with a list of one-liners I can use.'

'OK, happy to help.'

'I bet you've done yours, haven't you?'

Tom nodded.

'Goody-bloody-Two-Shoes,' growled Owen. 'Why do you always have to be so friggin' perfect? It's demoralizing.'

Tom sat down and pointed to the report at the top of the pile. 'Tell me what you want to say about the student and I'll dictate. I'm free before morning break.'

Owen smiled. 'Thanks. You're almost good enough to be Welsh.'

Tom sat back and stared out of the window. 'But before that I've got something to tell you . . . and it's important.'

Owen looked curiously at his friend. 'Go on then, man of mystery. Let's have it.'

'Inger and I have fixed a date for the wedding. It's March the twenty-third, beginning of the Easter break.'

Owen jumped up, skipped round the desk and shook Tom's hand. 'Brilliant, boyo. Great news. Well done.'

'Inger is letting everyone know this morning.'

Owen was still shaking Tom's hand. 'I'll ring Sue; she'll want to buy a new hat.'

'There's something else, Welshman. I want you to be my best man.'

For a moment Owen simply stared. Then he shook his head slowly. '*Diolch yn fawr, Tom, byddai'n anrhydedd.*'

'So was that a yes?' asked Tom.

Owen grinned. 'More than that, my friend. I said it would be *an honour*.'

'Right,' said Tom. 'Now that's sorted, let's get these reports finished.'

Owen sat back at his desk and for a moment looked as though he would burst into tears. 'You're a good man, Tom Frith,' he said quietly. 'I won't let you down.'

'I know that, Owen.'

Owen looked thoughtful. 'I'm really glad you didn't take that job in New Zealand.'

A party of teachers and headteachers from Australia and New Zealand had visited Eboracum earlier in the year. The headteacher of a school in Christchurch had offered Tom the post of deputy head but, after discussing it with Inger, he had refused.

Tom nodded. 'Yes, correct decision. It wasn't right for Inger.'

Owen picked up his pen. 'I'm going for a pint with my fourth years straight after lunch. Wait till I tell them the news.'

Pat had arrived at the Joseph Rowntree Theatre. He loved this art deco building. Built by the Rowntree family for the entertainment of its chocolate-factory workers, it had been providing entertainment for York since 1935.

The singers and members of the orchestra were good

friends and, on occasions, lovers. It was a lively start to the day, with coffee, home-made biscuits and local gossip, but with a communal desire to make this a special night. The programme included songs from the shows, Christmas carols and an audience sing-along. As Pat sipped his coffee he was happy in his world.

Six hundred miles away, Annika Sørenson was also happy in her world. She was drinking coffee in her favourite café in Oslo in the Grünerløkka district. She and Andreas loved this area, with its boutiques, vintage shops and flea markets. The locals called it 'hipster heaven'. Andreas was rehearsing this morning with the Oslo Philharmonic Orchestra but had promised to join her later. Meanwhile, she was enjoying a break away from her part-time secretarial work in a city centre publishing house. An accomplished guitarist, she sang in a folk group and enjoyed her life with the talented and caring Andreas Larson.

The café was full of the usual locals who had walked in from the street market. On the next table, a bearded and heavily tattooed man was expressing concern to his friends about the King of Norway. The former Prince Alexander had been on the throne, reigning as Olav V, since 1957, but his health was declining. Now that the ban on skateboarding had been lifted, the vociferous local had arrived on his multicoloured wheels and he continued to bemoan the state of the nation.

On the next table two young women were in discussion about *The Scream*, the famous painting by Edvard Munch, who had grown up in Oslo. One of them was explaining she had discovered the background to the painting depicted a view of Oslo. Conversations whirled like a carousel around Annika and she relaxed in the comfort of familiarity. That was until she noticed a swarthy, dark-haired man in his late thirties at a nearby table who was staring at her. This was not unusual. As a tall, slim, graceful woman with long auburn hair, she cut a striking figure. Annika was used to attention and ignored him. She stared at her coffee but was then surprised when he slipped into the seat opposite her.

'Please excuse me,' he said smoothly and with an engaging smile. 'I didn't mean to disturb you. It's just that I recognize you. We met briefly a few years ago. I used to know Andreas and his family. I'm an engineer. I work for Strukturas, building roads and bridges.'

'I'm sorry, I don't remember,' said Annika cautiously.

'How is Andreas? Still with the Philharmonic?'

'Yes, they're rehearsing this morning. He will be calling in later if you want a word.'

'Sorry, I have to get back to work but please pass on my best wishes. I recall his parents were very kind to me.'

'Yes, lovely people,' said Annika.

'And his sister, Inger . . . how is she? Another talented musician.'

'Inger has moved on. She teaches at a university in England now.'

'Oh, that's exciting. Which one?'

'Eboracum in York.'

'That's wonderful.' He looked at his wristwatch. 'Must go. Good to speak with you. Pass on my best to Andreas.'

He got up and hurried away.

Annika called after him, 'I didn't catch your name,' but it was too late and the bell above the door tinkled as he left.

Kai was deep in thought as he walked away. After all this time, Inger was suddenly back in his life. He recalled the fulfilment he had experienced with this beautiful woman. She had wanted him too, he knew, despite her struggles. It had been one of the most deeply satisfying experiences of his life and he smiled at the memory.

Richard Head was in the science department having a meeting with his two colleagues, Sam Greenwood and Selina Morton. It was the department's Christmas jumper day and the trio looked incongruous as they sat in their festive pullovers around a bench adorned with Bunsen burners and test tubes.

That morning, the perfectionist professor, after triple-locking his front door, had picked up his satchel and confirmed his lanyard was around his neck. Then he had placed his new jumper in a carrier bag and set off to walk from his home in Bootham to the university. The jumper was a gift from his fiancée, Dr Felicity Capstick. It had been carefully hand-knitted and featured Santa Claus on his sleigh flying across a sky studded with stars. Richard's fellow astrophile was the love of his life and she accommodated the vagaries of his obsessive-compulsive disorder with a calm acceptance. Felicity was due to arrive that evening in time for the Music Night concert at the Joseph Rowntree Theatre.

Sam Greenwood had dug out an old Christmas jumper that had somehow survived his student days. It had an image of a snowman drinking a pint of beer under the headline 'On the Piste'. Dr Selina Morton, or 'Sadistic Selina' as she was known, did not approve. A committed man-hater, she even seemed keen to have all men neutered. Her 'alternative' jumper merely sported the message 'I Hate Santa'.

Richard was carefully ticking off the list in his Filofax. 'So, are we all clear? We meet at the pub at twelve seventeen, ready to sit down at twelve thirty.' Richard always took his final-year students for lunch at the Cross Keys at the end of the autumn term. 'The table is booked until thirteen fifty and we can be back here for the stock check at fourteen fifteen.'

Sam merely nodded while Selina gave an exasperated sigh, looked up at the shelf of copper sulphate crystals and muttered, 'I hate bloody Christmas.'

'Fine,' said Richard. 'Now let's get these reports finished for Victor.'

Back in Oslo, Andreas was carrying a tray with another coffee for Annika and a glass beaker of *gløgg*. Made from red wine and spices and served hot, it was his favourite winter drink. Annika looked up in surprise as he placed two small plates on the table. On each was a *skolebrød*, a coconut bun with delicious vanilla cream inside.

Annika asked, 'What are we celebrating?'

'I have news,' he said. 'Inger is getting married on the twenty-third of March in York.'

Annika's eyes lit up. 'That's wonderful. I'm so pleased for them both.'

'It's at a register office. They're flying in next week to see us and then going back for Christmas.'

'I wonder how your parents will take it.'

'Happily, I think. Tom is a good man. It's just that my sister always said she didn't want a church wedding.'

'Understandable,' said Annika.

Andreas tucked into his *skolebrød*.

'So, how was your morning?' asked Annika.

'I've been asked to perform Mozart's Violin Concerto Number Five at the New Year Concert so I need time to perfect it. What about you?'

'A strange guy was in earlier.'

Andreas put down his spoon and sipped his *gløgg*. 'Who was he?'

'Didn't catch his name but it was someone who knew you and your family.'

'Maybe he'll come back,' said Andreas, looking around.

'Actually, I hope not.'

'Really?'

'He seemed too persistent,' said Annika with a frown. 'Can't say I liked him much, a bit over-familiar. To be honest I felt a little uncomfortable.' She paused and looked thoughtful. 'Maybe it's just *ugler i mosen*.'

Andreas smiled. *Ugler i mosen* was an old Norwegian expression that meant simply *owls in the moss*: a strange saying which suggested something suspicious had occurred, and he wondered what it could be.

'Oh, well,' said Andreas. He stretched out and held her hand. 'I'm here now.'

Suddenly, a group of friends from the string section of the orchestra arrived and sat down beside them.

Conversation flowed and Annika stopped thinking about her meeting with the stranger.

Snow was falling again as Inger hurried across the quad. She had asked Rosie and Zeb to meet her in the staff common room at morning break.

'Come on then,' said Zeb, 'we're all ears. What is it?'

Inger took a deep breath. 'Tom and I have got a date for the wedding. It's the day after we break up for Easter, Saturday, the twenty-third of March.'

'Congratulations,' said Rosie. 'I'm so pleased for you.'

'Great news,' said Zeb with a mischievous smile. 'About time you snared the handsome hunk. He's a lucky man.'

There was a pause as Inger looked at her two most trusted friends. 'The thing is, I want you two to be my bridesmaids. So, how about it?'

'Oh, yes, of course,' said Rosie. 'I should love to.'

'Do we get a say in the colour of our dresses?' asked Zeb. 'Peach is not my thing ... otherwise, brilliant!' She leaned over and gave Inger a hug. 'Thanks for asking. It's a first for me.'

'And me,' echoed Rosie.

'Well, that's settled,' said Inger. 'Let's seal it with a drink at tonight's concert.'

'Definitely,' said Zeb.

'Who else knows?' asked Rosie.

'Victor and Owen ... We're spreading the word,' said Inger, 'and I'm calling in to see the Vice Chancellor after lunch. Also, Tom's asking Owen to be best man.'

'My God!' said Zeb. 'Let's hope the scruffy sod smartens himself up.'

Rosie grinned. 'His best man's speech could be interesting.'

'Certain to involve sheep,' said Zeb.

They all laughed, finished their coffees and hurried away, excited by the news.

When Tom walked along Petergate towards the Guy Fawkes Inn he thought about Ellie MacBride. She had slipped a note under his door reminding him that English Three had organized their usual end-of-term Christmas drink and hoped he would join them. After all this time he still found her an enigma. She would probably hear on the student grapevine about his forthcoming wedding and he wondered if he ought to break the news to her personally, before it swept around Eboracum, but then decided against it.

As he walked in, on the jukebox Cliff Richard was singing 'Saviour's Day'. It was tipped to overtake Vanilla Ice to the top spot and become the Christmas number one. The Liverpudlian Billy Whitelock was standing at the bar. 'Hi, Tom,' he said. 'Can I buy you a pint?'

Tom smiled. 'Thanks anyway, Billy, but it's a tradition now for me to order jugs of beer and lemonade.' He waved to the barman and placed the order.

'Suits me,' said Billy. 'Thanks for calling in.'

Tom looked keenly at the young man before him. He had been traumatized by witnessing the Hillsborough disaster, but, following sessions of counselling arranged by Victor, he was now recovered. 'Are you going home for Christmas?'

'Yes. My mam needs me,' he said simply. These were words that would underpin the coming years of his life.

The students Tom knew so well had pushed some tables together at the far end of the pub and were sharing stories of Christmases past and present. Amy Field-house and Liz Colby were describing the wonders of Oldham market on Christmas Eve, while Ellie MacBride was regaling Tommy Birkenshaw with a story about the days she helped out in Santa's Grotto in Barnsley as a teenager. When she saw Tom she waved, and then stood up and hurried towards the bar to help him with the jugs of beer. 'Thanks for this,' she said. 'It means a lot to the group.'

'Good to wind down at the end of a busy term,' said Tom. 'Any plans for Christmas?'

Ellie sighed. 'The usual . . . Back to Barnsley and help-ing out my parents on the stall. It's manic on Christmas Eve morning.'

'I guess it is.' He paused, and then spoke quietly: 'Also, I haven't forgotten about that letter they received. We'll get to the bottom of it eventually.'

Ellie looked up at him expectantly. 'Thanks. It would be good to find out who's responsible. Anyway . . . what are your plans?'

'Oslo next week and Christmas Day with my parents.'

'Sounds good, Tom. I hope it goes well for you.' She squeezed his arm softly and then picked up one of the jugs of beer. 'Come on, the party awaits.'

*

Inger had enjoyed a relaxed Christmas lunch with her choir and then set off for the Lodge and her meeting with the Vice Chancellor. Hermione Frensham smiled when she walked in. 'He's expecting you, Inger.'

'Yes. I have some news for him. I'll share it with you when I've seen him.'

'About Vienna?' queried Hermione.

Inger shook her head. 'No, something even more exciting.'

'Can't wait,' said Hermione and stood up to open the door to Edward's study and announce her arrival.

'Good afternoon, Inger,' said the Vice Chancellor, immaculate as always in a three-piece business suit and his clerical collar. 'Do sit down. Would you care for some tea?'

'Good afternoon, Vice Chancellor. Thank you for seeing me and I'm fine, thanks. Just had lunch with my choir.'

'I imagine you will be rehearsing hard with them before Vienna.'

'Definitely. In fact we've already discussed a proposed programme.'

He settled back into his armchair. 'So, how can I help?'

'I'm here to pass on some news. Tom and I have arranged a date for our wedding and we were hoping you may be able to attend.'

Edward beamed. 'But of course. I should be delighted. Thank you for the invitation. What date have you chosen?'

'The first Saturday of our Easter break, the twenty-third of March.'

'Then I shall ask Hermione to put it in the diary.'

There was a slight pause. 'Vice Chancellor, it's in the register office on Bootham.'

'I know it well,' he said calmly. There was no judgement in his voice. 'I shall look forward to meeting your parents. I've already met Thomas's mother and father – shortly after his appointment. Lovely people.'

'My parents will be honoured to meet you. They are keen church-goers in their village in Norway. They are aware of your canon emeritus status.'

Inger immediately recognized that knowing look. The perceptive Vice Chancellor studied her for a moment. 'So how do they feel about your choice of a register office?'

'Disappointed, I'm afraid.'

'But this is what yourself and Thomas would prefer and it's your decision that is important.'

'Thank you for saying so, Vice Chancellor.'

Edward leaned forward and, with his usual patriarchal air, spoke with quiet authority. 'Inger, let's drop the formality for a moment. We know each other well and with every concert you enhance the reputation of Eboracum. Your talent is a gift for all of us to enjoy and share. So please call me Edward during a private conversation such as this.'

'Of course, Edward, that's kind of you.'

'I don't think Hermione would approve but that is another matter.' He stood up, walked to his bookcase and removed a slim volume entitled *The Zouche Chapel*. 'Take this with you, Inger. It makes interesting reading. Are you familiar with the Zouche Chapel in York Minster? It's really quite beautiful, named after one of the Archbishops of York in the fourteenth century.'

'I know of it and have walked past the entrance on many occasions.'

'In that case, there's a suggestion I should like to make that could appeal to your parents and enhance your wedding day.'

Inger smiled. 'I'm intrigued.'

Edward walked to the window and looked out. Beyond the trees and the city walls, the towers of the Minster were sharp against the winter sky. 'I'd be happy to organize a simple service, a blessing if you like, in the chapel to follow on from the register office. It would be a short walk down Bootham to the Minster for your friends and relations before you continue with the rest of your celebrations. Why don't you consider the proposal and let me know what you think? If you would like to accept I can make the necessary arrangements.'

'That's a kind offer, Edward. I shall do as you say, and I'll discuss it with Tom.' She stood up. 'I thank you for your time and your support.'

'Always a pleasure,' he said, 'and do share your news with Hermione. She will be thrilled.'

It was well known that Hermione had the directional hearing of a barn owl and conversations in Edward's study were always of interest to her. She looked up expectantly at Inger as she walked up to her desk. 'How did it go?' she asked, even though she knew already. Inger stayed a while to share her news before setting off to Cloisters corridor with the interesting proposal for Tom.

At seven thirty, Pat, elegantly dressed in a white suit and flaming red silk shirt, walked out in front of the curtain. Thunderous applause greeted him as he approached the microphone. 'Good evening, everybody, and thank you for supporting this very special concert of music and song. Tonight should definitely get you in the mood for Christmas, and if you have checked your programmes you will see we have included many of your favourites. So please welcome our ensemble of singers and our orchestra for the opening number. Join in, if you wish, to the number one Christmas song from a couple of years ago, "Mistletoe and Wine".' With a wave of his hand the curtains opened and the performance began.

Tom and Inger were on the front row of the dress circle along with Victor, Zeb and Vijay, Rosie and Sam, Owen and Sue, Richard and Felicity, plus many other colleagues. It was a perfect end to the term; the concert was excellent and the drinks party enjoyed by all. Victor felt proud as Pat was surrounded by admirers offering praise for a wonderful concert. Eventually hugs and good wishes were exchanged as taxis arrived and everyone drifted out into the cold winter's night.

It was late when Inger served up two glasses of *akvavit*, the traditional Norwegian flavoured spirit that she kept for special occasions. 'That was kind of Edward,' said Inger. 'My parents will love the idea of a blessing in York Minster.'

'Mine too,' said Tom. 'It makes the day really special.'

'And in the register office we could have some readings and music. I'll remind Andreas to bring his violin.' Then she put *A Classical Christmas* featuring Debussy, Vivaldi and Ravel on the record player and they relaxed at the end of a wonderful day.

*

For Annika it had been *almost* a perfect day as she and Andreas lay back in bed together. The afternoon had gone well at the publishing house, and an enthusiastic crowd had enjoyed her singing that evening in one of the city-centre bars. She was content with her life and was pleased Inger had finally decided to marry. She and Inger had always been close and often shared secrets. Except, of course, a few of the very private ones. Those remained hidden.

As a shaft of moonlight appeared through the scurrying clouds and pierced the shutters at the window, she reflected on her brief meeting with the strange man in the café. There was something uncomfortable, almost sinister about him. It had definitely been an *owls in the moss* moment. She also wondered about the vivid scar down his left cheek. He was not what he seemed.

Chapter Eight

Through a Glass Darkly

On the last day of December, Tom and Inger awoke to a frigid world of silence. Winter had closed in over the land. Pale sunlight flickered across the sleeping city and the bitter frost had created curved stitching patterns on the windowpanes. An eventful day lay ahead: Inger and Tom were hosting a New Year's Eve party and there was much to prepare.

Tom was frying eggs when the telephone rang. Inger, in her dressing gown, ran her fingers through her dishevelled hair and picked up the receiver.

'It's me,' said a voice.

'Hi, Rosie,' said Inger.

'When do you want us to help?' said Rosie. 'Sam's packing the car with food and drink as I speak. He's keen. I've not showered yet. We're picking up Owen on our way.'

'Come any time. There's lots to do. We need help to shift the furniture around, and Vijay and Zeb said they would call in before lunch. They're bringing plates and cutlery, plus some champagne glasses.'

'Sounds good,' said Rosie. 'OK, we'll be there around ten. Get the coffee on.'

'Will do,' said Inger. 'Thanks and see you later.' Tom was serving up eggs on toast and a large mug of tea when she walked into the kitchen. 'So . . . I see you have other skills,' she said with a wide-eyed smile and kissed him on the cheek.

'But of course,' said Tom with false modesty.

At that moment it seemed to be the start of a perfect day.

At nine o'clock in the Lodge, Hermione was at her desk, checking the weekend's mail prior to the bank holiday, when Edward walked in. 'Good morning, Vice Chancellor,' she said with a welcoming smile.

'Good morning, Hermione,' said Edward. 'You look busy.'

'Just a quick tidy-up so I'm ready for the new term.'

Edward smiled at his efficient PA. 'Is Gideon in?'

'Haven't seen him,' said Hermione. 'I'll check if you like.'

'If you would, please. I'm here until midday and then I'm having lunch with Professor Grammaticus.'

'Yes, it's in the diary,' said Hermione. 'Twelve thirty at the Dean Court Hotel.'

'That's right,' said Edward. 'In the meantime, please let the bursar know I wish to discuss something with him.' He glanced around Hermione's office. 'Remarkable, everything is so neat and tidy.' Hermione nodded in appreciation. It was good to be valued. 'Have you any plans for this evening?' he asked.

'Inger has invited me to her New Year's Eve party. I'm really looking forward to it. We've got to know each other well while planning for Vienna.'

'That's wonderful,' said Edward. 'She will be pleased to have your support.'

'Yes indeed,' said Hermione. 'We're both excited at the prospect.' She studied the cherubic figure before her, almost Dickensian in appearance. 'What about you? How are you celebrating the New Year?'

'I'm a guest at the Archbishop's Palace this evening,' said Edward with a smile. 'Just a clerical soirée.'

Hermione was aware that Edward held John Habgood, the Archbishop of York, in high esteem. A well-respected scientist, he had guided the Church of England through some difficult times. Although seemingly shy and retiring, he was a superb speaker.

'That's very special,' said Hermione. 'I hope it goes well.'

'Yes, indeed. Well, must get on,' said Edward and he ambled away to his private study.

Hermione walked out of her office and down the corridor to the back of the building, where Gideon Chalk had his office. She tapped gently on the door. 'Mr Chalk, hello, are you there?'

There was no reply so she opened the door and looked inside. It was empty and smelled of stale cigarettes. His Apple Macintosh SE/30 computer lay dormant on an untidy desk. She was about to close the door when she spotted a cupboard door slightly ajar at the far end of the room. To her surprise she caught sight of an old typewriter that she knew very well. Ten years ago she used to own an Olivetti Roma with its distinctive red trim and she wondered why Gideon would need one.

It was almost ten o'clock, as she was filing reports and updating Edward's diary for 1991, when she heard the bursar arrive. She opened her door and called after him, 'The Vice Chancellor wants to see you.'

He paused and glared at her. Without a word he turned back and headed for Edward's study.

By mid-morning Sam, Rosie and Owen had arrived outside Tom and Inger's apartment. Sam and Owen began unpacking the car while Rosie and Inger were in the kitchen sorting sausage rolls, pork pies and jars of pickle. Sam put a crate of beer on the worktop. 'I've emptied my fridge of this lot,' he said.

'There's an old table in the garage,' said Owen, 'and it's freezing. We could store all the beer in there and just keep nipping in to collect a bottle when we need it. There's no room in here with wine and food in the fridge.'

'Good idea,' said Sam. 'By the way, how's Sue?'

'Fine. Her mum and dad are with us looking after Gareth. She said thanks for the offer to take us back after midnight.'

Sam grinned. 'No problem.'

Then it was time to shift the heavy dining table against the wall. Tom and Sam took one end while the muscular Owen lifted the other effortlessly. 'Did you see the news this morning?' he asked. 'It's the end of an era in the Rhondda in South Wales. After one hundred years of coal mining it's all over.' He shook his head sadly. 'Three hundred miners have lost their jobs.'

'I'm sorry to hear that,' said Tom. 'It will have destroyed a community.'

'Too right,' said Owen. 'Dark times.'

Inger put her arm around Owen's broad shoulders. 'Maybe I can cheer you up. Would you like a coffee and one of my mother's festive *småkaker* biscuits? We brought plenty back from Norway.'

For a moment Owen looked dubious. He had never been a fan of what he called 'foreign' food.

'They're butter cookies covered in almonds,' explained Tom.

'Based on an old Welsh recipe,' quipped Sam. 'Well, maybe.'

Owen nodded. 'Why not? It will be an experience eating something I can't pronounce.'

Inger served up the coffee and soon Tom and Owen were sitting on the sofa while she covered the table with a white cloth.

'So, how was Norway?' asked Owen through a mouthful of biscuit.

'You would have loved it,' said Tom. 'Inger's dad brought forward his traditional Christmas dinner for us, pork belly served with sauerkraut and boiled potatoes along with meatballs and gravy.'

'Sounds OK,' said Owen unconvincingly. 'How did they respond to the wedding plans?'

Inger picked up her mug of coffee and sat down. 'Mixed, but generally good. It was the Vice Chancellor who saved the day with his offer of a blessing in the

Zouche Chapel. So now my mother is telling her friends we're getting married in the largest Gothic cathedral in northern Europe.'

'Impressive,' said Sam.

'Which reminds me,' said Owen. 'Sue's mum and dad said they would buy me a new suit.'

'That's great,' said Rosie pointedly, 'but make sure you take Sue with you when you choose it.' It was well known that the Welshman and sartorial elegance were not natural companions.

'OK, I've got the message,' said Owen as he picked up another *småkake*. 'Bloody good biscuits,' he mumbled.

It was just after ten o'clock when Gideon tapped on the Vice Chancellor's door.

'Come in,' said Edward.

Gideon walked in and Edward gestured towards a chair. 'Thank you for calling in,' he said. 'Do take a seat.' There was no offer of coffee and biscuits. 'I have a concern,' said Edward, his voice grave. 'We need to discuss the off-site properties we are offering to our students.'

'Yes,' said Gideon. 'I'm in the process of acquiring one more. It will be our ninth.'

'When you say "our" what exactly do you mean?'

'Well, clearly I action the lettings but the university benefits.'

Edward stared intently at the bursar. 'I think it would be unwise to proceed with this latest property.'

'Really, Vice Chancellor? Why ever not?'

'There have been reports about the poor quality of the accommodation you are subletting.'

Suddenly Gideon's face was as white as a tallow candle. 'I do hope you are not influenced by the nonsense I have read in the *Echo*.'

Edward leaned forward in his chair. 'Nonsense is too strong a word, Gideon. I think you ought to start improving the quality of the properties you have already acquired. As I have said many times, the reputation of Eboracum is paramount. I do hope I'm making myself clear.'

Gideon was shaking with indignation but trying to remain composed. 'My understanding is that the governors are delighted with my work.'

'This conversation goes beyond balance sheets,' said Edward sternly. 'Now, enjoy the Bank Holiday and ensure you do as I have instructed in the New Year.'

'Of course, Vice Chancellor. Will that be all?'

'For now . . . yes.'

Edward watched carefully as Gideon left and wondered if he had been too lenient in the past. He needed to understand more fully the nature of this problem. He stood up and walked into Hermione's office.

'Excuse me, Hermione, but I've had a thought and would appreciate your help.' Hermione looked up expectantly. She had been intrigued to see Gideon exiting, ashen-faced, following his meeting. 'I should like you to organize a review of the state of student accommodation, particularly the properties up the Hull Road. Employ an estate agent if you wish. Don't worry about the cost. I'll make funds available. Are you happy to take charge of this proposal?'

'Yes, of course.'

'Thank you, Hermione. I shall leave it in your capable hands . . . and please keep it confidential for the time being.'

Moments later she heard Gideon's car driving away.

By midday Zeb and Vijay had arrived at Tom and Inger's house and were unloading a selection of Indian snacks along with bottles of champagne and a box of glasses. Zeb was in the dining room helping Inger and Rosie cover plates of food with kitchen foil, while Vijay and Owen began washing and drying champagne flutes in the kitchen.

'Zeb tells me you're having some difficulties with the bursar,' said Vijay.

'He's a piece of work,' said Owen. 'Rents properties and sublets them to students at an exorbitant sum. I'm trying to find better accommodation for the men in my rugby team. They're in one of his properties that isn't fit for purpose.'

Vijay folded his tea towel neatly and placed it on the worktop. He looked thoughtful. As always, he analysed problems calmly and logically. 'Just an observation, Owen, but I may be able to help. I have a good friend, a fellow surgeon, who has just bought Homestead Manor, a huge property up the Scarcroft Road. He's intending to rent out the rooms. There's twelve of them over three floors.'

'I know where you mean,' said Owen. He flung his tea towel over his shoulder and nodded. 'I've passed it many times. It's near a school we use for teaching practice. Would he take students, I wonder?'

'I'm sure he would if I had a word with him.'

'Thanks, Vijay. I would really appreciate it if you could, but I guess it would depend on the rent.'

Vijay smiled. 'Sanjay is a fair man. Leave it with me.' Owen smiled and the two men walked back into the lounge.

'What have you two been plotting?' asked Zeb.

Owen gave Zeb a kiss on the cheek and nodded towards the handsome surgeon. 'Don't lose this one, Dancing Queen. He's special.'

Zeb grabbed the tea towel and whacked him round the head. 'Cheeky bugger!'

The atmosphere was much more sedate in the Dean Court Hotel. The Vice Chancellor and Professor Victor Grammaticus were seated at a private corner table and enjoying an excellent meal as conversation flowed. Following a starter of game terrine and a main course of roasted fillet of hake, they were looking at a selection of Yorkshire cheeses served with biscuits, fruit and home-made chutney while being served with filter coffee. Outside the bay window, they had a magnificent view of York Minster.

'You will have heard I've booked the Zouche Chapel for Thomas and Inger's blessing,' said Edward.

'Yes,' said Victor. 'A thoughtful gesture. It will add so much to their special day. I heard from Inger that her brother, Andreas, will be playing his violin. I'm looking forward to it.'

Edward dabbed his lips with a linen napkin and sat back. 'We shall need to decide upon a suitable gift from the university.'

'Yes. Any ideas?'

'I was about to ask you the same question,' responded Edward with a smile.

'You could ask Hermione,' said Victor. 'She would be good at something like that: feminine intuition and so on . . .'

'Precisely,' said Edward. 'Let's do just that. There is something else, Victor. How is Patrick these days? Is he fully recovered?'

A year ago Pat's diagnosis for prostate cancer had almost broken Victor's heart.

'Thank you for asking. He's fully recovered now. Obviously there's always the concern that symptoms may reappear. We're mindful of that but he is back to his usual ebullient self.'

'That's excellent news,' said Edward. 'He is such a wonderfully creative man.'

'I agree,' said Victor. 'I'm fortunate.' He leaned back in his chair and stared out of the window. 'Aren't we lucky to have the Minster on our doorstep?'

'My favourite building,' said Edward, smiling. He looked carefully at his academic friend. He noticed his hair was turning grey at the temples. He had always been intrigued by the professorial conundrum who sat before him. 'Tell me, Victor, when did you become an atheist?'

Victor paused and stared out at the crowds of tourists with their cameras. 'I think it was probably when I was a teenager and read about Nicolaus Copernicus and his heliocentric model of the universe. Then the declarations about the creation of man in Genesis began to puzzle me. Finally I read Darwin.'

'But isn't this where *faith* takes precedence, Victor?' Edward's voice was sympathetic. 'We have finite minds and will never understand the concept of infinity. The Apostle Paul in the First Epistle to the Corinthians, chapter thirteen, verse twelve, explains that at first we don't see things clearly but eventually we do.'

'I think I struggle with the idea of settling for an obscure or imperfect vision of reality.'

Edward was aware that Victor had a remarkable mind. 'So speaks the mathematician,' he said, 'and I have no wish to change you, Victor. Maybe I was hoping to expand your thought process,' he added with another gentle smile.

The waitress arrived at that moment. 'More coffee, gentlemen?'

'Perfect timing,' said Victor.

Twenty-five miles away, in the foyer of the Queen's Hotel next to Leeds railway station, a Norwegian engineer had also finished his lunch and was speaking to the concierge about hiring a car. During the past year he had become a highly paid consultant for a number of huge engineering works in England. They included the decision to complete the M3 motorway, bypassing Winchester by building a six-lane road cutting through Twyford Down. He smiled as he considered this was likely to cause controversy with environmental protesters. There was also work in the New Year at London Docklands. However, his current project involved the M621 motorway around Leeds known as the South West Urban Motorway. His first meeting was two days away and the Bank Holiday beckoned. Today he was free to choose and he had unfinished business of a different sort.

'Your keys, sir,' said the concierge. He looked up at the tall man before him, dressed for the cold weather in his stylish fur-lined parka and a distinctive hat similar to the one worn by Omar Sharif in *Doctor Zhivago*. It gave the impression of a visiting Russian general.

'So it's just for the day is it, sir? Are you going far?'

'York,' he said simply. He stroked the scar on his cheek and smiled.

Victor's car crunched over the frozen driveway outside their home in Easingwold. When he walked into the hallway, he hung up his coat and scarf and called, 'I'm back.'

'In the kitchen,' was the reply.

'You look busy,' said Victor.

'Party food,' said Pat.

There was a tray of potato skins topped with cheese, bacon and sour cream alongside some mini quiches filled with mushrooms and caramelized onions.

'These look delicious,' said Victor.

'Just a few simple extras,' said Pat. 'It's fun preparing for a party. So how did it go?'

'Edward is a generous host,' said Victor. 'We had a lovely meal. He asked after you. I told him you were fully recovered and back to your modest, retiring and unassuming self.'

'Oh yes?' said Pat. 'I'm sure you did.'

Victor leaned back against the kitchen cupboard. 'He mentioned my atheism. It just came right out of the blue.'

'Really? I wonder why?'

'Just curious, I suppose. He quoted the Bible at me.'

'Whatever for?'

'He said that the Apostle Paul declared at first we don't see things clearly but eventually we do.'

Pat looked up and grinned. 'A bit like us then.'

Victor smiled. 'You really are back to your old self.'

'Correct,' said Pat. 'Now go and sit down in the lounge, you silly old goat, and I'll bring you a hot toddy.'

Darkness had fallen when Kai pulled up on Lord Mayor's Walk and stared at the gates to Eboracum University. *So this is where she works,* he thought. He felt a surge of excitement. Inger Larson had been the perfect partner. The fact that she had struggled so violently on that memorable day four years ago merely added to the need to find her again. Since then there had never been anyone quite like her. She was unfinished business.

He stepped out of the car, wrapped his scarf a little tighter and walked across the road. Students were strolling into reception carrying bags of food and drink and chattering excitedly. He tagged on behind them and headed for the short corridor that led to the quad. The noticeboard was full of posters. The largest showed a wonderful image of Inger conducting her choir and his mouth went dry as he stared at her. The photograph, taken by someone called Ben Laverick, had captured her profile perfectly. Above it was a banner headline: 'The Eboracum Choir will be performing in St Stephen's Cathedral in Vienna, Saturday, 9 March 1991'. He knew Vienna well. It was one of his favourite European cities. After checking the date once again, he made a decision. The time was approaching when he would need to finish what he had started.

Next to the noticeboard was a wall-hung telephone with a shelf below it. On it was a directory. He opened it and sought out 'Larson'. There she was with an address next to the Knavesmire racecourse. He retraced his steps and climbed back in his car. He had driven past the racecourse on his way into the city so would be passing Inger's home on the way back to Leeds. The temptation was too great and he stared out into the darkness with anticipation.

Inger was busy making final preparations for the party. Coasters were scattered on the piano and serviettes placed on top of a pile of paper plates. Tom was in the kitchen giving the worktop a final clean while his little portable television was burbling away on the shelf in the corner.

It was a review of the year and an eclectic mix of news was being presented. There was an image of Tony Adams, the Arsenal captain, being sentenced to four months in prison for drink driving, followed by a report that a new supermarket chain, Poundland, had opened its first store in Burton-on-Trent. Viewers were reminded that on Christmas Day, following the great storms, one hundred thousand homes had been left without power. Finally, there was a picture of a beaming Duke and Duchess of York at the christening of their nine-month-old daughter, Eugenie Victoria Helena.

Tom glanced up at the kitchen window and was about to close the curtains when, for a brief instant – a fleeting moment captured by the streetlamp – he glimpsed a figure out there staring at the house. Then it was gone.

Puzzled, he walked into the hallway, opened the front door and peered out. There was no one there, but a car was pulling up outside. It was Sam's distinctive Citroën. He and Rosie climbed out, followed by Owen and Sue. They waved and yelled a greeting. They were in high spirits and Tom's moment of concern was forgotten.

By mid-evening the party was in full swing. Inger was playing the piano and Owen was belting out 'Land of My Fathers' in a strong Welsh accent. 'It's right what they say about Welshmen,' said Sam to Tom. 'They can all sing.'

Vijay and Victor were both smiling as they stood in the conservatory and looked back into the lounge, where Zeb was in animated conversation with Rosie. 'You won't find another like her,' said Victor. 'Her energy is boundless. It's sometimes hard to keep up when we're in meetings.'

Vijay sipped his iced water and smiled. 'I know what you mean. I'm a lucky man.' He looked across at the kitchen, where Pat was describing the art of making filo pastry to Felicity. 'As are you, Victor. Pat is astonishing, full of joie de vivre.'

'He certainly is. We are both fortunate.' He raised his glass of mulled wine. 'Cheers, Vijay. I wish you happiness.'

Vijay smiled. 'Likewise.'

'You've had an eventful life, by all accounts,' said Victor. 'I'm aware your specialism is arthroscopic surgery.'

'That's right, but I'm more interested in trauma. I did a fellowship in America and have researched it ever since.'

'I should like to hear more,' said Victor.

At that moment Zeb appeared. 'Darling, I hope I'm not

interrupting anything important but can you blow up a few balloons for me?'

'Of course,' said Vijay and winked at Victor.

It was getting close to midnight. Inger was pouring a glass of champagne and Felicity appeared by her side. 'One for you as well, Felicity?' she asked.

Felicity smiled and nodded. 'Thank you. I was so pleased to hear of your wedding news, Inger. Many congratulations.'

'Thanks, Felicity. Yes, we're both excited. The time seemed right. How about you and Richard?'

Felicity pursed her lips and thought for a moment. 'It will happen eventually but not yet. Richard needs more time to adjust than most men. He has *routines* in his life that are unbreakable. So he needs time to adapt. It's a slow process but we're getting there. I think he likes the fact that we're definitely seen as a couple now. We are engaged of course, but he has to feel comfortable to take the next step.'

'You're very patient.'

Felicity smiled. 'I have to be, but he's worth waiting for. Richard is a remarkable man and I do love him. Whatever the future holds, it's worth the wait.'

Suddenly Richard appeared. He sounded excited. 'I've just explained the "blue moon" anomaly to Owen,' he said.

'I bet he was thrilled,' said Felicity evenly.

'I wouldn't go that far,' said Richard, 'but he was certainly interested.' Then he readjusted his spectacles and wandered off.

'Go on then,' said Inger. 'What's the blue moon anomaly?'

'It's a second full moon in December and occurs once every two point eight years,' explained Felicity. 'So there are thirteen full moons in the calendar year rather than the usual twelve.'

'I see,' said a wide-eyed Inger.

'And that,' said Felicity, 'sums up my fiancé – the slightly off-kilter Richard.'

They clinked glasses, smiled and took another sip of champagne.

After 'Auld Lang Syne', a champagne toast, hugs and kisses, handshakes and balloons, Owen and Sam were in the hallway while Tom rummaged for their coats. 'I've just remembered something,' he said. 'Did you see anyone lurking around outside when you arrived? I'm sure I saw someone under the streetlamp staring at the house.'

'No,' said Sam.

'Too bloody dark,' added Owen. 'Probably kids.'

Rosie and Sue walked into the hallway and collected their coats. Inger was following behind. 'Are you sure you don't want to take home any food? There's stacks in the kitchen.'

Owen smiled. 'Maybe the strange guy was hungry.'

'Or checking out what's left of the Christmas cake,' added Sam with a grin.

'What strange guy?' asked Inger.

'Nothing to worry about. Gone in a flash,' said Tom.

'Owen's probably right,' said Sue. 'It will just be kids.'

Tom considered this for a moment. 'No, I'm pretty sure

this was a man. All muffled up in a parka. Oh yes, he had a funny hat like a Russian general.'

For a brief moment Inger froze. Her mind raced as she recalled a distinctive silhouette. *It can't be,* she thought. *It can't be.* Eventually everyone left for home and Tom and Inger turned out the lights and went to bed. It wasn't until the early hours that Inger finally drifted into a troubled sleep.

Chapter Nine

Wednesday's Child

Friday, 4 January was Inger's birthday, and Tom wanted to surprise her before they set off for the staff meeting. He placed on the kitchen table a neatly wrapped book of classical piano solos, a red rose and a birthday card. Then he boiled the kettle and began to whisk four eggs. On the radio, the Righteous Brothers were singing 'You've Lost That Lovin' Feelin'' but, after last night, he was certain he hadn't.

The kitchen was warm and cosy, whereas the outside temperature was minus five and diamond ice sparkled on the frozen windows. Inger was still in her dressing gown when she walked in. 'What a lovely surprise,' she said. Then she saw the gifts. 'Oh, Tom, thank you so much,' and she put her arms round his waist and gave him a hug. Tom served up the scrambled egg on toast and poured two mugs of tea. 'Happy birthday,' he said with a smile, and so began a few days of mixed fortunes.

At eight o'clock, Tom scraped the ice from his

windscreen before crunching the car out of the driveway. Snowflakes drifted down upon a white sepulchral
land that had been leached of colour and stripped of
warmth until, following a reluctant dawn, the sun was a
cool amber disc on the far horizon. After a slow journey
with busy traffic they hurried into reception and Perkins
was there to greet them.

'Happy Birthday, Dr Larson,' he said and placed a large
blue envelope on the counter.

'You remembered,' said Inger.

'I know everyone's birthday,' said Perkins with pride.
'I have a list in my Day Book. You're a Capricorn like my
Pauline. Did you know it's said that the goddess Venus
gave people born on this day both charm and beauty?'

'Really?' said Inger. 'I didn't know that.'

'And Venus knows what she's talking about,' said Tom
with a smile.

'I agree,' said Perkins.

'Well, thank you so much,' said Inger, picking up the
card. 'I'll open it in my study.'

'Have a good day,' called out Perkins as Tom and Inger
headed off for the quad. He had seen Dr Tremaine arriving earlier with an iced cake and guessed a celebration
was in store.

At ten o'clock, the staff common room buzzed with lively
conversations as colleagues gathered once again after the
Christmas holiday. Everyone was full of news and stories.
Tom was relating to Owen that he had received a hideous
multicoloured pullover from his Aunty Maureen that you
would only wear in a power cut, while Owen had spent

much of his holiday with his son, Gareth, watching a video of the great Welsh rugby team of the seventies. Richard Head was reciting to Inger the date of everyone's birthdays in the faculty. It was one of his idiosyncrasies and Inger marvelled at his power of recall. Finally, he wished her a happy birthday and took his seat next to Sam. Meanwhile, Rosie and Zeb crept back in from the music room where they had set up an impromptu birthday celebration for Inger.

Eventually everyone settled and Victor stood up and smiled. His ponytail was a little more grey these days but, as always, he commanded huge respect. His mustard waistcoat and magenta cord trousers, a gift from Pat, added colour to his presence. 'Good morning, everyone, and welcome back. I do hope you feel refreshed after the holiday. A demanding term awaits, not least the busy timetable for school-practice placements involving our students from all four years. Please make sure you check the list on the noticeboard, especially towards the end of this term during field week. This includes Richard and Sam's visit to the Science Museum, Owen's skiing trip in France and the invitation to the international choir concert in Vienna.' He paused and looked at Inger. 'So, well done, Inger. This is undoubtedly another accolade for Eboracum and the Vice Chancellor asked me to pass on his congratulations once again.' There was impromptu applause and Tom squeezed Inger's hand.

Victor glanced down at his notes. 'Also, next month, we have a one-day seminar that will provide an insight into new technology. Professor Jeremy Farquharson from Edinburgh will deliver the plenary lecture on the new Microsoft 3.0 operating system that is becoming a standard for many PC manufacturers. Richard has kindly offered to provide follow-up sessions with interested parties.' Victor turned to Zeb, who was sitting alongside him. 'That's all from me for now. Zeb and I will be available later this afternoon to deal with any queries.'

Zeb stood up and all eyes turned to the flame-haired Dance and Drama lecturer. In a beautifully tailored navy business suit, a present from Vijay, she looked to have moved on from her baggy sweatshirts and *Fame*-style leg warmers.

'Hi, everybody. Good to be back after the indulgence of Christmas; I noticed in the local paper that a record number of women joined one of the local Slimming World courses.' There were murmurs and general laughter at this announcement. 'So let me know if you are interested . . . male or female,' she added pointedly. Sam Greenwood patted his tummy and gave her a thumbs up.

'As Victor has mentioned, a busy term awaits and I would draw your attention to the list of academic meetings and events on the noticeboard. This includes the briefing at two o'clock this afternoon when the Vice Chancellor wishes to see all heads of department in the Lodge.' Then Zeb held up a colourful poster designed by Ben Laverick. 'There is also an important social event on the evening of Thursday, the fourteenth of February. It's a Valentine's Dance here in the senior common room, with members of Inger's orchestra providing the musical accompaniment. Proceeds go towards the students' emergency fund for those in greatest need, so do support if you can.'

She paused and smiled. 'Now, pin your ears back, everyone, because I have some exciting news. At long last, Tom and Inger have announced they will be married on Saturday, the twenty-third of March and I know you will join me in wishing them every happiness.' There was spontaneous applause while Inger blushed and Owen gave Tom a dig in the ribs. Zeb gestured towards the serving counter and the clatter of crockery. 'Meanwhile, the catering staff have organized hot chocolate and croissants, so happy new year to you all and best wishes for the new term.'

For the next thirty minutes the members of the faculty gathered around Tom and Inger to offer congratulations and enjoy the companionship of their colleagues. Victor made a point of circulating and catching up on news while Zeb and Rosie mysteriously hurried out into the quad. When Inger noticed she and Tom were almost the only ones left in the room, she picked up her shoulder bag and went to the pigeonholes to check for mail. 'I'll catch up with you later,' she said.

Tom followed her. 'I think you must be the most popular woman in the faculty this morning. It was kind of Zeb to make the announcement and the VC is clearly thrilled about Vienna.'

'Yes, and I'm meeting Hermione later today. She's been busy organizing flights and the hotel.' She turned to set off for the music room. 'Aren't you going to your study?' she asked.

'Not yet,' said Tom as he hurried ahead. When he opened the door, Inger was met by a group of familiar faces.

'Surprise!' called out Zeb. She was sitting at the piano and led everyone in a discordant chorus of 'Happy Birthday To You'. There was a cake with a candle, bottles of fruit juice and a card signed by everyone in the faculty. Inger was almost overwhelmed and Rosie gave her a hug.

'Hey,' said Hermione, 'remember the old nursery rhyme? It's Friday so it means you're loving and giving.'

'Sorry,' said Inger. 'I don't know it.'

Hermione recited:

> 'Monday's child is fair of face,
> Tuesday's child is full of grace.
> Wednesday's child is full of woe,
> Thursday's child has far to go.
> Friday's child is loving and giving . . .'

'I was born on a Saturday,' said Owen.

' "Saturday's child works hard for a living," ' continued Hermione.

'That's right,' said Victor. 'Owen definitely has a proclivity for hard work.'

'Too bloody true,' said Owen and everyone laughed.

'What about you, Tom?' asked Hermione.

'I'm a Thursday,' he said.

'So you have far to go,' responded Zeb, 'which means he's after my job.'

'No chance,' said Tom.

'What about me?' asked Sam. 'I think I was born on a Monday.'

'Oh dear,' said Rosie. 'It means you're fair of face.'

'Well, maybe it wasn't Monday,' said Sam with a grin.

'So, was anyone born on a Wednesday?' asked Hermione.

There was a shaking of heads. 'Good news then,' said Hermione. 'No one is full of woe and certainly not today.'

'Did you know that time speeds up as you get older?' said Owen to Tom while munching on a slice of cake. 'It's a well-known fact.'

Tom looked puzzled. 'Fact?'

Owen shrugged his shoulders. 'Well, the next best thing.'

Hermione approached Owen. 'Can we have a quiet word, please? Something's cropped up.'

'Of course,' said Owen and they walked over to the stage and sat down.

'It's about the off-site student accommodation,' said Hermione. 'I'm checking up on the quality we're providing on behalf of the university and I know you have concerns. I should like to visit the property up the Hull Road where your rugby players are placed.'

'That's good to hear,' enthused Owen. 'Thanks, Hermione. It's in a cul-de-sac called Lavender Close. Looks fine from the outside but inside it's dreadful. I can arrange a meeting for you with the scrum-half, Rod Parfitt. He's emerged as the spokesman for the rest of the men. Just let me know when you want to go there.'

'Sooner the better,' said Hermione. 'How about a convenient time next Monday, maybe at lunchtime or after lectures?'

'I'll sort it,' said Owen. 'I'm just pleased there may be a resolution in sight. In fact, I had a chat with Vijay at the New Year's Eve party and he's got a friend who has just bought a large property up the Scarcroft Road. So that might be useful.'

'That could be really helpful,' said Hermione.

Suddenly Owen looked concerned. 'Hermione, just a thought.'

'Yes?'

'Gideon Chalk can be vindictive. I wouldn't want you to come under any unnecessary pressure. He won't take kindly to any intrusion into his affairs. He's already given me a hard time about my costings for the Year Four skiing trip to France. Problem is, accountancy is not exactly my strength.'

Hermione studied him; she knew how well meaning he was. 'Maybe I can help, Owen. Keep every receipt carefully during your field week and give them to me for checking. Accountancy is part of my life. It would be no trouble.'

'That's really kind, Hermione. I'll do just that and thank you.'

'No problem,' said Hermione.

'So why are you getting involved in this off-site accommodation issue, if you don't mind me asking?' queried Owen.

'Simply following up some of the articles in the *Echo*,' she said cautiously.

Owen nodded. 'In that case I'll set up a meeting,' he said, 'and thanks again.'

She gave Owen a determined stare. 'Let's continue to liaise on this,' she said, and Owen realized this diminutive woman was someone to be reckoned with.

*

During afternoon break Inger tapped on Hermione's office door and walked in. Ben Laverick was already there.

'Inger, thanks for coming,' said Hermione. 'There's coffee here, if you wish.'

A cafetière of coffee stood on the table alongside china cups and saucers, a bowl of sugar lumps and a plate of Yorkshire shortbread biscuits.

'Yes, please,' said Inger and sat down. 'Hi, Ben. Pleased you will be recording our adventure.'

'I've been before,' said Ben. 'It's a wonderful city for photography and too good an opportunity to miss.'

Particularly as my mezzo-soprano, Alexandra Midwinter, will be among the party, thought Inger but said nothing.

Hermione opened a folder and handed out an itinerary. 'We're almost there,' she said. 'The organizers in Vienna say there are two other choirs from Switzerland and France and we shall all be performing twice on Saturday, the ninth of March in St Stephen's Cathedral. We have two thirty-minute recitals; one in the morning at eleven and an evening performance at seven.'

'That's perfect,' said Inger.

'Excellent,' said Ben enthusiastically. 'I was there with some students a few years ago studying the architecture. St Stephen's is a wonderful cathedral, the spiritual and geographical centre of Vienna . . . and they allow filming and photography.'

'That's great,' said Hermione and handed out a street map of the city centre. 'Also, I've managed to confirm three nights in a mid-range hotel near the cathedral. We've got eight twin-bed rooms plus three singles for us.

The flights are booked – we fly out on Friday, the eighth of March, and return on Monday, the eleventh. A coach has been hired for the return journey to Leeds Airport and I'll hang on to the tickets for the time being.'

'You've been busy,' said Inger.

'Thanks for this,' said Ben. 'Already looking forward to it. It was kind of the VC to let me come along.'

'He was determined we had a photographic record of such a memorable event,' said Hermione, 'and, like you, I'm keen to visit such an iconic city.'

When Inger and Ben had left, Hermione opened up her revolving card index of telephone numbers and picked up the receiver. Her mind had switched to accommodation that was closer to home and she had a friend in the environmental health department at County Hall.

Tom and Owen were in their study discussing the fact that Owen was going into York on Saturday morning to buy a new suit.

'The last suit I bought had flared trousers,' said Owen. 'I looked like a poor man's John Travolta.'

'Fashions have moved on,' said Tom. 'Buy something sensible that you can wear for weddings, funerals and formal occasions. Don't go for the *Miami Vice* look.'

'OK,' said Owen. 'I get the message. Just out of my comfort zone. I'd rather visit the dentist.'

The telephone rang and Tom picked up. 'Oh, hi. Yes, he's here.' He handed the receiver to Owen. 'It's Vijay.'

'Owen, good news,' said Vijay. 'Sanjay is happy to meet you at his Scarcoft Road property to discuss a rental agreement for your students. He suggested tomorrow some time, if you're free. I said I would get back to him with your decision.'

'Excellent,' said Owen. 'Many thanks. Maybe two thirty.'

'Fine,' said Vijay. 'I'll arrange that with him and good luck.'

'Thanks,' said Owen. 'Much appreciated.'

Owen replaced the receiver and sat back. 'Well, that's Saturday sorted,' and he smiled. Thoughts of a new suit were temporarily forgotten.

Darkness had fallen swiftly and by five o'clock everyone in the faculty had driven out of the university car park and headed for home. The weekend stretched out before them. In his riverside apartment Ben Laverick and Alexandra Midwinter were enjoying a hot meal of beef stew and a glass of red wine while discussing the arrangements for Vienna. Their relationship had progressed and Alexandra smiled when Ben told her he would be having a single room.

Close by, on Marygate, Felicity had arrived at Richard's house for the weekend and he had bought a fish and chips supper. When it was on the plate, Richard immediately adjusted the position of his fish so it pointed due north and then ensured there were an equal number of chips on either side of the fish. Felicity spoke up: 'Tell me, Richard, how is it that you can retain vivid images of information with such exceptional precision?' She had begun to use such questions as a distraction technique.

'I presume I got half of my DNA from my father. He

had a photographic memory too,' said Richard phlegmatically. 'Although, sadly, these days he is deteriorating rapidly.'

'I'm sorry to hear that,' said Felicity.

'Yes,' said Richard. 'Each day a few more words are lost to him, like grains of flour passing through a sieve. It's sad to see such a brilliant mind deteriorate. I wonder where it will all end.'

'What about your mother?'

'She's fine and perfectly normal,' said Richard, 'and enjoys her hobbies.'

'What are those?'

'Gregorian chant music, the poetry of Ferlingetti and the history of beekeeping.'

'As you say, Richard . . . quite normal.' He looked at her intently and there was a pause as if he was struggling for words. 'What is it, Richard? Is there something you wish to say?'

'Yes, but it's difficult.'

She gave a sympathetic smile. 'Go ahead. Just try.'

Richard put down his knife and fork and took a deep breath. 'It's just that I really do love you, Felicity . . . in my own way.'

There were tears in her eyes when she replied. 'I know you do, Richard . . . and I love you too.'

After a difficult journey Tom and Inger parked on their driveway. Snowflakes danced around them like wild dervishes and the land was a monochrome expanse of ice and skeletal trees. As they hurried to the front door, in the distance they heard the bark of a fox and, above their heads, the sound of an owl's wings passing by like a ghost in the night. It was good to relax in the warmth of their kitchen while Inger prepared a birthday supper. It felt like a perfect evening as they settled down to warming bowls of Norwegian fish soup followed by *kjøttkaker*, a dish of meatballs and potato.

Meanwhile, in the restaurant of the Queen's Hotel in Leeds, *kjøttkaker* was not on the menu. Kai Pedersen beckoned to the waitress and selected smoked salmon with baked potatoes and green beans. He had his black leather Filofax open beside him. From a pocket at the back he took out a photograph. It had been taken by Inger's father, Fredrik Larson, on the day he had driven to Inger's house in the tiny village of Langøy.

Her father had initially been impressed by the tall, confident engineer and took a photograph of the two of them next to Kai's VW Golf. On his next visit to meet Inger, Fredrik passed on a copy of the photograph and Kai had kept it ever since. However, by then Inger was having second thoughts about this new relationship and had decided to end it. Her perceptive mother, Hilde, had already made her mind up about this new man in Inger's life. She had concerns but kept them to herself.

Kai studied the photograph. There was something very special about the tall, blonde woman in her linen trouser suit and white blouse. Perhaps he had been too eager. He had enjoyed the pleasures of many women in his life, but the majority had been too subservient. Inger was spirited and had fought back. He liked that.

He flicked through the pages of his Filofax and made a decision.

On Saturday morning Tom and Inger drove into the city centre while Berlin's 'Take My Breath Away' played on the radio. They parked at the university and walked into the city centre. They had arranged to meet Zeb and Vijay at Bettys. In St Helen's Square there was a dusting of snow on the frozen pavements and they welcomed the warmth as they walked into the tea rooms. Beyond the display of handmade chocolates and art deco mirrors, they were guided to a table by the maître d'hôtel. A waitress in a starched apron and cap appeared with a notepad and pen to take their order just as Zeb and Vijay arrived. As always, when Vijay took off his woollen winter coat he looked immaculate in a dark blue suit, white shirt and tie. His silver cufflinks, a Christmas gift from Zeb, reflected the bright lights of the restaurant.

'I love this place,' said Zeb.

'I agree,' said Vijay. 'It reminds me of afternoon tea in the Taj Mahal Hotel in Bombay when I was a child.'

'Ah, but did they sell Fat Rascals?' asked Tom.

Vijay raised his eyebrows. 'Educate me,' he said simply.

Zeb smiled at him and kissed him on the cheek. 'We certainly shall. They're fruity scones filled with citrus peel, almonds and cherries; it's their speciality.'

'Sounds perfect,' said Vijay.

Zeb looked at Inger. 'So this is on us, Inger, a belated birthday treat.'

The waitress took the order and soon Zeb was pouring

tea from a silver teapot through a tea strainer and into the china cups.

It was a relaxed hour as Inger spoke of growing up in Norway and Vijay shared stories of his professional life abroad. He was particularly enthused about New York. 'I should like to go back there one day. It's such a vibrant city.'

'I can't see us moving,' said Tom. 'We both love York.'

'So, how are the wedding plans going?' asked Vijay.

'We have a first fitting for dresses next week,' said Inger. 'I promised to send photographs to my mother for approval.'

'And I've ordered a new suit from Clarksons,' said Tom.

'It will look good,' said Inger. 'Classic grey and specially ordered because Tom is so tall.'

Tom looked at his wristwatch. 'In fact, Owen will be there now. He had an eleven o'clock appointment to select his suit.'

Zeb looked concerned. 'I hope he took Sue with him. You know what he's like. Clueless about clothes.'

'He simply told me he was getting a three-piece suit,' said Tom, 'and he knows he needs to be smart.'

'Why don't we walk there now?' said Zeb. 'It's only up Stonegate, then round the corner.'

'Good idea,' said Inger.

Clarksons outfitters on High Petergate was a popular shop, famous for its high-quality suits and shirts and excellent service. Owen was in the doorway when they arrived. He was holding a suit carrier that was zipped up while thanking the owner.

He smiled when he saw Tom and Inger, with Zeb and Vijay close behind. 'Hi, this is a surprise! Guess what? I've just bought the perfect suit.'

'Where's Sue?' asked Zeb, looking over his shoulder into the shop.

'Couldn't make it. Gareth had an upset tummy so she stayed to look after him.'

The first hint of concern crossed Zeb's face. 'Let's have a look at it then.'

Owen began to unzip the suit carrier while everyone looked on. 'I told him I was Welsh and it was important I remained true to my roots. I'm particularly pleased with the waistcoat.'

'But I presume it's grey, isn't it?' asked Tom. 'Or maybe dark blue . . . something like that.'

'Not exactly,' said Owen and he slipped it out of its cover and held it up in triumph.

'Jesus wept!' said Zeb.

If the Vice Chancellor had been standing alongside he would probably have commented that this was the shortest verse in the Bible. However, this situation was significantly different. In the Gospel of John, chapter eleven, verse thirty-five, Jesus had wept when he heard of the death of his friend, Lazarus. Here, Owen's four friends felt like weeping because of the death of good taste. The Welshman's suit was bright red and the waistcoat was covered in a pattern of yellow daffodils.

At eight thirty on Monday morning, Hermione arrived at the Lodge and collected the morning mail from the metal box in the porch. She carried it into the hallway and scanned quickly through the huge pile. It was the usual bundle of advertisements for academic events along with private and confidential mail for the Vice Chancellor. However, on top was an official-looking letter for the bursar. It was at that moment he walked in, looking pale and exhausted.

'One here for you, Mr Chalk,' said Hermione with a distinct lack of enthusiasm.

She passed it to him; he nodded in curt acknowledgement but said nothing: he merely strode down the corridor. Hermione stared after him and noted the drooped shoulders. She had sorted the mail into letters for the immediate attention of the Vice Chancellor, postcards from office-equipment suppliers and junk mail for new guttering destined for the bin.

Incongruously, at the bottom of the pile there was another envelope addressed to Gideon, except this one was brightly coloured and was clearly a greetings card. She was looking at the spidery handwriting as she walked towards Gideon's office when she heard him cry out, 'Bloody hell!'

She was unaware that Gideon's letter was from the owner of three of the properties he rented. It stated clearly that the rent he would have to pay would be increased the following September.

She tapped on the door and walked in. 'What?' he said aggressively.

'You have more correspondence. Sorry, I didn't spot it earlier.' She placed it on his desk.

'It's nothing,' he grumbled. 'Simply a birthday card from my sister.'

'Is it today?' asked Hermione politely.

He shook his head with a face like thunder. 'Wednesday,' he muttered.

Hermione exited quickly. *It's right,* she thought. *Wednesday's child really is full of woe.*

Chapter Ten

The Master of Whispers

Gideon Chalk was incandescent. It was Monday, 28 January, and a weak winter sun filtered through his office window as he read the letter for the second time. Then he sat back and lit up another cigarette.

The envelope had a French postmark. Claude Sparrow, a retired London banker, resided in a large property in the Dordogne, where he looked after his mother. He also owned three properties in York and had been shocked to receive a warning letter from the York Environmental Health Authority. It stated quite clearly that there was an urgent requirement for essential repairs to make the accommodation fit for purpose. He had trusted Gideon Chalk to ensure there was no blemish to his property portfolio. The clever accountant had been persuasive and the subletting agreement for all three properties seemed an ideal solution. That was no longer the case. Mr Sparrow stated in no uncertain terms that he was considering ending their relationship.

Noting a reference to 'overcrowding', Gideon thought of Owen Llewellyn. 'Welsh bastard!' he muttered. 'He's been whispering behind my back.'

From Gideon's early days, perjury had become a way of life. He had become an expert in prevarication and deception. As a boy he had been despised by his schoolmates, and he had taken shelter beneath his cloak of deceit until lies became his default currency. Gideon had always been the master of whispers but the tables had begun to turn and he felt he was losing control.

Tom looked out of his study window that same Monday morning and saw Owen in the quad. He was in conversation with one of his rugby players and the young man appeared animated. It ended with a handshake and the student ran off. Owen stared after him and smiled.

Tom thought how fortunate he had been, sharing a study with this loyal and hardworking Welshman. They had become great friends and he was pleased that Owen had agreed to be his best man. His choice of a patriotic red suit for the wedding had caused considerable debate but Owen was proud of his purchase. Even his wife, Sue, had finally acquiesced and agreed it made him look not only smart but distinctive.

Over the weekend, Tom and Inger had driven to Kesgrave village on the eastern edge of Ipswich to meet up with his parents. They had discussed the wedding over Sunday lunch in a local pub. As Inger's parents were paying for the wedding breakfast in the Dean Court Hotel, Tom's father announced they would meet the cost of a honeymoon gîte in Brittany. It was a happy, relaxed time and his mother and Inger were soon in detailed discussion about her wedding dress while Tom's father was more concerned with the progress of Ipswich Town Football Club. They had beaten Blackburn Rovers the previous day and were riding high in Division 2. He also commented that his wife's choice of a hat for the wedding could be likened to an electrocuted flamingo but, wisely, had not shared this opinion with her. Late on Sunday evening, Tom and Inger had returned to York. A busy week of lectures and meetings lay ahead.

By ten o'clock Gideon had composed a reply to Claude Sparrow. He needed to get the millionaire property owner back on side. His letter read:

Dear Mr Sparrow,

I am in receipt of your recent letter and wish to reassure you that the problems to which you refer are entirely without foundation.

Here at the university a few malcontents among the staff regularly make complaints. Fortunately they are in a minority, along with the occasional activist student reporter who writes with bias in our monthly newspaper. The fact it merely whips up discontent is a common feature of many universities in the UK.

I've found it best to ignore them and get on with my job. In their last report, the governing body of the university praised my accountancy skills and congratulated me on our healthy finances.

*Regarding the unwarranted intrusion by a
local environmental officer into the properties I
am subletting, I would point out that the state of
the accommodation is degraded by the laziness of
the students who live there. I shall ensure this is
dealt with and am confident there will be no further
correspondence of this nature coming your way.
I trust this will satisfy your concerns.*

*With kind regards,
Gideon Chalk,
Chief Financial Officer, Eboracum University*

He folded the letter, placed it in an envelope bearing
the Eboracum crest and addressed it in bold print. Then
he headed for reception, where Albert, the junior porter,
was behind the counter.

'I want this posting today,' said Gideon in a command-
ing voice.

'Yes, Mr Chalk,' said a nervous Albert. 'It will go with
the lunchtime mail.'

'Make sure it does,' said Gideon. 'It's important.'

He strode away, leaving a thoughtful Albert staring at
the address.

At morning break Tom met up with Owen in the staff
common room.

Owen had spent twenty-five pence on a *Daily Mirror*
and was flicking through the pages. Tom put down his
mug of coffee and Garibaldi biscuits. 'So, what's the
news?' he asked.

'The usual,' said Owen phlegmatically. 'In the Gulf War, Saddam's oil pipeline has been bombed; cash-starved schools are begging for help from *Children in Need*; Thatcher the Milk Snatcher is planning a globe-trotting lecture tour; and, you'll love this . . . Liverpool's Tate Gallery has commissioned an artist to create two exhibits from a pile of rubble and River Mersey mud.'

'An eclectic mix,' said Tom.

'Exactly, boyo. What a world we live in.'

'I saw you talking to your scrum-half in the quad,' said Tom.

'That's right,' said Owen. 'Rod Parfitt, a great lad. I gave him the good news about the property up the Scarcroft Road. Vijay's mate has come up trumps and they can move in ASAP.'

'The bursar won't be pleased,' said Tom.

'He deserves everything that's coming his way. Rod told me he had checked the contract. They only needed to give a week's notice. At first they were worried that this could be used by Chalky to kick them out at any time. Now it's come back to bite him. Rod is seeing the rest of the team and they intend to move out next Sunday.'

'That's brilliant,' said Tom. 'What about the rent?'

'Less than they've been paying. So, happy days. The thing is,' added Owen, 'word will get round to the others who are renting his properties. Vijay told me he would keep his ear to the ground with some of his other property-owning mates.'

'I'd like to be a fly on the wall when the bursar finds out,' said Tom.

Owen grinned. 'Well, that will be this afternoon, so watch this space.'

In reception, Perkins had returned from his weekly meeting with Charlie the caretaker. 'Time for the post, Albert,' he said. 'Anything important?'

'A couple from Miss Frensham to London and one from Mr Chalk that's going to France.'

'France? Wonder who he knows there?' said Perkins. 'In fact, I can't recall the last time he handed in any mail.'

'There was one,' said Albert. 'It was last term. I remember because it was on my birthday.'

'Expect you would remember that,' said Perkins. 'OK. Off you go.'

At lunchtime in the refectory, Tom collected his meal and spotted Richard Head sitting alone. The studious professor was staring out of the window. 'Hello, Richard,' said Tom. 'Shall I join you?'

'Of course,' he said. He removed his spectacles and polished them furiously.

'You looked deep in thought.'

'Yes,' said Richard, 'it's because of Jupiter.'

'Is that the god of sky and thunder . . . or the planet?'

'Definitely the planet. It's at its closest point to Earth today.'

'That's interesting,' said Tom as he tucked in to his beef stew.

'Are you looking forward to your wedding?' asked Richard.

'Yes, only a couple of months now.'

Richard thought for a brief moment. 'Actually, fifty-four days.'

'I suppose it is,' said Tom as he watched Richard divide his semi-circular cheese omelette into four forty-five-degree segments.

'I imagine the planning takes time,' said Richard.

'Yes,' said Tom, 'but it's fun and we share the various tasks.'

'Really? How do you retain control of all the variables?'

'I don't,' said Tom with a smile, 'but, obviously, I trust Inger.'

'Why?' asked Richard, seemingly perplexed.

Tom put down his knife and fork and stared at his friend. 'Because I love her, Richard, in the same way as I guess you love Felicity.'

'Ah, love,' said Richard. 'It's intriguing, isn't it?'

'But surely you feel it, don't you?'

'I suppose I do. At first I thought it was dyspepsia.'

Tom raised his eyebrows. 'Indigestion?'

'Yes,' said Richard. 'Exactly like that.'

'Have you mentioned this to Felicity?'

'Not in so many words.'

'Probably wise,' said Tom as Richard stared out of the window again.

It was afternoon break when Rod Parfitt rang the bell outside the Lodge and walked into the hallway. Hermione popped her head around her office door and saw a young man staring in awe at the splendour of the surroundings.

'Good afternoon,' said Hermione. 'Can I help?'

'Hello, Miss Frensham, I'm Rodney Parfitt, Year Two

PE. I'm sorry to trouble you but I have a letter for Mr Chalk.' He held up a slightly grubby envelope.

'Of course,' said Hermione. 'I'll pass it on now.' The stocky scrum-half looked nervous. 'What is it?' she asked, glancing down at the envelope. 'Is there a problem?'

'I'm wondering if I should wait.'

'I suppose it depends on whether you require a prompt response.'

Rod considered this for a moment. 'It's just that we're giving him a week's notice. Me and the other lads in the rugby team are moving out of his Hull Road property.'

Hermione was intrigued. 'And why is that?'

'It's the house we're living in. It's in a really poor state and the bursar isn't interested. The rent is high and the facilities are hopeless . . . leaks, no heating, overcrowding. We've had enough. Now we have a chance to move on, thanks to Mr Llewellyn's support.'

'I see,' said Hermione quietly. 'I wish you luck. I'm sure Mr Chalk will reply at some stage.' She glanced down the corridor towards Gideon's office. 'I don't see any need for you to stay.'

The young man was clearly relieved. 'In that case, thank you for your help.'

'You're welcome. Now tell me,' she said brightly. 'I gather the rugby team is doing well?'

Rod beamed. 'We're unbeaten. Mr Llewellyn says we're the best team he's had in years.'

'That's wonderful,' said Hermione. 'And good luck in your new accommodation.'

'Thank you,' he said as he turned towards the door. 'We're looking forward to it.'

Moments later she tapped on Gideon's door and looked inside. 'Letter for you, Mr Chalk.'

He didn't look up. 'Put it on the desk.'

Hermione left quietly, walked back into her office, waited and listened. Then there was the crash of a slammed door, loud footsteps and, out of the window, she saw Gideon heading for reception with a face like thunder. She grabbed her coat from the hanger behind the door and hurried after him.

'What's happening?' asked Perkins as Hermione skipped through reception.

'I don't want to miss this,' she called out as she headed for the quad.

Perkins looked at Albert. 'You stay here,' he said and followed Hermione.

Owen was on his way back from the gym. Wrapped up in his warmest tracksuit and carrying a clipboard, he was looking forward to a hot drink in the staff common room. He had just entered the quad when he saw Gideon Chalk striding towards him. 'You!' shouted Gideon. 'I want a word.'

The diminutive bursar stopped in front of Owen. His stacked heels raised him to five feet six inches but he was still shorter than the tough Welshman. He wagged his finger in Owen's face. 'What gives you the right to interfere with my business?'

Owen guessed the man must have received the letter giving a week's notice. 'I'm going for a coffee and you're in my way,' he said, trying to remain calm.

'You've picked the wrong opponent this time,' said

Gideon. Acid tones spilled from his lips and he sneered at Owen. 'Anyone who crosses me is made to suffer.'

'So who's rattled your cage?' said Owen.

'That environmental check on my properties was cowardly.'

'Environmental check? I know nothing about that but I'm pleased you've been found out.'

Gideon leaned forward and was almost spitting in Owen's face. He grabbed Owen's collar. 'Typical of a Neanderthal from the valleys.'

'Piss off,' said Owen. He grabbed Gideon's wrist and shook him off. Gideon stepped back, stumbled and fell on to the frozen lawn.

'That's a dismissal offence,' shouted Gideon. He waved his fist and looked over his shoulder for witnesses while Owen strode away into the staff common room.

Life was more peaceful in the music room. Inger was sitting in the large annexe that doubled up as an instrument store and an occasional office. She was on the telephone to her brother in Oslo, who was in good spirits. 'I was thinking about what I should play for your wedding. We need something soft and meaningful and I have an idea.'

'That's kind, Andreas. What have you decided?'

'How about Adagio for Strings by Samuel Barber? It's a beautiful piece. What do you think?'

'Sounds perfect,' said Inger. 'Thank you so much. Our parents will be pleased.'

'I mentioned it to Father. He said it would add gravitas.'

'That's good. What did Mother say?'

'She told me to get my suit cleaned.'

169

'Predictable,' said Inger. 'Anyway, how's Annika?'

'Lively as always. Her singing with her folk group is going well.'

'Has *she* ever mentioned marriage?'

Laughter came down the phone. 'She's a free spirit. I'm not sure I should ask.'

'Try it some time, little brother,' said Inger. 'She may surprise you.'

A bell sounded in the background. 'Back to rehearsal,' he said.

'Be good,' said Inger.

'I'm always good,' said Andreas and ended the call.

A telephone call had summoned Owen to the Lodge and he was welcomed by Hermione. 'Don't worry,' she said. 'The VC is just following up the incident in the quad. He's already spoken to Mr Chalk.'

Edward gave Owen a beatific smile and gestured towards one of the armchairs. 'Would you like a hot drink, Owen?'

'Yes, please,' responded Owen in surprise and Hermione smiled and hurried away.

'We have an outstanding first XV this year,' said Edward. 'A great shame young Christopher Scully could not be a part of it. However, I've heard of his progress with wheelchair rugby and your visits. His parents are most grateful to you.'

'He deserves the best we can offer,' said Owen.

'Quite so,' said Edward.

Hermione returned with a tray and placed it on the mahogany coffee table.

'Thank you, Miss Frensham, I'll pour,' said Edward.

'Brontë biscuits, Mr Llewellyn,' she said cheerfully and returned to her office.

Edward served the tea, sat down and looked at Owen. 'I'm afraid there has been a complaint about you from Mr Chalk. Thought we ought to have a word. There's nothing to be concerned about. The matter has been dealt with. Fortunately, Miss Frensham witnessed the incident.'

'I see,' said Owen. 'I appreciate you letting me know. Mr Chalk approached me in the quad. He appeared very angry.'

'Yes, so I understand. He came to me claiming a physical assault.'

Owen looked surprised. 'That's not true.'

'Quite so,' said Edward. 'In fact Perkins also witnessed the incident and he concurs with Miss Frensham.' The Vice Chancellor sipped his tea and sat back in his chair. 'However, I'm aware harsh words were exchanged and I'm reminded of Proverbs. "A soft answer turneth away wrath."'

Owen was munching on a biscuit and looked bemused. 'Ah, yes,' he mumbled. 'I'll watch what I say in the future.'

'And the tone in which you say it,' added Edward with a knowing look. 'Now tell me, Owen, what do you think of the Welsh rugby team this season?'

Darkness had fallen when Richard picked up the telephone and made an impulse call to Felicity. There was no preamble. 'I've been thinking,' he said.

'Oh yes,' said Felicity, 'and I can guess what about.'

'Really?'

'Yes, probably last week's conjunction of the Moon and Mars.'

'Not exactly.'

'Then it must be that today Jupiter is at its perigee, its closest point to the Earth.'

'Actually, no . . . although, of course, it is.'

'You surprise me. So what is it?'

'I was talking to Tom today about their wedding.'

'Yes, only two months away.'

'Their organization is impressive.'

'I see,' said Felicity, while wondering where this conversation was heading.

'They appear to have coped with all the variables without the need of a complex spreadsheet. It's remarkable.'

'Perhaps when it's our turn, Richard, we won't need a spreadsheet.'

There was a long silence. 'Is that because we love each other?'

There was an even longer silence. 'Yes, Richard, I think it is.'

'I wish you were here,' he said.

'So do I,' said Felicity quietly.

'Then we could look at Jupiter together. It's only three hundred and sixty-seven point three million miles away today.'

'And here in Sheffield, I'm only fifty-two miles away.'

'I know,' said Richard.

'And there's a full moon on Wednesday,' said Felicity. There was another pause while she waited to see what might come next.

'Are you definitely saying we don't need a spreadsheet for when we get married?'

'Yes, I am saying that, Richard.'

'It's just that when we got engaged I developed a spreadsheet macro with intricate calculation strings and multiple variable expressions.'

'I thought you might,' said Felicity.

'Would you like to see it?' he asked plaintively. 'It's meant to eliminate stress.'

'Yes, Richard. I'll come over on Friday night.'

'I'll polish my telescope in readiness,' he said.

'And I'll cook my cheese-topped shepherd's pie.'

'That's what love is,' he said suddenly.

'Oh, Richard. What a wonderful thing to say.'

'I mean it,' he said. 'I read it somewhere. The critical variable is the cheese.'

It was five o'clock and Victor and Zeb had just finished going through the list of students who were causing concern.

'Hot drink?' asked Zeb.

'Yes, please,' said Victor.

'Tom told me what happened in the quad earlier with Owen and the bursar,' said Zeb as she filled the kettle.

'Yes, he met with the VC. Edward rang to say it was all in hand and nothing to worry about. Fortunately Hermione witnessed the whole fracas.'

'Doesn't miss a trick, that woman.'

'Definitely,' said Victor.

'The bursar is an evil bastard,' said Zeb. 'There is enough bitterness in that man to conquer hell itself.

There are times when Gideon appears to be Satan's right-hand man.'

'You have a wonderful turn of expression, Zeb,' said Victor.

She nodded as she selected two packets of herbal tea. 'That's exactly what Vijay said last night.'

In his office Gideon was simmering after his reprimand from the Vice Chancellor. He opened his costings file for the various departments and began to scrutinize Owen's estimates for the forthcoming skiing trip to France during field week. Then he underlined several of the items on the list. His mood was sombre and the room swirled with cigarette smoke. Like a vulture he stared down at the list of figures. Time to seek retribution.

It was nearly six o'clock before Tom and Inger had completed their final tutorials of the day and tidied their desks. They said goodnight to Perkins and Albert in reception and walked out into the darkness. Fingers of moonlight caressed the frozen earth and Inger was quiet and held tightly on to Tom's hand.

She was aware that she had always carried within her a tendency towards melancholy. Until she met Tom she had been cocooned in grief and shame, and during the past year the journey from true pain to true love had proved difficult. Now she had found peace and happiness with Tom. She knew the threads of their lives were bound as one.

Beneath the firmament of stars she pulled her hood over her head as snowflakes caressed her cheeks like a whisper of the night.

Chapter Eleven

Beneath a Broken Moon

It was pitch dark when Tom crept out of bed, leaving Inger sleeping peacefully. From his satchel in the hallway he took out a Valentine card, a box of Terry's All Gold chocolates and a bottle of Dior's Poison eau de cologne. At the kitchen table, he quickly scribbled 'I love you' on the card and arranged the gifts. Then he filled the kettle and found a box of herbal tea in the cupboard. While he was waiting for the water to boil he stared out of the window. In the dark sky, beyond the scudding clouds, there was a waxing moon, a crescent that appeared broken. It scattered pale reflected light on a world where the stillness of winter lay heavy on the land. Another bleak and bitter day was about to dawn.

North of York, in their kitchen in Easingwold, Victor and Pat had risen early and were sharing gifts. Victor had given Pat a selection of artists' brushes and a Valentine card depicting Van Gogh's *Sunflowers*.

'Your turn,' said Pat.

Next to the cafetière of coffee was a beautifully wrapped gift and on top was a single red rose. Victor opened the parcel. It was a book, *A Mathematician's Apology* by G. H. Hardy. He held it up. 'This is wonderful and most thoughtful. Thank you so much.'

Pat gave Victor a gentle smile. 'I went to Walter Popple's Book Emporium.'

'A lovely man,' said Victor. 'I know him well.'

'I gathered that when I spoke to him,' said Pat. 'I asked him if he could recommend a book for a brilliant mathematician and he found this. He said it was an extended essay on why people study mathematics which, to be perfectly honest, is still beyond my comprehension.'

'It's well chosen and a perfect gift. I'm most grateful.' Victor riffled through the pages. 'This man is one of my heroes, an absolute genius, and his work in number theory helped advance mathematics beyond my wildest dreams.' He glanced down at Pat's collection of brushes. 'It makes my gift look rather mundane.'

'And we musn't forget the rose,' said Pat proudly, 'appropriate on this special day.'

'Actually, you're right,' said Victor. He held it up, appreciating the scent. 'The rose is special. In fact, it has its roots in Greek mythology.'

'Really?'

'Yes, it was believed to have been created by Aphrodite, the goddess of love and mother of Eros. Rose is an anagram of Eros so she named it in his honour.'

Pat shook his head and looked bewildered. 'How do you know all this stuff, Victor?'

'I've said it before, Patrick,' said Victor with an affected stern expression. 'I paid attention at school.'

'Oh well,' said Pat, 'as my dear, departed mother used to say, life is not a bed of roses nor a bed of thorns. It's what you make it.' He lifted the cafetière. 'More coffee, brainbox?'

Tom and Inger were driving steadily past the railway station towards the university. A huddle of commuters trod warily on the frozen pavements, heading for the early-morning train to Leeds. It had been a reluctant dawn as grey light filtered through the mist. On the car radio, Madonna was singing 'Justify My Love' and Tom was considering the day ahead. Inger had loved her gifts, even if she thought they were a little excessive. For her part, she had merely passed over a card at the breakfast table. Their life had settled into a pattern and they were content.

'Let's get a taxi tonight,' said Tom. 'Neither of us will fancy driving in this.'

'I agree,' said Inger, 'and I'll have a word with my musicians. Some of them live off-campus and it could be late when we finish.'

Zeb had organized a Valentine's Dance for members of the Education Faculty and many of the admin staff along with their partners. Around a hundred were expected to attend. Tickets had sold quickly with the proceeds going to the emergency fund for students in greatest need. It was a worthy cause that had been created a year ago by Zeb and Victor.

A poster advertising the event and designed by Ben

Laverick was on display in reception where young Albert, the attentive porter, smiled up at them.

'Good morning, Dr Larson, Dr Frith,' said Albert. He looked very smart in the new green blazer Perkins had bought him with an Eboracum badge on the breast pocket: a heraldic shield that included the eagle of St John the Evangelist and the cross keys of the Archdiocese of York. Beneath was the Latin motto *Ut Vitam Habeant et Abundantius.*

'Good morning, Albert,' said Inger, 'and how dashing you look this morning.'

Albert beamed. 'Thank you. Mr Perkins said first impressions are important.'

Tom glanced at Inger and recalled the time he had met her on his first day at Eboracum. 'Very true, Albert,' he said with a smile.

'Are you going to the dance this evening?' asked Inger.

'Yes, I'm helping on the bar.'

'But will you be dancing?' She was wondering if he had a friend to accompany him.

He shook his head sadly. 'Mr Perkins said it will be *proper* dancing with steps. I can't do that.'

'Then we'll have to teach you,' said Inger.

Tom and Inger headed for the quad, leaving behind a bemused Albert.

Hermione Frensham arrived at the Lodge as a new flurry of snow cascaded around her. She was surprised to see Gideon Chalk's car parked outside. *Early bird,* she thought. *I wonder why?*

In her office she hung up her hat, scarf and coat and

propped her umbrella in the stand. It was a distinctive one with a sturdy bone handle, a present from her mother. She grinned as she gripped it in both hands and swung it in a gentle arc as she recalled her younger days as a fierce hockey player. Then she settled at her desk for another day of letters, filing, meetings and shorthand. She began by checking the Vienna file. The visit was only three weeks away and she wanted her itinerary to be perfect.

Meanwhile, down the corridor, Gideon Chalk was busy studying the costings for next month's field week activities. He was altering the figures relating to Owen Llewellyn's skiing trip to France. It now appeared there was £200 unaccounted for and it was time to point the finger at the irritating Welshman. Gideon had always been a devious and irascible man and it was important for him to come out on top.

Rosie Tremaine was driving her two-door Opel Manta carefully towards Thirsk. Year Three students were out on teaching practice and a morning of school visits in two North Yorkshire villages had been timetabled. Snow pattered against the windscreen and she was concerned about the state of the roads. Beyond the frozen hedge-rows, the ploughed fields had been transformed into a washboard of smooth folds.

On the car radio the newsreader was reporting on the recent troubled times. A week ago the Provisional IRA had launched a mortar attack against 10 Downing Street. She decided to lift the mood by inserting a cassette of Elaine Paige's *Cinema* LP. As she listened to 'The Way We Were' she reflected on the emotional rollercoaster of the past year. Life was happier now, more secure. In Sam Greenwood, the shy scientist, she had found a trusted companion and the future looked bright.

He had sent her a Valentine card. Typically he had not left it anonymous; neither had he gone down the conventional route of writing 'I love you'. In his rapid scrawl were the words: 'Albert Einstein said that when you are courting a girl, an hour seems like a second – that's relativity.' She had smiled and placed it on her mantelpiece.

At morning break, following a lecture on the work of Edgar Allen Poe with his Year Two English group, Tom was enjoying a coffee in the staff common room when Owen joined him. 'I just passed Chalky in the quad,' said the Welshman with a grin. 'He looked like death warmed up.'

'That's usual these days,' said Tom. 'He's got real problems now with his off-site accommodation.'

'They're gathering momentum,' said Owen with determination. 'Vijay has been in touch again. He's definitely on the case, checking out properties owned by his affluent friends. There may be another one coming up in New Earswick. Chalky was livid when my rugby lads moved out. I've heard the Hull Road property is still empty.'

'You need to be careful,' said Tom. 'He could be dangerous.'

'Don't worry . . . I've got the measure of that evil bastard.' He sat back and drank his coffee with a grin on his stubbly face.

Tom looked at the clock. 'Time to go. School visit coming up.'

'It's Year Three this week, isn't it? Who are you seeing?'
Tom nodded. 'Poppy Hartness and Ellie MacBride.'

Owen gave a mischievous look. 'Interesting. What a combination . . . the socialite and the seductress.'

Tom groaned. 'Come on . . . they're both OK and will make great teachers. By the way, I've heard Ellie is going out with Jonny Halliday.'

Owen leaned forward. 'She'll always hold a candle for you, Englishman. Problem is, you don't understand women like I do. It's all down to saying the right thing at the right time. That's why they're putty in my hands.'

Tom shook his head, muttered, 'Bollocks,' picked up his satchel and left.

Richard Head was in his study, marking essays titled 'The Benefits of Tim Berners-Lee's World Wide Web'. Outside, a weak sun was sinking over the rooftops and the cold weather seemed endless. The wind rattled the leaded windows and beneath him the quad was still as a stone under a new fall of snow. Then the phone rang. It was Felicity.

'Just confirming I'll be at yours tonight by six,' she said, 'and I'm coming in my new car. It's a Peugeot 205 Trio. I'm really pleased with it.'

'It was voted *Car Magazine's* Car of the Decade,' said Richard. 'So a good choice. Was it expensive?'

'A bargain at £5,795,' said Felicity.

'Well done.' He paused for a moment, recalling that he had spent five pounds on a box of chocolates as a Valentine gift. 'That's equivalent to one thousand, one hundred and fifty-nine boxes of chocolates.'

'Really,' said Felicity, somewhat bemused. 'That's interesting.'

'Yes, I thought so too,' said Richard enigmatically.

It struck Felicity that conversations with Richard were always a circuitous journey into the unknown. 'I'm looking forward to the dance,' she said.

'So am I,' said Richard with enthusiasm. 'I went to Walter Popple's bookshop and I bought Robert Brandon's book, *Ballroom Dancing Made Easy*. It's the 1955 edition so I can introduce you to some classical steps.'

Felicity, an accomplished dancer, had her doubts but knew the pernickerty professor meant well. 'That's lovely, Richard.'

'Do be careful on the roads,' he added.

'Yes, I will. But I don't want to drive back to Sheffield this evening, so I should like to stay over.'

'Excellent,' said Richard. 'We can discuss the lunar cycle. The moon is very interesting at the moment. It's twenty-nine point three one days since the last new moon. I had better set up my telescope under the skylight in the spare room for you.'

Felicity sighed. She had been considering a different scenario. 'That sounds exciting, Richard,' she said with subdued politeness.

At eleven o'clock Tom drove out of the car park to visit a local York school. It was only a mile away and two of his Year Three students had been placed there. Poppy Hartness was teaching a class of seven-year-olds and Ellie MacBride was in the top junior class of ten- and eleven-year-olds. He parked outside the Victorian building.

Above him, the rooks in the high elms squawked their danger cries as the wind rattled their nests. Sparrows and chaffinches were busy in the hedgerows while a lonely robin perched forlornly on the school gate.

He walked into an entrance that was filled with light and colourful displays of children's work. The head-teacher, Miss Carol Mountjoy, a tall, imposing woman with a purple rinse and the demeanour of a Girl Guide leader, welcomed him. 'You have some outstanding students this year, Dr Frith. I would have no hesitation in employing them both when they have completed their degrees.'

'That's good to hear,' said Tom. He glanced up at the timetable on the noticeboard. 'Please can I start with Miss Hartness, then see Miss MacBride at half eleven?'

'That's fine,' said Miss Mountjoy, 'and would you like to stay for lunch? I'm afraid it's spam fritters, but our cook is very good.'

'Thank you but sadly I can't. I have lectures this afternoon.'

Miss Mountjoy led him to a lively classroom full of vibrant artwork and activity. Poppy Hartness had forsaken her usual tie-dye outfits and was dressed soberly in a navy suit and a cream blouse. London rave parties fuelled by ecstasy seemed a world away for this young woman as she worked with a group of young children who were weighing and measuring. She smiled up at Tom and looked content in her world. The class teacher, a cheerful thirty-something, was hugely impressed. 'A natural,' she said quietly to Tom as they observed her at work. 'Great to work alongside someone like her.' Tom wrote a positive summary in his carbon-copy notebook and left the page on the teacher's desk.

At the end of the corridor was the largest classroom, where thirty-three ten- and eleven-year-olds were in the middle of a history lesson about celebrations in the annual calendar. Predictably, Valentine's Day was being discussed when Tom walked in. The deputy head, Mr Peter Maddocks, a grey-haired traditionalist and only two years from retirement, waved from his seat at the back of the classroom. He had written 'Love Thy Neighbour' in neat, cursive handwriting on the blackboard and invited Ellie to continue the discussion.

'I know what love is, miss,' said an eager ten-year-old, Stevie Backhouse, with his hand in the air.

'Really?' said Ellie. 'Go on, Stevie. Share it if you wish.'

The thoughtful little boy considered this for a moment. 'It's when my big brother puts on his aftershave and his girlfriend wears perfume and they go to the pictures and smell each other.'

'Good answer,' said Ellie with a smile in Tom's direction. 'Anyone else?' More hands were waved in the air. Ellie pointed towards a cheerful blonde-haired girl with neat pigtails. 'Amy, what do you think?'

'Well . . . I know my big sister loves me.'

'That's good to hear, Amy,' said Ellie.

'And I know why,' said Amy.

Ellie gave an encouraging smile. 'Go on.'

'It's because she always gives me her old clothes when she's grown out of them and that saves money for my mum.'

'And so it does. Well done,' said Ellie and turned to the

group of expectant faces. 'Now I want you to write a short story in your English books.' For a moment she glanced at Tom. 'Think about caring for someone or something, your best friend or a favourite pet or maybe one of the grown-ups at home. Why are they special? If you're stuck on a word, raise your hand and I'll help.'

The lesson progressed well and, once again, Tom was impressed with this confident woman. The deputy head shook Tom's hand as the bell went for school lunch. 'Thanks for calling in, Mr Frith,' he said. 'I've helped with many students over the years but this young woman is the probably the best.'

'I appreciate that, Mr Maddocks,' said Tom, 'and thank you for your support.'

Out in the corridor the children hurried away for their school dinner while Tom and Ellie walked together to the entrance hall. 'Thanks for coming, Tom,' she said. 'I've been fortunate with this placement, a great school and a short journey each morning.'

'Both the head and deputy are singing your praises,' said Tom. 'In fact, there could well be a job here when you've got your degree.'

'Really? That's encouraging, but the likelihood is I'll go back home. I'm hoping for a job in Barnsley and then I can still help my parents on the stall at weekends.'

'How are they?'

She lowered her voice. 'Fine but, like me, they would still like to know who sent that letter.'

'We'll find out eventually,' said Tom.

Ellie looked thoughtful. 'Hope so. Fortunately, very few know about it.' She glanced up at Tom, her green eyes searching for a reaction. 'It was a difficult time for me, mainly because I thought the letter would affect your work. You must know I would never do anything to hurt you.'

'I understand,' said Tom quietly.

Suddenly they were a point of stillness in a moving world. Members of staff hurried by and, beyond the hall doors, countless children were eating spam fritters, chips and peas. 'I had better go,' said Ellie. 'I have preparation to do for this afternoon's art lesson.'

'I'll call by again next week,' said Tom. 'Good luck and well done.'

'I may see you briefly tonight,' said Ellie. 'Zeb and Victor asked me to do an article for the *Echo* on the Valentine's Dance. The money raised is really helpful to those students from challenging home backgrounds.'

'OK,' said Tom. 'See you then.'

Ellie walked with Tom to the entrance door. 'And don't worry,' she said. 'I won't ask you for a dance this time.' She watched him walk away and considered what might have been.

It was shortly after six o'clock, and Tom and Inger were sitting at the kitchen table after a warming meal. The portable television on the worktop was on in the background and the newsreader was summarizing the items of the day. A scary film called *The Silence of the Lambs*, based on the Thomas Harris novel of the same name, had been released in America and the movie star Kirk Douglas had survived a helicopter crash. Meanwhile, Princess Diana had slipped out of Kensington Palace to visit the homeless who were sheltering from Britain's big freeze in Westminster Cathedral's Parish Hall.

'A special lady,' said Inger. She picked up the plates, turned off the television and headed for the sink.

'How do you feel about Vienna?' asked Tom.

There was a clatter of crockery. 'Fine. Rehearsals have gone well and Hermione has organized everything to perfection. The hotel is well chosen, only a short walk from the cathedral. Ben will be there with his camera, of course. I'm looking forward to it.'

'I wish I was coming with you,' said Tom.

'You'll be busy with your students. It's only a few days.' She dried her hands, glanced at the clock and smiled. 'Come on, time to get changed. Get your dancing shoes on.'

By seven thirty the staff common room was full of colleagues sharing news and relaxing in the warmth. Richard Head had set up a microphone and, following Zeb's welcome, Jonny Halliday had made a brief speech thanking everyone for supporting such an important cause. He reminded everyone it was the first of two fundraising events, the second being an inter-department 'It's a Knockout' tournament in May. Alongside him Ellie MacBride was making notes, Ben Laverick was taking photographs and Albert was busy helping behind the bar.

On a raised stage in the corner of the room, Inger was chatting with her musicians, who included a saxophonist, a bass guitarist, a flautist, Adam Kite on his violin, and a wonderfully talented pianist. The singer, Arabella Esposito, was checking the songs as Inger moved towards the microphone. 'Welcome, everybody, to our Valentine's Day event and many thanks for your support. Tonight's music is a little different from our usual DJ and popular records. It's an opportunity to brush up on your dance steps. So we have members of my orchestra performing, along with Arabella providing vocals. They've planned three sets throughout the evening, beginning with a gentle waltz to get you in the mood. So please take to the floor as our musicians create a beautiful and romantic atmosphere and entertain us with Johann Strauss and his "Blue Danube" waltz.'

There was applause and Peter Perkins and his wife Pauline were the first to take to the floor. They were quickly followed by Sam Greenwood and Rosie, and Sue Llewellyn dragging a reluctant Owen. Inger headed for the bar, took a surprised Albert by the hand and began to take him slowly through a few simple dance steps.

Pat was collecting two glasses of wine at the bar for himself and Victor while many of the women were openly admiring this sartorially elegant man. Pat was dressed in a beautifully tailored blue cord suit. Once each year he travelled down to Petworth in West Sussex to visit his favourite gentleman's outfitter's. There he received superb service and the clothing on offer was of the highest quality.

In earlier times, Pat had secretly admired the flamboyant Italian owner, Davide Antonio Collardo, an elegant and sophisticated entrepreneur. However, the handsome Italian was married to the dynamic aristocrat and socialite

Lady Linda Devine, who took him on world cruises, and Davide knew which side his ciabatta was buttered.

The Vice Chancellor had spotted that Gideon Chalk was sitting alone. 'Good evening, Gideon,' he said and sat down beside him. 'I'm pleased to see you are supporting this important event. The funds raised will help those in greatest need.'

'Good evening, Edward. Yes, I agree and I felt I needed to be here.'

'Incidentally,' said Edward, 'the account for this event will be handled by Mr Halliday and myself. I'll pass on the details to Miss Frensham. You can check them if you wish.'

'Of course,' said Gideon. 'I'll do that. I'm busy with the field week accounts at present.'

'And how is that progressing?'

'It's all in hand, although I've had to make a few suggestions to members of staff regarding use of transport. Other than that it's fine, although Mr Llewellyn's costings are a concern. I've checked them thoroughly and there's two hundred pounds that cannot be accounted for.'

Edward gave Gideon a knowing look and stood up. 'Oh well, *veritas numquam perit*,' and he walked away.

Gideon was puzzled. Latin had never been one of his subjects. If it had, he would have known that the Vice Chancellor had said, 'Truth never dies.'

Arabella Esposito approached the microphone following the orchestra's wonderful renditions of 'Moon River' and Judy Garland's 'Puttin' On The Ritz'. 'OK, everybody,' she said. 'Time for a change of mood and pace. The quickstep is a fun and energetic dance and has the fastest tempo of all our ballroom dances. So put down your drinks, show us what you can do and please enjoy our version of Abba's 'Waterloo'.'

Sue Llewellyn grabbed Owen's hand once again and pulled him to his feet. 'Come on, God's gift to women,' she said. 'If your mate Tom can do it, so can you.'

What followed was frantic but fun. Felicity in particular was impressed. 'Well done, Richard,' she said. 'You've clearly been practising.'

'There's lots of space in the spare bedroom,' he said rather breathlessly, 'and I've gone through the steps there.'

'I've been thinking,' said Felicity. 'We're both tired and it's a cold night. I think we ought to share your room tonight.'

'Oh, I see,' said Richard hesitantly. 'I suppose the lunar cycle will save until the weekend.'

'I'm sure it will, my darling man,' and she took his hand and led him to the car park. It meant they missed the final dance. The lights were dimmed as the orchestra played 'Are You Lonesome Tonight?' and couples smooched around the floor followed by hugs and farewells. It had been a successful evening.

Tom and Inger's taxi drove them home carefully along the frozen roads and their apartment, with its light over the porch, was a welcome sight. As they hurried towards the front door their breath steamed before them and they stumbled into the warmth of the hallway. 'A lovely evening,' said Inger and kissed Tom on the cheek.

'Happy Valentine's Day,' said Tom, 'and many more

to come.' As he closed their bedroom curtains he stared out at the frozen world. Across the road, the crust of snow on the Knavesmire reflected a ghostly light beneath a fractured moon.

Meanwhile, 225 miles away in the Winchester Royal Hotel, Kai Pederson was staring at the same sky. It had been a long day. His planning meeting for the M3 motorway had gone well. Meanwhile there were other considerations on his mind.

He stared out of his bedroom window at the frozen streets and streetlamps. Above, only the broken crescent of the moon was visible in the dark sky. In two weeks he was taking a European holiday, visiting France, Switzerland and Austria. He stroked the scar on his cheek and smiled.

Chapter Twelve

Miss Frensham's Apple Strudel

'It's the flaky pastry,' said Hermione. 'Absolutely perfect!'
There were nods of agreement.

It was early Saturday morning, 9 March, and Hermione, Inger and Ben Laverick were in a coffee shop in Vienna. Hermione had ordered single Mokkas and three generous slices of classic Viennese apple strudel. It helped that she spoke fluent German: the language had been one of her A Level courses at York College for Girls in the early 1970s.

'This is the best apple strudel I've ever tasted,' said Ben.

Hermione nodded in agreement. 'The finest in Europe, so I'm told.'

'Delicious,' agreed Inger. 'And the coffee is excellent.'

'It's their *Kleiner Brauner*,' said Hermione. 'Always served in a glass. By the way, I read the hotel's guidebook last night. It said Austria is credited with introducing coffee into Europe. Apparently bags of coffee beans were left behind by the retreating Turkish army after the Battle of Vienna in 1683.'

'I've been here before, in my student days,' said Ben, 'but I didn't know that. Good to have a tour guide while we're here,' he added with a grin. It was followed by a muffled yawn and Hermione knew why.

Inger was sipping her coffee appreciatively. 'And thanks for your organization, Hermione,' she said. 'Everything has gone to plan. Love the hotel. It's really handy for the cathedral . . . and the apple strudel is a delight.'

Yesterday's early-morning flight had been on time and the coach at the airport had been waiting for them. After settling into the hotel and enjoying a light lunch, the choir had had a brief rehearsal in the cathedral, which had gone well. Inger had selected an *a cappella* arrangement of 'Ave Maria' followed by Beethoven's 'Ode to Joy'. Countless hours of practice had gone into this and she knew her choir was close to perfection.

In the cathedral, Inger, Hermione and Ben had also met up with the other two conductors, Herr Christian Steiner from Fribourg in Switzerland and Monsieur François Lavigne from Dinan in France. Both were supportive and looking forward to the prestigious concerts. It was noticeable that Christian Steiner quickly engaged Hermione in conversation and Inger thought she had rarely seen Hermione so animated.

Last night, the sixteen members of the choir, six men and ten women, had left the hotel in Innere Stadt and wandered off to explore Vienna. Hermione remained in the lounge reading her guidebook while Inger was feeling very tired and decided on an early night. Later that evening, the fact that twenty-two-year-old Alexandra Midwinter had crept into Ben's room had not gone unnoticed by Hermione as she stepped out of the lift.

On Saturday morning, shortly before 9.30 a.m., Inger selected the first of her two long black dresses from her hotel wardrobe. She put it on, added a red silk scarf and stood back to check the ensemble in the mirror. After ensuring her hair with its French plait was perfect, she wrapped up warmly in her long woollen coat. Then she picked up the leather satchel containing her music and walked out to the lift. Downstairs in the foyer, the sixteen excited members of the choir were dressed in their formal outfits. The women all wore long black dresses and a red silk scarf around their necks. The men wore black trousers, black shirts and red bow ties. Each one of them had added a warm coat and scarf.

'OK, everybody,' said Inger. 'This is it. The concert starts at eleven and we're performing after the choirs from Switzerland and France.' She held up the satchel and smiled. 'Don't worry, I haven't forgotten the music.' There was laughter and a rumble of appreciation. 'I'm told that, while we wait our turn, seating has been reserved for us near the pulpit. Also, I met briefly last night with the other two conductors, Herr Christian Steiner and Monsieur François Lavigne. They are both very supportive and keen that you get to know the members of their choirs. So look upon this as an exceptional cultural opportunity. Make the most of this special time. Good luck, everybody, and let's go.'

Hermione walked beside Inger as they left the hotel on Bauernmarkt and strolled down Jasomirgottstrasse towards St Stephen's Cathedral. It was a cold clear day and the sky was as blue as a starling's egg. Hermione put up her umbrella as occasional snowflakes fluttered down from the heavens. Before them was revealed the breathtaking sight of the cathedral with its four imposing towers and multicoloured tiled roof. Ben Laverick was already outside the main entrance, known as the Giant's Door, taking photographs of the group as they approached.

When they walked inside they were greeted by the organizers and a petite woman showed them to their seats next to the pulpit, a masterwork of Gothic sculpture. The audience was arriving in large numbers and finding their places while the two other choirs were already seated. The Swiss choir in their white shirts and blouses were at the front near the altar along with members of their orchestra. In their striking blue outfits, the French choir were assembled to one side on the front row; like Inger's choir, they were singing *a cappella*.

The concert was a triumph. All three choirs performed their two pieces beautifully. The harmonies were exceptional and filled the void of the cathedral. The audience was spellbound and, at the end, they jumped to their feet to show their appreciation. All three choirs took a bow and Inger, Christian and François were each presented with a huge bunch of flowers.

Gradually the audience made their way outside to the vast spaces of Stephansplatz. Inger gathered her choir together at the back of the cathedral. 'Listen, everybody.

We meet again at five forty-five in the hotel foyer, dressed and ready to go. I'm told it's a sell-out audience for the seven o'clock performance this evening, so we need to concentrate and perform with the same professionalism as we've just shown. I have to say it was a privilege to hear you singing.' She paused and looked at the far side of the cathedral where the members of the other choirs were receiving a similar message from their choirmasters. 'I know you have met up with the members of the other choirs so do enjoy your afternoon and remember . . . no alcohol please and be very careful what you eat. Relax, of course, but be sensible. We need to be perfect again this evening. Until then, we all know that our hard work has paid off. So thank you all and I'll see you later.'

There was impromptu applause and then the students drifted away to mingle with the other choirs and lay the foundations of new friendships, some of which were destined to last a lifetime.

A few minutes later, Hermione and Herr Christian Steiner were chatting outside the cathedral. Inger called out to Hermione: 'Ben and I are going for a late lunch. Are you joining us?'

Hermione glanced back at Christian and then turned to smile at Inger. 'Thanks, but Christian wants to show me a restaurant he has discovered and it's a chance to brush up on my German.'

'Fine,' said Inger. 'We'll catch up later at the hotel.'

There was no doubt Hermione was intrigued by the tall, beautifully dressed Swiss choirmaster with his greying wavy hair, chiselled good looks and charming manner.

'I know the perfect place and it's nearby,' said Christian. 'We arrived on Thursday because, unlike you and the French choir, we brought our own orchestra and needed to rehearse before you arrived.'

'So how many students have you brought?' asked Hermione.

'Thirty including the orchestra. We are very experienced and perform all over Europe.'

'That must be wonderful,' said Hermione. 'Do you know Vienna well?'

'Yes, it's one of my favourite cities. Please follow me. I'm sure you will enjoy my choice of restaurant.'

They wandered off towards Josefsplatz, where Christian stopped outside a very smart restaurant. He took Hermione gently by the arm and led her inside. The tall maître d' in his black suit and bow tie welcomed them, and Christian requested a table with polite authority. They were led to a table for two in the window and were soon enjoying a glass of Pinot Blanc as Hermione scanned the menu. 'All this is fine for me,' she said.

'In that case, may I order for both of us?'

Hermione raised her glass and smiled. 'Of course.'

Christian ordered *Strozzepreti mit Melanzane, Pinienkernpesto und veganem Feta*. 'The cheese is a delight,' he said.

'So, Christian, tell me about Fribourg.'

'You would love it,' he said. 'It's a beautiful place and sits on a small rocky hill above the valley of the Sarine. We're on the cultural border between German-speaking and French-speaking Switzerland so it is normal for us to speak both languages . . . as well as English, of course,' he added with a twinkle in his eyes. 'In fact you would be most welcome to visit.'

Hermione enjoyed relaxing with this charismatic man. The meal was perfect and the conversation was enlightening. Christian was fascinated by the extent of Hermione's skills as the personal assistant to the Canon Edward Chartridge.

'What a busy life you must lead,' he said. He glanced at her empty glass. 'More wine?'

'No, thank you. A demanding evening lies ahead and it's important I'm there to support.'

'Very well, but I absolutely insist that, before we leave, you join me in one of Vienna's true specialities.' He walked over to the counter where lots of pastries were displayed behind a glass case.

Moments later, the waiter appeared with two plates. On each was the largest slice of apple strudel Hermione had ever seen.'

'You must try this, Hermione. It's a classic in Vienna.'

Hermione didn't want to burst his bubble and, for the second time that day, worked her way through a mountain of flaky pastry and huge, delicious and very sweet pieces of apple. By the end she felt fit to burst.

Back at the hotel, Ben carried Inger's leather satchel into the foyer while she held her bunch of flowers. To her surprise, when she arrived, the young lady in reception called out, 'Miss Larson, you have a delivery.'

It was a bunch of red roses, beautifully wrapped. 'That's a nice surprise,' said Ben. 'Who are they from?'

Inger removed the card but the typed message simply read: 'Good luck this evening.'

'Anonymous,' said Inger.

'Probably from Tom,' said Ben.

Inger looked thoughtful. 'Yes,' she said, 'but strange he didn't add his name.'

'Maybe he did,' said Ben, 'and they misheard or forgot.'

She left the flowers in reception while she and Ben walked into the hotel restaurant and ordered *Rindergulasch* that arrived with a bread roll and butter. They were drinking apple juice when Inger suddenly asked, 'How's Alexandra?'

Ben didn't miss a beat. 'She's fine. You'll gather we're good together. I spoke with the Vice Chancellor and he was more relaxed about it than I imagined he would be. Alexandra is over twenty-one. She's heading for a first – her work is outstanding – and our relationship isn't affecting that.'

'That's good to hear,' said Inger. 'I wish you both happiness.'

'Likewise,' said Ben. 'Your wedding is getting closer. Are you excited?'

Inger smiled. 'I am, in a way. To be honest I wanted something quiet and low-key but parents tend to get involved.'

Ben smiled. 'I know what you mean. I heard Edward has offered a blessing in the Minster. That sounds special. I'm sure your parents will love that.'

'Too true. Knowing my mother as I do, the whole of Oslo will have heard by now.'

Inger enjoyed relaxing with Ben: he was an interesting

and talented man. They discussed photography tech-
niques, life beyond Eboracum and the fact that Hermione
had been whisked away by a handsome stranger. When
they finally left the dining room, Inger collected her flowers and took them upstairs.

By six o'clock the sun had set and, in the darkness, Inger,
Ben and Hermione left the hotel once again and walked
to the cathedral, followed by the choir.

When they entered it was Monsieur François Lavigne's
turn to approach Hermione. He was a similar height to
her, a stocky man with a swarthy complexion, long black
hair and a dashing moustache. His French beret and long
overcoat with a belt and epaulettes would not have been
out of place in wartime Europe.

'Your choir was magnificent this morning,' he said.
'Beautiful *a cappella*. It makes a performance very special
and your soloist is a gift from heaven.'

'Thank you,' said Hermione. 'Miss Esposito has a
remarkable voice but all the praise must go to Miss
Larson. She has worked so hard during recent weeks.'

'Yes, and the results were there for all to see.' He paused
and gave Hermione an admiring glance. 'I was wondering if you know the city well?'

'No, this is my first visit but I've read a few of the
guidebooks.'

'Have you any plans for tomorrow?'

'Actually, yes. I've decided to visit the National Library
in the morning. I'm told the paintings on the ceiling rival
those in the Sistine Chapel.'

'You are quite right and you have made a perfect choice.

I wonder . . . would it be inappropriate for me to ask to join you? The young people in my choir have their own plans.'

Hermione smiled. 'It would be a pleasure, Monsieur Lavigne.'

'François . . . please.'

'And I'm Hermione.'

'A beautiful name,' he said. 'Hermione was the daughter of Helen in Greek mythology. She was also the loyal wife of King Leontes in Shakespeare's *The Winter's Tale*.'

'You seem very well read, François.'

He gave a shy smile. 'Books are my friends.'

'Mine too,' said Hermione.

Meanwhile, in the darkness, Kai Pedersen removed his Russian fur hat and walked into the cathedral. There was a long queue and he handed his ticket to the assistant and paused to take in the surroundings. There were hundreds in the audience. Bright lights hung from huge chandeliers above the altar and the choir stalls, where members of the Swiss orchestra were tuning their instruments and arranging their music on stands. The choir had taken their seats and were waiting patiently.

He had enjoyed his holiday in Paris, Bern and now Vienna. During his time in France and Switzerland, there had been fine dining and occasional female companions who were too eager. He preferred those who were not.

He chose his seat carefully on the back row, almost behind a stone pillar, and sat in the gloom. There he could watch from a distance. When Inger approached the rostrum under the bright lights and arranged her music on the lectern, once again his mouth went dry. Suddenly those moments of excitement back in Norway, when she was completely within his power, were vivid in his mind. Yet for now, the thrill of following Inger from a distance and her not knowing was enough. Sending the anonymous bunch of flowers to her hotel was yet another act that had given him pleasure.

Kai turned briefly, aware of a figure behind him, and heard the click of a camera. It was simply a long-haired hippy dressed like a tramp and Kai ignored him.

Ben Laverick wanted a long-distance view of Inger and her choir from the back of the cathedral. Satisfied, he headed back to the pulpit and used his zoom lens to capture special moments of the performance.

When the audience rose to give a standing ovation it was time for Kai to leave. A brief flurry of snow greeted him as he walked outside and he was smiling as he set off for his hotel beyond St Peter's Church.

At some time in the future he would confront her. It would be his decision, and his alone, when that would be. He imagined the surprise and fear on her face and smiled again. Then he touched the scar on his cheek. She would pay dearly for that. Inger had no idea he was close by once again and that's how he liked it. He was invisible, and therein lay his power.

In front of the altar rail, Inger, Christian and François were centre stage holding hands and taking a bow. Once again, Inger received a bunch of flowers and Ben recorded the moment.

As the audience departed, the choirs mingled at the front of the church and made arrangements to meet up in one of the city's many bars. A late night was in store for them. Ben and Inger had arranged to explore the city the following morning and shared a secret smile when Hermione told them she was meeting Monsieur François Lavigne in order to visit the library.

'You appear to have rivals for your company, Hermione,' said Ben.

Hermione's cheeks flushed slightly. 'They are both interesting men and I get little chance these days to practise my language skills.'

'Well, enjoy your morning,' said Inger. 'The library sounds to be a fascinating visit. Ben and I have decided to get a taxi to the Schönbrunn Palace, whereas our students are more interested in the bars and cafés. But it will be good for them to relax and celebrate the success of the concert.'

It was late when, after dinner, Inger finally climbed into bed. She had telephoned Tom, who was delighted everything had gone so well. They spoke about the forthcoming wedding and, during the conversation, it became clear to her that he had not sent her any flowers. They were in a vase now on the dressing table, alongside her two other bouquets, and, as she ended the call, she wondered who her mystery admirer might be.

On Sunday morning François arrived in the hotel foyer, where Hermione was waiting for him, clutching her guidebook. 'I thought we could get a taxi outside the cathedral to take us there,' he said. 'Then we can maybe have a bite to eat afterwards.'

'Perfect,' said Hermione.

As they left the hotel, Hermione pointed to the cathedral and opened her guidebook. The bells were pealing. 'This is interesting, François,' she said. 'Did you know that Ludwig van Beethoven was standing right here when he suddenly discovered the extent of his deafness. The bells rang out and when startled birds flew away he realized he could hear nothing.'

'Remarkable,' said François as he stared up at the bell tower. 'A wonderful story.'

Hermione's French was as good as her German and they drifted from English to French as the morning progressed.

She was thrilled with her visit to the Österreichische Nationalbibliothek. It was the largest library in Austria, containing millions of books. She was full of awe as she stared at the marble statues of emperors and the countless manuscripts from almost every literate culture. 'Astonishing,' she whispered.

'A wonderful experience,' said François. 'The glory of books.' Yet as captivating as the library was, he found he was more intrigued by this fascinating woman. He gestured towards the tall, decorated wooden shelves that soared above them. 'The Grand Hall is one of the most beautiful library rooms in the world.'

'Oh, François,' she said. 'Just look at the ceiling.' Above was a huge dome decorated with a colourful fresco depicting 'becoming a God' and for a brief moment she felt she had been transported to the heavens. However,

François was not staring up at the ceiling, he was looking at Hermione and wishing he could enjoy more time in the company of this gentle yet vibrant woman.

During the walk back to the city centre François would have loved to have held Hermione's hand but he felt that would be too presumptuous. It was the happiest he had felt for many years. Likewise, Hermione was aware of a new freedom, walking through this remarkable city with a caring and cultured companion.

Together they chose a likely restaurant, busy with locals, which François believed was always a good sign. They shared stories of their professional lives, Hermione at Eboracum and François as the choirmaster at the Basilica of Saint-Sauveur de Dinan.

'Hermione, you really must come to visit,' he said. 'Dinan is one of Brittany's best-preserved medieval towns and you would love my beautiful church.'

Hermione studied this gentle yet eager man. The two of them had spent only a short time together, yet it was clear they had made a connection, a connection she had not felt with Christian. In fact, as much as she had enjoyed Christian's company, he had been eclipsed by the Frenchman.

'I should like that very much,' she said softly.

They had enjoyed a light and simple lunch full of carefree conversation when François suddenly stood up and took a few paces towards the waiter. Moments after their brief exchange the waiter returned with two slices of apple strudel. 'I thought we could finish with a special treat,' said François. 'No one should visit Vienna without sampling their classic apple strudel. It's the best in the world.' Hermione was too polite to refuse.

François walked alongside her back to the hotel and they stepped into reception. There was a writing desk beneath a painting of Mozart, and François sat down and wrote out his address. 'This is where I live with my sister, Juliette. Please remember, Hermione, you are always welcome and there is an excellent hotel close to the church. I do hope we meet again.' He took her hand and kissed it gently. There was sadness in his eyes as he left and Hermione watched him walk away.

Darkness had fallen and at seven o'clock Inger, Ben and Hermione met in reception and headed for the hotel restaurant. They all perused the menu. 'May I make a suggestion,' said Hermione. 'I've just spotted their iconic dish is here.'

'Go on,' said Inger.

'It's Wiener Schnitzel,' said Hermione. 'I'm sure we'd all enjoy it. It's usually veal or pork, coated in flour, egg and breadcrumbs and then fried to perfection. François was telling me about it earlier. They serve it with potato salad and a slice of lemon.'

'Perfect,' said Ben.

Inger smiled. 'It sounds as though your French companion made an impression.'

Hermione blushed slightly. 'I've certainly made a good friend.'

'I'm sure you have,' said Ben. He glanced back at the menu. 'So it's Wiener Schnitzel all round, is it, and maybe a bottle of wine?'

'Let's order,' said Inger. 'I don't know about you, but all this fresh air has made me hungry.'

All three were happy: Inger knew her concert had been a success; Ben had taken countless photographs which he was sure would be good; and Hermione had the prospect of a new man in her life. They enjoyed their meal, drank wine and then discussed the arrangements for the journey home. Hermione knew their itinerary off by heart.

Ben suddenly stood up and spoke to the waitress. When he returned to the table he gave a big smile. 'Let's end this time together as we began,' he said. 'My treat.'

Three plates of apple strudel were served along with three Mokkas. Ben stood up, stepped back a few paces and recorded the moment with his camera. It was much later that Inger and Ben finally saw this photograph and wondered why Hermione was staring at her plate with a slightly forced smile.

Chapter Thirteen

The Music of Life

The Students' Council meeting in the Lodge had ended. It was six o'clock on Friday, 22 March. The Vice Chancellor took Gideon and Jonny Halliday to one side. 'Excellent,' he said. 'That went well. All that's left is for us to sign off the accounts.' The Valentine's Dance had proved to be a huge success and the funds raised were going into the students' emergency fund. Edward signed the relevant document and Gideon and Jonny both added their signatures.

Edward smiled. 'So, any plans for the Easter holiday?'

'I have work to do here in York,' said Gideon, 'but I'm hoping to spend a few days in Herefordshire, fishing on the River Lugg.'

'Splendid!' said Edward. 'It will do you good.' He turned to Jonny. 'And what about you, young man?'

'I'm meeting up with Ellie MacBride in Sheffield,' said Jonny. 'She's got tickets for Shakespeare's *All's Well That Ends Well.*'

For a moment Gideon frowned, whereas Edward's eyes lit up. 'I know it well,' he said. 'A wonderful play. "Love all, trust a few," and so on. One of my favourites.'

They walked along the corridor to the brightly lit porch. 'Well, thank you for your attendance,' said Edward, 'and enjoy your well-earned break. In the meantime I have some preparations to make for tomorrow's wedding.'

Gideon followed Jonny out into the darkness. He was curious. 'Jonny, just a thought. You mentioned Miss MacBride. I did hear there was some doubt about her returning this year. I presume that's all resolved.'

'Yes, I was so pleased,' said Jonny. 'Apparently someone wrote a letter to her parents saying she was in trouble.'

'Oh, yes?'

'The powers that be are investigating to see where the letter came from, given its intent was clearly malicious.'

'How will they do that?' Gideon enquired.

'It was handed back to college and those higher up than us are looking into it.'

'I see. Sounds sensible,' said Gideon uneasily. 'I expect that will be a job for the Vice Chancellor or Victor.'

'Probably,' Jonny replied, a little suprised at Gideon's sudden interest. 'Anyway, I must go. Have a good break.'

Gideon watched Jonny leave, knowing that he had to act, and sooner rather than later.

'Wake up, sleepyhead,' said Rosie. 'It's your wedding day.' She was wearing a silk dressing gown and her usually immaculate hair looked like a bird's nest in a high wind. She had popped her head around Inger's bedroom door. It was very early on Saturday morning and there was much to do.

Inger sat up in bed and for a moment was surprised Tom was not beside her. 'Oh, hi, Rosie. What time is it?'

'Six o'clock and Zeb's hairdresser is due here at seven so get your skates on. The shower's free.'

'OK, thanks,' said Inger.

Rosie closed the door and hurried away.

Inger stretched, walked over to the window and drew the curtains. She smiled as she looked out across the Knavesmire. Spring was in the air and the promise of light and colour stretched out before her. Blue-grey bullet heads of daffodils speared through the grassy banks while snowdrops, aconites and crocuses brightened the misty morning. Sticky buds on the horse chestnut trees were bursting open while, close by, winter jasmine clung to the wall.

She took a deep breath. As she looked at her wedding dress hanging on the wardrobe door she thought of Tom.

Tom and Owen had stayed overnight in the Dean Court Hotel. It was the height of luxury. Owen was lying back in the jacuzzi. 'This is the life, Englishman. You picked a winner here for your last night of freedom. Look at all these fancy soaps and shampoos. I could get used to this.'

Tom had stepped out of the shower in the ensuite. 'Where's my toothpaste?' he shouted.

'Sorry, forgot mine,' said Owen. 'It's in there somewhere.'

'I don't know how Sue copes with you,' grumbled Tom. He found the tube of toothpaste on the floor minus its screw top.

Owen climbed out of the jacuzzi, picked up a large towel and stood in front of the full-length mirror. 'God's gift to women,' he said as he flexed his muscles. He dried himself off, wrapped the towel around his waist and wandered over to the huge bay window. Outside a fitful sun pierced the iron-grey clouds above the Minster. The season was changing and the first breath of spring was tantalizingly close. 'Looks like you've got decent weather,' he said. He glanced back at his red suit draped over a chair and smiled.

Hermione had taken on responsibility for the flowers. As always she was organized and efficient. The local florist had delivered them to her home and, just before seven o'clock, she was in her car heading for the Knavesmire. For the buttonholes, Inger had requested carefully wired white roses and dainty gypsophilia. Hermione had already dropped two of them off at the reception desk in the Dean Court Hotel for Tom and Owen. In a separate box was Inger's beautiful bouquet. It featured red and white roses with blue hyacinths, the colours of the Norwegian flag.

As Hermione pulled up outside Inger's home the hairdresser had just arrived and they walked in together. Rosie opened the door and welcomed them. 'Hi, Hermione, wonderful flowers.'

'I'll put them in the kitchen, shall I?'

'Yes, please,' said Rosie. 'And you must be Brenda.

Thanks for coming so early. Inger is ready for you. Meanwhile, anyone for a Buck's Fizz?'

Zeb's hairdresser, Brenda Duckworth from Crayke village, was a very experienced stylist. Within minutes she was unpacking her huge bag of scissors, combs, a host of bottles and her favourite Clairol 1200 hair dryer.

She sat Inger down on a chair in the conservatory and covered her shoulders with a towel. 'Your hair is beautiful! Zeb mentioned you had great hair,' she said as she began to comb Inger's long blonde locks. 'Vijay's paying, so it's anything you want: up high or over the shoulders . . .'

'Thanks,' said Inger. 'I always just put it into a French plait; then it looks tidy. So, if you can come up with something more interesting, I'd appreciate it!'

Brenda got to work. 'Don't worry,' she said. 'You'll look a million dollars when I've finished.'

Owen had left Tom trying to get the creases out of his new white shirt. After taking a call from reception he made his way downstairs. The young receptionist passed over a box with two buttonhole flowers. 'They're beautiful,' she said. 'Congratulations.'

'I'm the best man,' said Owen with an engaging smile. 'The groom is upstairs struggling with his cufflinks.'

'Good luck,' she said.

With flowers in hand, Owen wandered back to the lift. The receptionist watched him walk away and wondered why he was wearing a suit that would stop traffic.

At ten thirty Tom and Owen set off for the short walk to York Register Office. They paused under Bootham Bar when they saw a large crowd gathering up ahead. 'Bloody hell,' said Owen. 'Big turnout.'

Friends and family were standing outside on the pavement along with a crowd of students. Inger's parents were engaged in conversation with Tom's mother and father. They were smartly dressed, the men in dark-grey three-piece suits and the two women in fashionable outfits with very different large-brimmed hats. Both would have been perfect for Ladies' Day at Royal Ascot.

'Your mum has pushed the boat out with that hat,' said Owen. 'In a high wind she'll fly away.'

'I know,' agreed Tom. 'My dad said the same.'

'I've met *your* parents,' said Owen. 'What's Inger's family like?'

'Remarkable,' said Tom. 'You've met her brother, Andreas, the violinist ... great guy. Her dad is Fredrik, a Norwegian economist ... very serious. Her mother, Hilde, was an Olympic skier back in the fifties, a very perceptive woman. She'll weigh you up in seconds ... so behave,' he added with a grin.

Owen studied Hilde Larson appreciatively; she was tall, slim and blonde. 'Inger definitely takes after her mother,' he said.

They were spotted from the other side of the road. Victor and Pat were chatting with Richard Head and Felicity while Sam Greenwood began a round of applause as they crossed the street. It was a scene of celebration and Ben Laverick was capturing every highlight on his camera.

Some of the students were holding boxes of confetti and Arabella Esposito was clutching a bag of rose petals.

The increasingly confident Adam Kite was busking nearby with his violin and being applauded by Andreas and Annika, while collecting coins from passers-by in the open violin case at his feet. As Owen stepped on to the pavement Sue Llewellyn grabbed hold of him and began to straighten his tie and turn down the lapel of his red suit, which he had already crumpled. 'Good luck today,' she said and gave him a kiss. Meanwhile, on the other side of the street, Ellie MacBride was standing alone. She cast a wistful glance at Tom as he was surrounded by his colleagues.

Suddenly a serious, pale-faced man opened the door of the register office and beckoned everyone in. 'This way, please,' he said, 'and take your seats.'

Owen led the way with Tom and then ushered everyone inside; the excited chatter ceased as they settled down to wait for the bride. Fredrik Larson stood quietly to one side, looking out for the arrival of his daughter.

At that moment Vijay's Jaguar XJ, newly cleaned and sporting white ribbons, pulled up outside. Vijay, in an immaculate charcoal-grey three-piece suit, opened the doors. Rosie and Zeb, as bridesmaids, stepped on to the pavement. They were dressed in mid-calf blue satin dresses and carried a small posy of flowers along with Inger's bouquet. Then Inger appeared, looking stunning in an ivory halter-neck wedding dress covered in lace with floral beading. Ben Laverick took another photograph.

Vijay jumped back in the car. 'Catch you later,' he shouted and drove off to the nearest car park.

Fredrik stared at his daughter and stood back in admiration. 'You look beautiful,' he said. 'Love the dress.'

'Thanks,' said Inger. 'Rosie and Zeb helped me choose it.'

'And you too, Rosie and Zeb,' said Fredrik. 'You both look lovely.'

'Thanks.' Rosie smiled. 'You don't look too bad either!'

Zeb turned to Inger. 'How do you feel?'

'OK, I think,' said Inger and smiled in her turn. 'Don't forget we've got to survive Owen as best man.'

Zeb grinned. 'He's a good friend.'

'I'll make sure everyone is seated before we go in,' said Rosie, and hurried inside.

'Well, this is it,' said Inger. She took her bouquet from Zeb. 'And thanks for everything.'

'Always a pleasure,' said Zeb. 'You look radiant.'

Rosie reappeared. 'Everyone is sitting down now. The front row is reserved for us and Sam is saving a seat at the back for Vijay.'

'So ... we'll follow you in,' said Zeb. 'Enjoy the moment.'

Fredrik Larson took his daughter's arm and they walked in together.

At that very moment, Gideon Chalk was working out a plan to retrieve the letter that had been sent to Ellie MacBride. It would be helpful for it to mysteriously disappear. He paced his room, knowing that everyone would be at the wedding and only the young and not-too-observant Albert would be on duty at the porters' lodge. Gideon would have time to search the Vice Chancellor's room, and Victor's if needed, and should their office doors be locked, there were other ways to get round that problem.

An expectant audience on either side of the central aisle of the room glanced up as the sound of footsteps signalled the arrival of Inger, Fredrik, Zeb and Rosie. The silence was disturbed only by the wonderful sound of a solo violin. Andreas was sitting in the far corner, deep in concentration and playing Samuel Barber's *Adagio for Strings*. It set the scene beautifully. But all eyes were on Inger. As she approached the front of the room for a moment she felt in a daze. The crowd appeared to swirl and coalesce around her as she took her place. Inger's mother on the second row dabbed away a tear as she looked in wonderment at the spectacle of her husband and beautiful daughter. At the same moment, Tom's mother clutched her husband's hand.

Tom looked at Inger. 'I love you,' he whispered.

Owen beckoned to Rosie and Zeb to sit down next to him. He looked up at the clock. It was eleven o'clock. The Superintendent Registrar, a cheerful woman in a smart navy business suit, was clearly very experienced. She smiled at Tom and Inger, leaned forward and whispered, 'I'm Jacqui from Malton. I've done this a hundred times so don't worry. Just follow my lead.'

'Thanks,' said Tom while Inger began to relax.

The registrar made a short statement about marriage and invited a statement of vows. The ceremony went smoothly; the rings were exchanged and Jacqui invited Tom to kiss the bride. This was greeted by cheers and applause. Finally, after signing the marriage certificate, everyone stepped out on to the pavement and, once again, Ben Laverick recorded the scenes before him.

Tom and Inger led the way down Bootham to the Minster, followed by an excited group of their friends and relations, until the great west door loomed above them. Predictably, it was quiet as they walked inside the awe-inspiring expanse of one of the world's most beautiful Gothic buildings. Off the south aisle of the choir was an old wooden door and a few steps that led into the Zouche Chapel, a peaceful space beneath fine stone vaulting.

Everyone took their seats. This was the part of the celebration that meant so much to Inger's mother. She had hoped for a traditional church wedding in Norway but this was beyond her wildest dreams. In front of her sat Tom with Inger by his side. Fredrik Larson leaned forward in his chair and nodded towards Tom's father. Meanwhile Tom's mother was dabbing away tears with her lace handkerchief and remembering a little boy full of life and questions.

In front of the altar stood Canon Emeritus Edward Chartridge in his magnificent attire. Over his clerical black shirt and white collar he wore an alb, a white robe. He had added a beautiful chasuble, a green-coloured outer vestment, over the alb. The finishing touch was his stole, a long narrow scarf with threads of white and gold. Edward smiled. 'Welcome, everyone, to York Minster and particularly to Inger's parents, who have flown in from Oslo, and to Thomas's parents, who have travelled here

217

from the county of Suffolk.' He spoke clearly and with solemnity. 'Since the seventh century, the Minster has been at the centre of Christianity in the north of England and it was built for the glory of God.' Inger's mother took out a silk handkerchief and wiped away a tear.

Edward's pause was perfect as he scanned the chapel and those listening in rapt attention. 'We are in the Zouche Chapel, named after its founder, William de la Zouche, Archbishop of York in the middle of the fourteenth century. These days it is mainly used for prayer and meditation, but today we are gathered to bless the union of Inger and Thomas.'

He looked down at them and smiled. 'May God bless this marriage with hope that is sure and with love that endures.' And then, speaking to everyone seated, Edward continued, 'As we rejoice and celebrate the commitment that our friends, Inger and Thomas, have declared, bless the bond they have made here today.'

He turned to the huge Bible resting on the lectern beside him. 'In Corinthians, chapter thirteen, verses four to seven, we are reminded of the meaning of love.' He touched the Bible gently and raised his eyes. He knew these words by heart. ' "Love is patient. Love is kind. Love is not envious or boastful or arrogant or rude. It does not insist on its own way. It is not irritable or resentful. It does not rejoice in wrongdoing but rejoices in the truth. It bears all things, believes all things, hopes all things and endures all things.' Then he turned towards Victor and stood to one side.

Victor rose and walked confidently to stand before the altar. In an immaculate grey suit and a red bow tie, he surveyed the faces before him that he knew so well. 'It's both a pleasure and a privilege to be part of Inger and Tom's special day as they set out on a new journey together.' He paused, took a dog-eared paperback from his pocket and held it up. 'One of my favourite poets is Kahlil Gibran, a Lebanese-American. He was an insightful man and he reminded us that tears and smiles make the music of life. Life without tears is as incomplete as a life without happiness, but embracing both can lead to a much more meaningful existence.'

Then he glanced at Pat on the back row. 'However, life is sometimes a rocky road.' Pat nodded briefly in acknowledgement and then bowed his head. 'So, as Tom and Inger set out on this new journey together, the duality of human emotions lies before them with occasional sorrow but mainly joy.' He gestured towards Inger and Tom and gave a gentle smile. 'We wish them well as they create their own music of life.'

For a moment there was silence and Victor's eyes were moist with tears. The stillness of the tableau ended with Edward gripping Victor's arm. 'Perfect,' he whispered and Victor returned to his seat.

Then Edward invited Tom and Inger to stand up before him. 'And now our newly-weds will lead us out as we make our way to the gardens at the back of the Minster for the official photographs. From there we move to the Dean Court Hotel and the wedding breakfast.' There was a rumble of appreciation as the spell was broken and normality resumed. Tom and Inger stood up, bathed in a kaleidoscope of sunlight from the stained-glass windows. They soon processed from the Minster, through the metal gates to the spacious lawns, where they were showered with confetti and rose petals.

In the gardens Ben Laverick photographed the usual sequence of groupings: Inger and Tom with their parents, then the bride and groom with Zeb, Rosie and Owen. Finally, colleagues from the faculty, along with a few of the students, gathered around the happy couple. It was over in what seemed like a few minutes, and everyone walked to the Dean Court Hotel.

At Eboracum University, Albert was tidying up the porter's lodge. He was grateful that Perkins had trusted him to be on call for most of the morning on his own. Nothing much had happened, although he was surprised to see Mr Chalk almost running into the university buildings earlier on. 'Hello, Mr Chalk,' Albert had called out, trying to emulate the friendliness and welcoming comments always made by Perkins, even to people like Gideon Chalk. It did not surprise Albert that the bursar didn't bother to reply or even appear to notice him. But Gideon *had* noticed him and was pleased that Perkins was not on duty.

At the Dean Court Hotel, the maître d' in his black suit and bow tie welcomed the married couple and their guests and soon they were being served with an excellent meal. Wine flowed and conversations filled the room while Tom and Inger circulated and thanked everyone for their cards and gifts.

Finally, Fredrik Larson rose from his seat, tapped his wine glass and said a few words, followed by a toast to the bride and groom. Then it was Tom's turn; he was grateful that his father-in-law's address had been friendly and short. He stood up, and, in reply, thanked Inger's parents for the wonderful meal and his own parents for the gift of their honeymoon gîte in France. He turned to Inger. 'You will be aware that my beautiful wife was brought up in Norway: fishing with her father, skiing with her mother and making music with her brother. It was clearly a special childhood. Likewise I have to thank my parents for giving me opportunities in life and supporting me every step of the way.'

There was applause and a few more tears. 'Inger and I wanted a quiet wedding' – everyone laughed and clapped again – 'but today has been remarkable, thanks mainly to our Vice Chancellor, who provided us with such a memorable ceremony in the Minster.' Edward nodded in acknowledgement. 'So thank you, Edward, for the blessing you bestowed upon us and thanks to Andreas for your music. We shall carry the memory through our lives together.' He turned to Zeb and Rosie. 'Our thanks go to our friends and colleagues, Owen as my best man, along with Zeb and Rosie as Inger's bridesmaids. They have provided wonderful support. So I ask you to charge your glasses and join me in a toast to . . . our bridesmaids.'

After a few cheers and thunderous applause there was a rumble of anticipation as Owen got to his feet. His wife, Sue, called out, 'Behave!' and everyone laughed.

'Good afternoon, everybody,' said the Welshman. 'I'm so pleased to be part of the only five minutes that were not planned by Rosie and Zeb.' There was polite laughter. Owen grinned. 'As you are aware I'm the best man but I guess you have all known that for a long time.'

Zeb shook her head and muttered, 'Typical.'

Owen was enjoying his few minutes of fame. 'It's been an emotional day. Even the cake was in tiers.' There was a groan from everyone. Undeterred, he looked down at Tom: 'Loyal, caring, honest and a great man . . . but enough about me. As a Welshman living in Yorkshire people say to me, "You miss Wales?" I say, "No, I look nothing like her. She has long blonde hair and wears a sash."' So it went on but at least Owen kept his promise to avoid jokes about sheep. Finally he raised his glass and called out, 'To Tom and Inger,' and everyone drank a toast and applauded. Tom breathed a sigh of relief. Everything had gone well.

Gideon Chalk was in a state of distress. He was back in the Lodge and searching Hermione's office for the letter he had sent to Ellie MacBride's parents. The door to Edward's study was locked and he was hoping Hermione would have a spare key in her desk. This was a perfect opportunity while everyone was attending the wedding.

Except everyone wasn't. Perkins had cheered Tom and Inger as they walked into the register office and then he had returned to the porters' lodge where young Albert was holding the fort. 'I'll do my rounds,' he said and took the master keys from the cupboard. He had done this many times, always beginning with the Lodge when he knew it was empty and then moved on to the study rooms on Alcuin and Cloisters corridors.

When he entered the Lodge, he was surprised to see Miss Frensham's door was open. He walked in and Gideon leapt back from her desk, clearly very shocked. 'Good afternoon, Mr Chalk,' said Perkins evenly. 'Sorry to alarm you. I'm just doing my rounds, checking doors for the weekend. Was there anything in particular you were looking for? Miss Frensham is at the wedding breakfast in the Dean Court at the moment.'

Gideon scowled at Perkins. 'I'm merely delivering the accounts for the Valentine's Dance,' he said quickly. 'The door was unlocked and I thought it would be helpful to pass them on before I go on holiday.'

'I see,' said Perkins. 'In that case I'll lock the door as you leave,' and he walked out to check the Vice Chancellor's door.

Gideon fumed. He could have done without the interference, but he had no option but to leave. There would be another opportunity.

'Good afternoon,' called Perkins as Gideon swept out of the front door. He didn't bother to reply.

'Shifty,' mused Perkins. 'Definitely shifty.'

It was late when Tom and Inger returned to their home on the Knavesmire. Vijay and Zeb had delivered all the presents and they were packing their suitcases ready to leave for France in the morning.

'Well, we've done it,' said Inger. 'A really lovely day.'

'We're lucky, aren't we?' said Tom. 'So many special friends.'

Inger zipped up her case and sat down on the bed. 'I was really touched with Victor's words. They meant a lot . . . the music of life.'

'That's what lies ahead,' said Tom.

'Almost perfect,' said Inger with a smile.

'Almost?' queried Tom, looking puzzled.

'Yes,' said Inger. 'You still need to learn how to use the washing machine.'

Chapter Fourteen

Wind of Change

Hermione had arrived early at Eboracum. It was Monday, 8 April, the first day of the summer term, and she was full of optimism. The scent of wallflowers hung in the air and the blackthorn trees, the first to blossom, had woken from their winter sleep. The ground beneath her feet was covered in white petals while, in the far distance, the hills were rimmed with golden fire. She had enjoyed a holiday with her sister, Cordelia, in Oxford and felt refreshed. They had visited the Ashmolean Museum and spent hours in the Bodleian Library, where her sister was a curator. Cordelia was fascinated by Hermione's visit to Vienna and secretly hoped her sister would take up the offer of a visit to Dinan by the charming Monsieur François Lavigne, but Hermione was reluctant to commit.

The sun was shining as she walked under the porch and into the Lodge. She knew that Perkins would have locked her door when the university went down for Easter. However, when she turned the key and opened her office door, she stopped and stared at her desk, puzzled and concerned. It wasn't as she had left it.

Tom and Inger walked into reception, where Perkins greeted them. 'Good morning, Dr Larson, Dr Frith. Welcome back. How was your honeymoon?'

'Perfect,' said Inger. 'The gîte was lovely and there are so many beautiful fishing villages in Brittany.'

'And we visited most of them,' quipped Tom. He patted his tummy and smiled. 'Especially the ones with crêperies serving their famous *galettes*.'

'Sounds wonderful,' said Perkins. Then he took a bunch of eight red roses from behind the counter. 'These were delivered earlier for Dr Larson.'

'How lovely,' said Inger. 'My favourite flowers.'

'There's a card attached,' said Tom and handed it to Inger.

'It says "Best Wishes for the New Term".' She turned over the card. 'No name. I wonder who sent them?'

'It was just a courier who delivered them,' said Perkins.

'A kind thought,' said Tom. 'Maybe your parents.'

'Oh well, we'll soon find out,' said Inger.

'Have a good day,' said Perkins. 'And, by the way, are you Mr and Mrs Frith now?' He looked at Inger. 'I've got used to calling you Dr Larson.'

'I'm still Dr Larson at work, Perkins. It's easier that way.'

'Fine,' he said. 'Enjoy the new term.'

Tom smiled. 'Thanks, Perkins,' and he and Inger set off for Cloisters corridor.

*

Owen was at his desk when Tom walked into their study. He was reading a letter and held it up with a big grin on his face. 'Good news,' he said. 'Vijay's worked his magic again. There's another property available for students.'

'Brilliant,' said Tom.

'I've already sounded out Zeb,' said Owen. 'Some of her first-year drama students are struggling with over-crowding. All this will definitely backfire on Chalky. He thought giving a week's notice in the contract would suit him and not them.'

'Be careful,' said Tom. 'You know what he's like.'

'The evil bastard can crawl back into his shell for all I care,' said Owen. He jumped up. 'Anyway, come on, let's grab a coffee before lectures and you can tell me all about your honeymoon and why you look so knackered.'

Tom smiled. His Welsh colleague was in good humour and it was reassuring to be back.

At eight thirty Hermione walked out of the Lodge and followed a group of students into reception. Perkins gave a cheery wave. 'Good morning, Miss Frensham, I hope you have had a good holiday.'

'Yes, thank you. I spent time with my sister in Oxford.'

'A wonderful city,' said Perkins. 'One of my favourites.' He noted a slight hint of concern on her face. 'So . . . how can I help?'

'I was just thinking back to the end of term. I intended to return to my office after the wedding but it went on much later than I thought. Usually I would finish up with some filing before starting my holiday but I had to leave early the next morning.'

'Yes,' said Perkins. 'No problem. When I do my rounds

after the end of term I always start with the Lodge and then move on to the tutor corridors. So I went to your office first.' Then he paused. 'Although, come to think of it, Mr Chalk was in there. Said he was delivering some accounts. Then he left and I locked up.'

'I see,' said Hermione neutrally. She was annoyed but didn't want it to show. 'Thanks, Perkins. As always, I appreciate you looking after our security.'

'A pleasure,' said Perkins. 'Although I must say it was unusual to see Mr Chalk behind your desk. I presumed you had made an arrangement with him.'

Hermione looked at her watch and frowned. 'Oh well, things to do. Thanks again.'

'Any time, Miss Frensham,' Perkins called after her. Then he shook his head. 'Something's going on,' he muttered to himself.

In his office Gideon was staring at a letter in disbelief. Another group of students had given him a week's notice, stating they were moving out of one of his properties. If this continued he would be facing serious financial trouble. 'It's that bastard Welshman,' he muttered.

He unlocked the bottom drawer of his desk and took out a manila folder. Then he opened it, studied the figures once again and smiled.

Hermione was back at her desk when Gideon walked in. 'I need to see the Vice Chancellor. It's important,' he said abruptly. 'Let me know when he's free.'

'Can I tell him what it concerns?'

Gideon gave her a cold stare. 'No,' he said. 'It's a formal financial matter, way above your pay grade.'

'I see,' said Hermione as he turned his back on her and returned to his office.

A few minutes later Hermione tapped on Gideon's door and entered. The room stank of cigarette smoke and she stood there waiting for the bursar to acknowledge her presence. Finally he looked up. 'What?'

'The Vice Chancellor is free to see you at ten thirty.'

He gave an abrupt nod, glanced at his watch and returned to a list of figures in his manila folder.

Tom had completed his first lecture of the term with English Three and the morning coffee break beckoned. The students began sharing their Easter holiday news as they packed up their notes on twentieth-century American literature.

Amy Fieldhouse and Liz Colby had returned from their annual job in Bridlington, where they had sold ice creams from a kiosk on the seafront. Poppy Hartness, still wild at heart, had gone to another Orbital rave in London. Meanwhile, Ellie MacBride had helped on her parents' market stall in Barnsley and then gone on a walking holiday in the Yorkshire Dales with Jonny Halliday.

As they stepped outside, Ellie caught up with Tom. 'How did it go?' he asked.

'Loved it,' said Ellie. 'Just what I needed. Wonderful scenery. Stayed over in Kettlewell. Great village.'

'I know it well,' said Tom. 'I'm pleased you managed to take a break.'

'Yes,' she said. 'I just needed to sort out a few things in my life.' Then she caught up with the rest of the group and headed for the refectory.

*

At precisely ten thirty Gideon tapped on the Vice Chancellor's door. After hearing a familiar 'Come in' he entered the study. He gave his usual subservient smile while Edward gestured towards one of the armchairs. To his surprise Hermione was perched on a carver chair next to the mahogany table by the bay window. She was holding a spiral bound notepad and a pen.

'Oh, I thought it would be just the two of us,' said Gideon.

Edward gave a calm smile. 'I got the impression it sounded sufficiently formal to warrant a record of the meeting.'

Although ill at ease, Gideon pressed on. 'As you wish, Vice Chancellor. I have no wish to detain you longer than necessary, but I have discovered an unsettling anomaly that I consider important enough to share with you.'

'And what might that be?'

'It concerns the accounts for field week.'

'Go on,' said Edward. Hermione, head bowed, began to write shorthand notes.

'I've double-checked this as you would expect but I've discovered a significant shortfall in Mr Llewellyn's accounts. A sum of two hundred pounds appears to have gone astray. Sadly, this will need investigating.'

'Have you a copy of the accounts in question?'

'Yes, Vice Chancellor,' and he held up a manila folder.

'Thank you, Gideon. If you will leave it on my desk I'll get to it in due course. I won't detain you any longer.'

Gideon stood up. 'Thank you for your time, Vice Chancellor. I'll get on with my work.' He gave Hermione a curious glance as he walked out.

When the door closed Edward looked thoughtful. 'What do you make of that?' he asked.

Hermione closed her pad, put down her pen and shook her head. 'There's something you should know, Vice Chancellor.'

At morning break in the staff common room, Ben Laverick collected a mug of coffee and sat down next to Inger. 'Just thinking about the collection of Vienna photographs,' he said. 'I've been working on them in my spare time. There's a lot to process.'

'Thanks, Ben,' said Inger. 'I'll look forward to seeing them.'

He nodded. 'So I began thinking that it merits an exhibition. I know the VC would be keen, so maybe one evening in your music room? It's a big space. Larger than my art studio. What do you think?'

'Good idea,' said Inger. 'When is a good time for you?'

'I'm really busy up to the end of May, so maybe early June. We could make an event of it. Wine and nibbles. Maybe a short recital if you wish.'

'A lovely idea, Ben. Yes, let's do it. When you've firmed up a date we can check it out with Victor and the VC.'

'OK, I'll get on to that. How was France for you and Toni?'

She smiled. 'Perfect.'

He grinned. 'Enough said. Catch you later,' and he hurried off to the art studio.

Gideon was summoned to the Vice Chancellor's study shortly before lunchtime. He was surprised when

Hermione followed him in and took her seat once again next to the table by the bay window. It was covered with a neat row of receipts and invoices.

'Hello again, Gideon,' said Edward. 'You'll be pleased to know the shortfall in Mr Llewellyn's accounts has been checked carefully.'

'That's reassuring,' said Gideon. 'Thank you for dealing with it so promptly. Did you want me to contact him and ask him to join us?'

'That won't be necessary,' said Edward. He turned to Hermione. 'Miss Frensham will explain.'

Hermione gently patted Gideon's manila folder. 'I have here the accounts you passed on to the Vice Chancellor this morning.' Next to it was a detailed list of expenditure. 'Fortunately Mr Llewellyn took my advice and collected receipts for every single transaction during the skiing field week in France. So everything we need is here and has been recorded.'

The colour left Gideon's face as he sat there transfixed by the unexpected turn of events. Edward was watching his reaction carefully.

'I've checked your accounting,' said Hermione firmly, 'and you will be relieved to know I've found the error.'

'Error?' spluttered Gideon.

'Yes,' said Hermione. 'It was obvious. You have added two hundred pounds to the cost of the Courchevel ski lodge. So I've corrected your figures.' She picked up the folder, stood up and gave it back to him.

'I don't understand,' said Gideon. 'My accountancy is always excellent.'

'As is Miss Frensham's,' added the Vice Chancellor. 'So

I won't detain you any longer, Gideon, and I'll discuss this with you later.'

Gideon stood up, gave Hermione a look of pure hatred and departed.

When the door was closed Edward smiled at Hermione. 'Well done.'

Hermione began collecting the receipts. 'Always glad to help. I'll leave you to your lunch.'

'No need to depart,' he said with an engaging smile. 'I've ordered lunch to be delivered on a tray . . . for the two of us. You've earned it.'

An excellent sandwich lunch had also been prepared in Victor's office.

'Scrumptious,' said Zeb. 'Pat really is a marvel. These are delicious.'

A collection of Tupperware containers containing sandwiches, pastries and flapjack was displayed on top of the bureau under the latticed window and Rosie was preparing mugs of coffee. When Inger and Ben arrived their eyes lit up at the unexpected treats. After a few minutes of convivial banter and sampling Pat's offerings, they sat down in the armchairs around the coffee table.

Victor opened the meeting. 'I appreciate your time, everybody,' he said. 'Zeb said this won't take long. It concerns this term's annual drama festival in the quad, which involves us all.' He turned to Zeb. 'Over to you.'

'First of all,' said Zeb, 'thanks to Victor, and Pat of course, for arranging the delicious lunch. Much appreciated.' She looked down at her notes. 'I've done some work over the holiday and I thought we could do another Shakespeare play.'

'Excellent,' said Rosie.

'Inger will recall we did a version of *The Merchant of Venice* a couple of years ago and it was successful. I sounded out my final-year drama group about this before we went down for Easter and they're all keen. So we could start rehearsals next week.'

'Good idea,' said Inger.

'I've spoken to Victor and Edward,' continued Zeb, 'and they're happy for a dress rehearsal on Friday, the twenty-first of June, followed by two performances on the Saturday. Richard isn't here but no doubt he will do his stuff with the lights and sound.'

'So, what's the play?' asked Rosie.

'*Twelfth Night*,' said Zeb, 'and there's some background for this. Over Easter I was given a script from a friend in Stratford.' She turned Rosie. 'Here's a copy. I was hoping you could adapt it like you did last year.'

'Of course,' said Rosie.

'And you'll want my musicians,' said Inger.

'Yes, please,' said Zeb.

Inger was scribbling on her notepad. 'In that case we need to discuss the pieces we need to practise.'

Zeb turned to Ben. 'I recall you arrived last summer as we were about to perform *The Importance of Being Earnest.*'

'That's right,' said Ben. 'So I'm guessing my job is building the stage in the quad.'

Zeb grinned. 'Yes, please.'

'Consider it done,' said Ben. 'Just tell me what you need.'

'Wow!' said Zeb. 'What a team.' She took a sip of her coffee. 'There's something else. My friend said the Royal Shakespeare Company are on tour in Oxford with *Twelfth Night* and offered me some tickets for the end of this month.' She glanced down again at her clipboard. 'It's on Saturday the twenty-seventh. So I wondered if any of you might be free to come along? Have a think and let me know. I intend to go down there on the Friday evening and stay a couple of nights.'

'Sounds to be a good plan,' said Victor. 'Thanks, Zeb. Any questions, anybody? If not let's meet again next week.' He paused and smiled. 'And I'll persuade Pat to provide the food.'

They all immediately engaged in vibrant conversation as they finished their lunch and then left for afternoon lectures.

Over lunchtime, Tom was having a stern conversation with one of his first-year English students. He was both angry and disappointed. Sally Latimer had done well on her early teaching practices and, up to now, her essays had been exemplary. It was the recent one on Steinbeck that had upset him. Tom was familiar with most of the current books of criticism, particularly those relating to *The Grapes of Wrath*, which summed up the desperate times of America's great depression.

'It's simply plagiarism,' said Tom. 'Do you understand?'

Sally looked distraught. 'I think so. I was just using the books in the library to help me.'

'But, Sally,' he said. 'You've lifted complete paragraphs. It's theft, the dishonest appropriation of another person's property.'

'I'm sorry, Tom,' she said. She looked as if she would burst into tears.

'I'm afraid you will have to repeat the essay. I'll give you a week. Don't make this error again. You're a good student and this was unnecessary. If you're stuck or confused, come to me and I'll help.' He tapped the top of the filing cabinet. 'There's lots of research material here that you can use.'

'It won't happen again,' she said.

Tom looked at this bright nineteen-year-old. One day she would become a fine teacher. This was a tough lesson but it looked as if she understood the gravity of the situation.

'OK,' said Tom and softened his approach. He looked at his wristwatch. 'Have you had lunch?'

She shook her head. 'Not yet.'

'When is your next lecture?'

'I'm with Rosie at two.'

Tom opened the door. 'Get some lunch. Let's put this behind us and move on.'

Sally hurried away while Tom reflected on the vagaries of youth.

In the staff common room at afternoon break, Zeb and Inger were deep in conversation when a delighted Rosie joined them. She was clutching a letter. 'Exciting news,' she said. 'Perkins has just passed this on to me. My

Oscar Wilde book has been accepted for publication. I've just had confirmation from my agent in London, so I'm going down there at the weekend for a meeting. She says it will be out in the autumn.'

'That's wonderful,' said Inger.

'Wow! Brilliant,' said Zeb. 'We must celebrate.'

'I have to sign a contract,' said Rosie, 'and she wants to know whether or not we might think about going for a two-book deal.'

'Have you got an idea for a second book?' asked Inger.

Rosie looked thoughtful. 'Probably, not sure.'

Zeb grinned. 'How about *Confessions of a Chess Champion*? It could be a racy Jilly Cooper-inspired thriller with a character like Rupert Campbell-Black from her *Rivals* novel in a power struggle with a handsome Russian grandmaster.'

Inger smiled and joined in. 'Perfect,' she said, 'and they both fall in love with the enigmatic and super-intelligent Cornishwoman who is their threat to chess supremacy.'

'Could be a bestseller,' said Zeb eagerly.

'Definitely . . .' added Inger, a whimsical note to her voice.

Rosie gave them a stare. 'Sounds wonderful but I was thinking more along the lines of the poetry of Elizabeth Barrett Browning.'

'Did she have any affairs?' asked Zeb.

Rosie considered this for a moment. 'Well, she did elope to Italy with Robert Browning.'

'That's a good start,' said Zeb. 'Just add a few lovers – maybe the Russian grandmaster.'

At that moment Tom and Owen arrived and sat down beside them.

'You all look animated,' said Tom. 'Have we missed something?'

'Rosie's book on Oscar Wilde is to be published,' said Inger.

'That's great,' said Tom. 'Congratulations.'

'Zeb had a few ideas for a follow-up book,' said Rosie.

'All you need is a tough Welsh hero,' said Owen, 'and all the women in the village want to marry him. A guaranteed bestseller.'

'Typical,' muttered Zeb.

'Well, thanks everyone for your ideas,' said Rosie. 'I'm off to tell Victor. I promised he would be one of the first to know.' She left with a smile on her face. It was good to have supportive and creative friends – even when they were pulling your leg.

Late in the afternoon, Owen found Tom and Inger sitting in the corner of the staff common room near the television set, drinking tea. The news was being reported.

'Hi, Owen,' said Inger. 'Had a good day?'

'Fine thanks,' said Owen. 'I've just arranged to go down to visit Chris Scully in Hampshire.' Owen's rugby protégé was adjusting to life in his wheelchair. 'I'm meeting up with his parents and taking Maddy Defoe with me. Apparently she and Chris are an item now.' Maddy was a Year Two science student and very bright, according to Richard. She and her brother, Josh, had been victims of a hit-and-run accident, and Josh was now competing for a place in the England wheelchair rugby team and Owen was doing his best to support him.

Owen nodded towards the television. 'So what's happening?'

'You'll be interested in this,' said Tom. 'They've just announced plans for a "super league" of eighteen clubs to replace the football league First Division.'

'It's all about money,' grumbled Owen.

A report followed concerning the inquests into the fatalities during the Hillsborough disaster. It had recorded a verdict of accidental death, much to the dismay of the families concerned. Many had hoped for a verdict of unlawful killing along with criminal charges to be brought against police who patrolled the match. Tom reflected on how one of his best students, the Liverpudlian Billy Whitelock, would take this news. Apparently his mother was still traumatized.

It was a sombre trio who walked back to their studies after finishing their tea.

Lectures had ended for the day and Zeb had called into the science block to meet up with Richard. He was busy writing a heading on the chalkboard: 'Calculating Moments of Inertia'. Richard was pleased to see her. 'Hi, Zeb. Just getting ready for tomorrow.'

'Glad I've caught you, Richard. I was hoping you could help out again with this summer's drama festival. We're doing *Twelfth Night*.'

'Excellent choice,' said Richard. ' "Some are born great, some achieve greatness . . ." '

' " . . . And some have greatness thrust upon them," ' added Zeb with a smile. 'You know your Shakespeare.'

'I was in *Twelfth Night* at my boarding school.'

'Really? What part did you play?'

'Viola. It was a boys' school so a few of us had to play the female characters. It was OK though, as Viola had to dress up as a boy.'

'Well, that's impressive, Richard. I had no idea you had played dramatic roles. Have you told Felicity? She would be impressed.'

'Do you really think so?'

'I'm sure,' said Zeb.

'So, when are you planning the performance?'

'June the twenty-first.'

Richard nodded. 'It's the summer solstice, of course.'

'Oh, does that make a difference? Are you and Felicity going to Stonehenge?'

'Not really. The conjunction of Mars and Venus around that time would be of more interest.'

'Ah, yes. I suppose it would,' said Zeb. 'So, how about it, Richard? Can you do the sound and lighting?

'Of course . . . and we must remember that Tom is a useful assistant.' He paused and polished his spectacles on his shirt. 'He now understands the psychoacoustics of loudspeakers.'

'Good to know,' said Zeb. She glanced up at the chalkboard. 'In that case, many thanks and I'll leave you to your inertia.' She hurried away while contemplating the world that Felicity had to share with this brilliant but quirky academic.

*

It was almost six o'clock when Tom and Inger were driving home. On the radio, Gloria Estefan was singing 'Coming Out Of The Dark' and Inger suddenly said, 'I wonder who sent those roses?'

'Could it be your brother?' asked Tom.

'Not like him,' said Inger.

'Has to be someone who attended the wedding,' said Tom.

'Probably,' murmured Inger.

'What are we having for our meal tonight?' asked Tom.

'I'm tired,' said Inger. 'How about a takeaway?'

Twenty-five miles away in the Queen's Hotel in Leeds, Kai Pedersen was happy with life as he ordered room service in his bedroom. A steak salad would be perfect after a long day. His consultancy work was going well, the pay was good and he enjoyed the occasional commute from London back up to Yorkshire.

He wondered if Inger had been puzzled when she received her flowers that day at Eboracum University. The thought of unsettling her from a distance appealed to him. Paying cash to the florist in the city centre retained his anonymity and the young assistant would not remember him. He would choose a different shop next week. It was a delicious game and he was the puppet master.

He had driven past Inger's house on several occasions and considered breaking in. It was tempting but not wise. *Slowly but surely* had to be the mantra. When the day came, he would finish what he had started.

The radio was on in the background. It was Scorpions,

the German rock band, with their power ballad, 'Wind Of Change', and he smiled. It reminded him that the important elements in his life were his to control and Inger Larson was one of them. Then he sat back, lit up a Rothmans King Size cigarette and opened his Filofax. With deliberate care he circled a special date two months hence. Anniversaries were special. They were significant. Just as the number of roses was significant.

Chapter Fifteen

A Font of Knowledge

It was early morning on Monday, 22 April, and the Vice Chancellor was standing by his window. A new dawn had swept across the sleeping land and darting swallows had returned to their nesting sites in the eaves of the Lodge. He loved this time of year. The almond trees were in blossom and the cherry trees would soon awaken too. Bright yellow forsythia lifted the spirits as did the sight of his personal assistant, Miss Hermione Frensham, walking down the path towards the front door. There was a spring in her step and a smile on her face. A few paces behind her walked Gideon Chalk, appearing downcast and preoccupied. The contrast was remarkable but, Edward reflected, unsurprising given recent events.

By 8.30 a.m. Owen was in the staff common room drinking an early-morning mug of tea before lectures and reading his *Daily Mirror*. Zeb arrived, collected a coffee and sat down beside him. She glanced over his shoulder at the newspaper. Next to a picture of Stormin' Norman Schwarzkopf's return to America with a hero's welcome, following victory in the Gulf War, was a photograph of David Owen, former leader of the Social Democratic Party.

'So . . . what's the news, my Luddite friend?' asked Zeb.

Owen shook his head. 'Bloody politics gone mad,' he muttered. 'David Owen is cosying up to John Major about joining the Conservative Party.'

'He's trying to save himself from political oblivion,' said Zeb.

The Welshman sipped his tea and shook his head. 'His credibility would be zero. Thank goodness the Labour Party don't want him.'

Zeb looked around as members of staff wandered in. 'Where's your handsome friend?'

'On the road. School visits.'

'By the way,' said Zeb, 'Inger had a chat with Hermione. Word has it she did you a big favour with your receipts for the skiing trip.'

Owen smiled. 'It was that bastard, Chalky, trying to stitch me up. The VC called me in to confirm what had happened. He's definitely on his case now.'

'He'll get his comeuppance one day,' said Zeb. 'You can't continue living a life of secrets and lies.'

'Too true, Dancing Queen.'

She ruffled his curly hair. 'So, how are Sue and Gareth?'

'She's enjoying work and her mum and dad are a big help. Gareth is growing fast. Twenty-three months now and really energetic: running, jumping, opening doors. When he's up, it's all systems go. He can catch a rugby ball now and run with it.'

Zeb smiled. The pride of this tough little Welshman was there for all to see and she thought of her own life with Vijay. 'I'm pleased for you, Owen,' she said and glanced at her watch. 'Anyway, must go. I need a word with Victor.'

Owen grinned. 'I heard about your time in Oxford with Inger and Rosie. While you're away Tom and Sam are coming to our rugby dinner on Saturday night. So, not exactly Shakespeare.'

Zeb stood up and smiled. ' "Dost thou think, because thou art virtuous, there shall be no more cakes and ale?" ' Owen looked puzzled. 'It's a line from *Twelfth Night*,' said Zeb. 'In other words, enjoy yourselves but stay sober,' and she hurried away towards the quad.

In his office in the Lodge, Gideon's mind was in turmoil. A trickle had become a torrent. There were three more letters on his desk from students giving him notice to move out of one of his properties. He would have to write to the owner again. His money-spinning subletting scheme was no longer viable. It felt as though he was in a Kafkaesque nightmare and his world was disintegrating. Little did he know it was about to get worse.

At lunchtime in the refectory, Inger and Rosie each collected a tuna salad and found a quiet table at the far end of the dining hall. 'I asked Hermione to join us,' said Rosie. 'A girls' catch-up.'

'That's lovely,' said Inger. 'We don't see enough of her.'

'I wonder if she'll visit that charismatic Frenchman you mentioned,' said Rosie. 'I heard on the grapevine he had made an offer.'

'He was certainly very attentive,' said Inger as Hermione appeared and gave them a wave. She collected her meal and sat down beside them.

'Thanks for joining us,' said Inger.

'A pleasure,' said Hermione. 'Makes a nice change. By the way, I was on the phone to my sister in Oxford over the weekend and told her you were coming down to see Griff Rhys Jones's production of *Twelfth Night*. Her husband is a journalist and he's attending the Press Night on Wednesday. He said the play is likely to receive rave reviews, so you're in for a treat.'

'Looking forward to it,' said Rosie. 'Zeb is driving us down. Ben has other commitments so its just the three of us.'

'Actually, there's room if you want to join us,' said Rosie.

'Thanks anyway,' said Hermione, 'but I've got other plans with a friend.'

Inger gave a mischievous smile. 'Is Monsieur Lavigne paying a visit?'

Hermione blushed. 'No, it's a girlfriend from my book club.'

At that moment Jonny Halliday and Ellie MacBride walked in holding hands. They were discussing plans for next month's 'It's a Knockout' tournament to raise money once again for the students' emergency fund. Rosie spoke quietly. 'I'm pleased she's found someone.' She gave Inger a knowing glance, who responded with a gentle nod.

Hermione looked thoughtful. 'I recall there was some problem about her returning for this year.'

'Yes,' said Rosie. 'Some nasty piece of work sent an

anonymous letter to her parents saying she was causing trouble.'

'So we went to her home to persuade her to return,' said Inger.

'Well done,' said Hermione. 'Do you know who sent the letter?'

'Sadly, no,' said Rosie. 'It was on Eboracum notepaper. We asked Perkins but he had no recollection.'

'She certainly looks happy now,' said Hermione as they watched Ellie and Jonny engage in animated conversation in the lunch queue.

Inger sat back in her chair. 'We ought to do this more often.'

'I usually take my lunch break in the Lodge,' said Hermione.

'Try to join us whenever you can,' said Rosie. 'It's good to catch up with all the gossip.'

'Thanks,' said Hermione. It had certainly made a change for her and she had enjoyed relaxing with friends.

It was twelve forty-five when Hermione was walking through reception on her way back to the Lodge and Albert was behind the counter. Presumably, Perkins was having his lunch. 'Good afternoon, Miss Frensham,' said the young assistant porter.

'Hello, Albert, how are you?'

'Fine, thank you, and learning a lot from Mr Perkins.'

'I'm sure you are,' said Hermione. She liked this young man: he was willing and friendly. Suddenly she stopped and turned. Something had occurred to her. Rosie had

said that Perkins had no recollection of a letter being sent
to Ellie MacBride's parents. There had been no mention
of Albert. 'Just a thought, Albert,' she said, 'but do you
handle the mail each day?'

'Yes, Mr Perkins sends me to the post office, morning
and afternoon.'

'So when he is not here, you receive mail for posting.'

'Yes, that's right.'

'Do you recall a letter being sent to Ellie MacBride's
parents at the end of last summer term?'

Albert's cheeks went red. Ellie MacBride was the girl of
his dreams. 'Yes, I remember because it was my birthday.
Mr Perkins wasn't here.'

'Albert . . . who gave you the letter?'

'It was Mr Chalk, miss, and he told me to get a
move on.'

There was a pause as Hermione recognized the import
of this statement. Then she quickly retraced her steps to
the quad. Inger and Rosie were about to enter the door
marked 'Cloisters'.

'Inger, Rosie,' she called out.

They stopped in surprise. 'Hello again,' said Inger.

'Can you tell me what happened to the letter that was
sent to Ellie MacBride's parents?'

'We brought it back with us,' said Inger.

'And I gave it to Victor,' added Rosie.

'In that case we need to knock on his door.'

'Whatever for?' asked Inger.

Hermione gave them a look of steely-eyed determination. 'I think I know who may have sent it.'

*

In Victor's study Zeb had completed a list in the faculty diary. 'So, to summarize,' she said, 'apart from all the usual dates, we've got final teaching practice in May, examination dates for the first and second years sorted, plus Ben's Vienna exhibition on Friday, the seventh of June.'

'There's one more,' said Victor. 'Edward wants to host a garden party for the faculty in the Lodge on the sixth of July.'

'Sounds good,' said Zeb. 'He always does these in style, professional caterers and no expense spared.'

There was a hurried knock on the door. 'Come in,' said Victor. Hermione walked in with Inger and Rosie close behind. 'Hello,' he said. 'How can I help?'

Inger stepped forward. 'Apologies, Victor, for bursting in . . . but it's important.'

'Of course,' said Victor in measured tones.

'Excuse me,' said Rosie, 'but have you got the letter that we brought back from Ellie MacBride's parents?'

'Yes, I have it filed.'

'In that case,' said Inger, 'could you please show it to Hermione?'

'Why?' he asked.

'I think I know who might have sent it,' said Hermione.

Victor nodded thoughtfully and walked to his filing cabinet. He opened the lower drawer and took out a manila folder. Then he placed it on his desk and took out the letter. Everyone was still as he passed it to Hermione.

She studied it for a few moments. 'As I thought,' she said. 'I now have a strong suspicion who sent this letter. I used to own an Olivetti Roma typewriter. It was a favourite of mine with a distinctive red trim and a very particular typeface. I recognize this font and would know it anywhere.'

'Go on,' said Victor quietly.

Hermione took a deep breath. 'Gideon Chalk has the identical typewriter in a cupboard in his office. I saw it quite by accident last term. Also, I've just spoken to young Albert on reception. He received a letter from Gideon Chalk for Mr and Mrs MacBride at the end of last academic year. It was his birthday so he remembers it well.'

For a few moments everyone present froze into a tableau of stunned surprise, and then Victor spoke with calm authority. 'We need to handle this with great care and nothing of this conversation must be shared outside this room.' He paused. 'This includes speaking to partners,' he added gravely. 'Thank you, Hermione, for this information and I should be grateful if you would accompany me to the Vice Chancellor's office and bring the letter with you. We can progress this matter from there.' He turned to Zeb. 'In the meantime, can you complete those diary dates and leave the list on my desk? I'll let the rest of you get on but perhaps we can meet up again at five o'clock, after lectures. Can we do that?'

There were nods and murmurs of agreement and Victor strode out with Hermione in attendance.

Zeb leaned back against Victor's desk. 'Well, that's it. Victor will nail the evil bastard to the wall.'

Rosie turned to Inger. 'We never thought to ask Albert.'

'Exactly,' said Inger with a deep sigh. 'We missed the obvious.'

'OK, everybody,' said Zeb. 'Silence is golden. See you at five.'

Hermione walked into her office while Victor waited in the corridor outside. She telephoned Edward. 'Vice Chancellor,' she said. 'Sorry to disturb you but I have Professor Grammaticus with me and, if convenient, we should both like to speak to you. It is a matter of some urgency.'

'Of course, Hermione, come on through.'

Edward smiled up at Victor and Hermione as they walked in. 'Good to see you both,' he said. 'Do take a seat. How can I help?'

'Thank you, Edward,' said Victor. He turned to Hermione. 'Perhaps you could give the letter to the Vice Chancellor and share what you have discovered.'

Edward scanned the letter. 'Yes, Victor . . . I recall our discussion about this. So, Hermione, what has occurred?'

Hermione took a deep breath. 'I believe it was Mr Chalk who sent this letter to Mr and Mrs MacBride. I recognize the typeface. The font is one with which I am very familiar. It's an old Olivetti typewriter. I used to own one and last term I spotted the identical model in Mr Chalk's office.'

Edward pondered this for a moment. 'Yes, Hermione, but that doesn't necessarily mean it was the bursar who typed it.'

Hermione pressed on. 'I have also just spoken with Albert, the assistant porter, in reception. He recalled being given a letter by Mr Chalk addressed to Mr and Mrs MacBride on the date coinciding with the letter. He told me he remembered because it was his birthday.'

There was a long silence while Edward looked again

at the letter and then up at Hermione. 'I'll keep this letter for now, Hermione, and thank you for your diligence. I must emphasize that this conversation is confidential. I'll let you continue your work while I discuss it further with Victor.'

Hermione stood up. 'Of course, Vice Chancellor,' and she closed the door behind her as she left.

'A bad business,' said Victor. 'I'm afraid Gideon has always been a disciple of obfuscation.'

'Sadly, yes,' agreed Edward.

'So what next?' asked Victor.

'I'm going to bring in Elizabeth Glendenning to represent the governing body and discuss this with her. It's a dismissal offence, of course, if proven without doubt, but we must handle it with extreme care. In the meantime who else knows?'

'Hermione brought Dr Larson and Dr Tremaine with her into my office while I was meeting Dr Peacock. I've emphasized that this matter is extremely confidential and asked them to meet me again after lectures at five o'clock.'

'That's fine, Victor. Thank you. Once again, the reputation of Eboracum is at risk so please ensure they say nothing at all about this.' He got up and walked with Victor to the door. 'I'll keep you informed.' Then, after seeing Victor out through the porch, he called into Hermione's office. 'Please could you ask Elizabeth Glendenning if she is free to call in at her earliest convenience.'

Minutes later Hermione rang Edward. 'Miss Glendenning is on her way.'

*

At one thirty, Elizabeth Glendenning was met by Hermione and shown into Edward's study. 'Good afternoon, Edward,' she said. 'It sounded urgent.'

'Thank you for coming so promptly,' said Edward. 'Would you like some refreshment?'

'Tea would be welcome.'

Hermione nodded and went to the kitchen, where she sought out the fine china and superior biscuits.

Edward studied the calm composure of his most trusted governor, who was an academic of the highest order. 'While we're waiting for the tea, could you read this letter, please?'

Elizabeth sat down and studied the letter. 'Unusual,' she said. 'Not signed. Obviously mischievous.'

Hermione returned with a tray and served the refreshments.

When she had left, Edward sipped his tea and nodded towards the door. 'It's that young lady we have to thank,' he said. 'She's done some detective work. It seems likely that our bursar, Mr Chalk, sent this letter under the name of Professor Grammaticus. I'm also aware that he had issues with Miss MacBride, who is now in her third year and an outstanding student. As co-editor of the *Eboracum Echo*, she had begun to expose the unsatisfactory state of the off-campus accommodation that the bursar was subletting.'

'And you have evidence that Mr Chalk was responsible?'

'Yes. Mr Chalk owns a particular Olivetti typewriter with a distinctive font that is known to Miss Frensham. She caught sight of such a typewriter in his study.'

253

Elizabeth looked thoughtful. 'Edward, that does not necessarily mean he wrote the letter.'

'However,' said Edward, 'we have proof that Mr Chalk handed a letter to the assistant porter which was addressed to Mr and Mrs MacBride on the date printed on the letter.'

'I see,' said Elizabeth, 'and are we certain of this?'

'We are,' said Edward. 'The young man remembered because it was his birthday.'

'I know your first thought in these cases is the reputation of Eboracum.'

'Definitely.'

'I suspect there may be other issues you have yet to share.'

He smiled at his analytical friend. 'Correct. There is evidence that he tried to implicate a member of staff in false accounting. It was disproved, thanks once again to Miss Frensham. Also, there's the issue of his subletting scheme, which would appear to be detrimental to the students but extremely profitable for him.'

'I see,' said Elizabeth. 'In that case I presume you are considering dismissal.'

'Initially he would be suspended pending a full investigation.'

'Presumably on full pay?' queried Elizabeth.

Edward nodded. 'Yes. It would have to be.'

'What would you like me to do?' asked Elizabeth.

'Have you had lunch?'

'Yes, before I received your call.'

'I propose to locate the typewriter in his study and I should be grateful if you and I could discuss the matter further with Mr Chalk. Miss Frensham will record the meeting.'

'Very well,' said Elizabeth. 'After which I can draft a letter to the governing body.'

Edward picked up the telephone. 'Victor, it's Edward here. Are you free for twenty minutes?'

'Yes, I can be.'

'Can you return to the Lodge and meet Miss Frensham? I need you to find the Olivetti typewriter in Mr Chalk's office and bring it into my study. I'm currently in discussion with Miss Glendenning.'

'I'll be there directly.'

Edward tapped another number. 'Miss Frensham. Professor Grammaticus is on his way to meet you. I want you to show him where you saw the typewriter in Mr Chalk's study.'

'Of course. I'll look out for him.'

Elizabeth removed her half-moon spectacles and polished them carefully. 'And so it begins.'

Edward lifted the teapot and tea strainer. 'More tea?'

Elizabeth smiled and nodded.

Minutes later Victor knocked on Gideon's door and walked in. The room was, as ever, dense with cigarette smoke and Gideon looked up in surprise. 'What is it?' he asked.

'We're here to collect a certain typewriter you have stored away,' said Victor.

'I don't know what you're talking about.'

'I think you do,' said Victor. He turned to Hermione, who pointed to the far corner of the room.

'I saw it in that cupboard,' she said.

'Open it now please, Gideon,' said Victor firmly.

'I certainly shall not. How dare you come in, invading my privacy!'

Victor turned to Hermione. 'Please could you look, Miss Frensham?'

Hermione walked to the far end of the room and tried to open the cupboard. 'It's locked.'

Victor stretched out his hand. 'The key, please.'

'I have no key,' said Gideon.

Victor turned to Hermione. 'Go and fetch Perkins and ask him to bring his set of master keys for the cupboards in the Lodge.'

'Stop!' said Gideon. 'Very well.' He rummaged in a drawer and pulled out a bunch of keys. He walked over to the cupboard, unlocked it and there it was, an Olivetti typewriter.

Victor bent down and took it out.

'I know nothing about it,' said Gideon. 'It must belong to the previous bursar.'

Victor didn't reply. He swept out with the typewriter, quickly followed by Hermione. Once in Edward's office, he placed it on the table next to the bay window. 'Hello, Miss Glendenning,' he said. 'Good to see you again.'

'Likewise,' said Elizabeth. 'I've been hearing excellent news of the work you are doing in the Education Faculty.'

Victor gave a gentle smile. 'You're too kind. I'm fortunate in having an outstanding team.' He turned to Edward. 'I'll leave you to it, shall I?'

Edward nodded. 'I'll be in touch.' He turned to Hermione. 'You're certain this is the typewriter?'

'I'll type a sentence, shall I?' She picked up a sheet of paper, fed it into the typewriter and, with lightning speed, typed 'The quick brown fox jumped over the lazy dog'. Then she tugged the paper out and put it alongside the letter on Edward's desk. 'As you can see, Vice Chancellor . . . an identical font.'

'Thank you,' said Edward.

'So it is,' added Elizabeth.

Edward checked his wristwatch and looked at Hermione. 'Please will you ask Mr Chalk to come in at two thirty? And I should like you to record the meeting.'

Hermione tapped on Gideon's door. There was no reply. She opened the door and Gideon looked up in anger. 'I'm busy,' he snapped.

'The Vice Chancellor would like to see you,' she said quietly.

'When?'

'Two thirty,' said Hermione and closed the door behind her.

Meanwhile, Tom had returned from his school visits. As he walked through reception, Perkins called out, 'Good afternoon, Dr Frith. You'll never guess. There's another bunch of flowers for Dr Larson.'

'Really? Do we know who they're from?'

'No, just like the others. A courier turns up and leaves them here. There's a card attached but this time it's blank.'

'Maybe you can follow it up,' said Tom. 'The courier might know which shop sent them.' He looked at his watch. 'I've got a tutorial now so I'll see you later.'

Perkins smiled and nodded as Tom hurried away. Then he looked under the counter. *Strange,* he thought. *It's the same again. Eight roses.*

At afternoon break, Tom met up with Inger and Owen in the staff common room. He collected a mug of tea and sat down beside them. 'You've got some flowers again,' said Tom. 'I spoke to Perkins when I got back.'

'You're definitely popular,' said Owen.

'Who are they from this time?' asked Inger. 'That's the second time this month.'

'No idea,' said Tom. 'Perkins said it's a different courier every time.'

'Was there a card?'

'Yes, but it was blank.'

'Well, it's a mystery,' said Inger.

'I thought it might have something to do with Vienna,' said Tom. 'You were a huge success over there and maybe picked up a few admirers.'

Inger was curious. 'There was a German choirmaster but I can't imagine it's him. We spent very little time together.'

Owen grinned. 'Might be him. Could be feeling guilty after their football team beat us on penalties.'

Inger shook her head and smiled. 'Insightful as always, Owen.'

At two thirty, Gideon knocked on the Vice Chancellor's door and looked alarmed when he saw Edward sitting behind his desk and Elizabeth Glendenning in a chair alongside. Hermione, notepad in hand, was sitting in front of the bay window. The formality was obvious.

'Vice Chancellor,' said Gideon with a forced calm. 'You wished to see me.'

'Sit down, Gideon,' said Edward. 'I've asked Miss Glendenning to be in attendance on behalf of the governing body and this meeting is being recorded by Miss Frensham.'

Gideon looked around him cautiously but said nothing.

'Miss Frensham, could you show Mr Chalk the letter?'

Hermione passed it to Gideon, who scanned it quickly.

Edward leaned forward in his chair. 'Gideon ... did you write this letter?'

There was a pause as a sudden April shower pattered against the window. 'I've never seen it before,' said Gideon and handed it back to Hermione.

Edward pressed on. 'The letter is dated the fourteenth of July 1990. A noteworthy day. The end of the summer term. It would appear you handed this letter to the assistant porter.'

'This is the word of a boy,' exclaimed Gideon.

'It happened to be his birthday,' said Edward. 'He remembers it well. So I ask you again ... did you send this letter?'

'No.'

'In that case, let us move on to another concern,' said Edward. 'I refer to the accounts you presented implying Mr Llewellyn had appropriated a sum of two hundred pounds.'

'That's right,' said Gideon.

'However, this was entirely disproved.'

'I would need to check the receipts again,' said Gideon.

Hermione glanced up from her shorthand. She was surprised Gideon was putting up a show of defiance.

'I also recall that Mr Llewellyn reported to you the unsatisfactory state of the accommodation you are subletting.'

'Entirely the fault of untidy students,' declared Gideon.

'That may well be in dispute, Gideon, based on the recent environmental report which concluded the students were correct.'

'That's a matter of opinion,' said Gideon guardedly.

'Correct, Gideon,' said Edward, 'which is why Miss Glendenning will be scrutinizing it.' Edward paused and then continued, choosing his words carefully. 'In order to protect yourself, Gideon, and the university, it is necessary to conduct a full investigation into these matters.'

'This is an outrage,' spluttered Gideon.

Edward spoke with authority: 'You are therefore suspended from duty on full pay until the investigation is concluded. Should there be no issues proven you will then be able to resume your work.'

Gideon glared defiantly. 'And at that time I shall demand an apology.' He stood up. 'And when will this so-called suspension begin?' he demanded.

'Now,' Edward said quietly. Then he turned to Miss Glendenning and Miss Frensham. 'Please accompany Mr Chalk to his office while he collects his belongings. In the meantime I shall contact Perkins to escort him from the premises.'

Elizabeth stood up, opened the door and led Gideon back to his study.

Hermione was about to follow on when Edward glanced up at her. 'Did you get all that?'

'Every word.'

'Please let me have a copy at your earliest convenience.'

'Of course, Vice Chancellor.'

He looked at his trusted PA. 'And, Hermione . . . thank you.'

Back in his study Gideon stared around him, his rheumy eyes uncomprehending of the sequence of events. His world was a crazed mirror: the previously smooth equilibrium of his life was now cracked and shattered. Elizabeth Glendenning stood calmly in the doorway while he packed his belongings, and as he left he looked at her with hatred in his eyes.

Shortly before five o'clock, Zeb, Inger and Rosie were heading for Victor's study while chatting about arrangements for next month's 'It's a Knockout' tournament. 'It should be fun,' said Rosie.

'I heard it's between some of the departments in the faculty,' said Inger.

Rosie grinned. 'Owen was boasting the PE department will walk it.'

'Typical,' muttered Zeb.

'And wait for it,' said Rosie, 'Sam told me Richard has prepared a spreadsheet.'

'Oh dear,' said Inger.

'Exactly,' said Zeb.

When they arrived in Victor's study, Hermione and Victor were drinking tea. 'So . . . what happened?' asked

Rosie eagerly. 'The bursar was seen carrying a couple of cardboard boxes, loading them in his car and driving away.'

'That's correct,' said Victor. 'However, you will appreciate this is a delicate matter so confidentiality is key. Suffice to say matters are in hand and I thank you for your support.'

Zeb looked curiously at Victor. 'So you're saying you can't reveal what has just happened.'

Victor nodded. 'Exactly that.'

Zeb looked at Hermione and smiled. 'And you presumably are also sworn to secrecy.'

'Correct,' said Hermione.

'In that case,' said Inger, 'we fully understand and we won't press you further.'

'Absolutely,' said Zeb. 'I'm just hoping he's got what he deserved.'

Victor took a sip of his tea. 'Tell me,' he said quietly. 'Are you looking forward to Oxford and *Twelfth Night*?'

Zeb rolled her eyes at Victor. 'That's one way to change the subject.'

'The answer is yes, Victor,' said Inger.

'"And thus the whirligig of time brings in his revenges,"' quoted Rosie. 'Act five, scene one.'

'And let's hope revenge will be sweet,' said Zeb. 'And if our inscrutable professor shares out Pat's scrumptious flapjacks, we shall be sympathetic.'

And with a smile, Victor reached for the Tupperware.

Chapter Sixteen

Spreadsheet Knockout

'I love spreadsheets,' said Richard Head. There was a blissful look on his face as he admired the final draft.

'Looks perfect,' said Jonny Halliday, politely but with hidden reservations.

'Almost,' said Richard, shaking his head. 'There are sixty-five variables but only two I can't control.'

Jonny looked puzzled. 'What are those?'

'The weather and the height of the netball posts.'

'The forecast for tomorrow is fine,' said Jonny. 'So what's the problem with the netball posts?'

'The rings are welded to the posts at a height of ten feet and I wanted to make it easier for the vertically challenged competitors to score a goal.'

'Is that important?' asked a bemused Jonny.

'It would be to them,' said Richard.

It was early morning on Friday, 17 May, and they were in the science block. Jonny was Richard's star student and heading for a first-class degree. He was also the President of the Students' Union and his idea for an entertaining 'It's a Knockout' tournament to raise funds for those students in greatest need had gathered momentum in recent weeks. Teams of four, including staff and students, from various departments in the Faculty of Education were looking forward to a Saturday afternoon of fun and games.

'OK,' said Richard, 'let's put this on the faculty noticeboard and then set up the pipettes for the first session.'

At eight fifteen, in reception, Perkins beamed when he saw a familiar figure walking in. 'Good to see you back, Mr Bottomley. Never been the same since you left.'

The rotund, cheerful Frank Bottomley, in his familiar creased three-piece suit, smiled at his old friend. 'Thanks, Perkins. It sounded as though Eboracum was in a fix after Mr Chalk got his marching orders. All very sudden. So I answered the call. The Vice Chancellor was very persistent. He needed a new bursar at short notice. It's only temporary until they appoint a replacement.'

'Well, here's your mail and my Pauline thought you would like these.' He put a packet of chocolate eclairs on the counter.

'Perfect,' said Frank. 'She knows me so well. Tell her she's an angel.'

'She already knows,' said Perkins. He smiled as his old friend ambled away towards the Lodge and the office that Perkins had personally fumigated.

Meanwhile, on this perfect morning, Tom and Inger had decided to walk into work. They strolled along holding hands in the soft balmy air while pink petals from the cherry trees drifted across the pavements like springtime confetti.

'I'm going to call in to see Frank Bottomley before my first lecture,' said Tom. 'He's returning to his old bursar's office today.'

'A perfect choice,' said Inger. 'The Vice Chancellor will be pleased to have him back.'

'He was really helpful to me when I first arrived at Eboracum,' said Tom. 'Victor told me Frank would be holding the fort until a new bursar is appointed.'

'Good to see the back of Gideon Chalk,' said Inger. 'Hermione told me he eventually resigned. Apparently, even at the end, he was claiming he had been victimized.'

'He got what he deserved,' said Tom. 'Good riddance.'

As they walked past the railway station, commuters were hurrying by. 'I'm glad we can do this,' said Inger. 'We're fortunate to be living close enough to the university.'

'Maybe we ought to buy bicycles,' said Tom. 'Owen does it every day. Keeps him fit.'

'As he reminded me yesterday,' said Inger with a smile. 'He told me he would wipe the floor with us in the "It's a Knockout" tournament. It's Owen plus three of his athletics students. I've heard one of them is in the British students' female tennis team.'

'Good to know,' said Tom, 'but there're other skills involved.' He tapped the side of his nose. 'I have inside information.'

'Really, what's that?'

'Ellie MacBride is in my English department team along with Rosie and Billy Whitelock. She told me Jonny Halliday has been preparing the tournament alongside Richard and there are netball posts involved.'

'Excellent,' said Inger. 'I'll tell my music team. Alexandra Midwinter is a county standard netball player.'

'Oh, damn!' said Tom. 'Don't tell Owen.'

When they finally arrived at Eboracum, above their heads a flock of starlings wheeled in close formation and rooks hovered lazily among the tall elms. Inger felt happy and relaxed as they enjoyed the early-morning sunshine and, apart from wondering who the secret admirer was who kept sending flowers, life was perfect. 'See you later,' she said to Tom as they headed for their first lectures of the day.

In the Lodge, Edward and Victor were enjoying a cup of tea. 'So is Elizabeth Glendenning still pursuing Gideon's case on behalf of the governors?' asked Victor.

'She is,' said Edward, 'and ensured his contract was terminated with immediate effect.'

'I can understand that,' said Victor.

'So long as there is no further action from Gideon, then we need to keep this out of the local press.'

'Reputation,' said Victor.

Edward nodded. 'Exactly.'

Gideon had finally gone. The tsunami of lies and deceit had finally engulfed him and swept him away. Even in abject defeat he had clung to deluded outcomes. His letter of resignation stated he was disappointed senior management had not supported him and recognized the excellence of his accountancy.

'I thought Hermione handled everything well,' said Victor. 'You're fortunate having her watching your back. She's an absolute gem.'

Edward smiled knowingly. 'Ah, Victor, "For wisdom is better than jewels and all desirable things cannot compare with her." Proverbs, chapter eight.'

Victor grinned. 'A quote for all seasons, Edward. Well said.'

Edward finished his tea and sat back. 'I'm hoping this so-called "Knockout" event tomorrow will be one of decorum.'

'That I can't guarantee but it's in the quad and out of sight of the public. Also Richard is assisting with the organization, so whatever is planned will no doubt run smoothly. It's for a worthy cause and should be good for morale.'

'I'm suitably reassured,' said Edward as he stood up. 'And now I shall call in to see our temporary bursar to ensure he has settled in.'

At morning break in the staff common room, an over-confident Owen was waxing lyrical to Tom, Rosie, Inger and Zeb. 'The Physical Education team will win of course,' he said with absolute confidence. 'I've got a lad from my rugby team and two women who are superb athletes; one of them is in the British students' tennis team.' He flexed his muscles. 'Plus me, of course.'

Tom nodded. It was a fact that, in any sort of competitive sport, Owen combined a win-at-all-cost mindset with the charm of a determined Rottweiler. For the unassuming Welshman, tomorrow's result was a foregone conclusion.

'Don't be too confident,' said Inger. 'We don't know what the tasks are yet and my music team is ready to go.'

'As are my dancers,' said Zeb. 'We've got speed and grace.'

'And Ellie MacBride is in our team,' said Rosie. 'And I can't imagine her wanting to come second in anything.'

'The dark horses might be the science team,' said Zeb. 'I know Jonny Halliday has been working closely with Richard setting up the events.'

'Just a thought,' said Rosie. 'On my way here I saw Charlie the caretaker stacking a few netball posts just outside the entrance to the quad . . .' Owen frowned.

'Meanwhile,' said Tom, changing the subject, 'I called into the bursar's office this morning to see Frank Bottomley. He looked pleased to be here.'

'A good man,' said Zeb. 'I know Edward moved quickly to bring him back.'

'So that's the end of Gideon, is it?' queried Rosie. 'He collected his belongings and hasn't been seen since.'

'He was an evil, conniving bastard,' muttered Owen.

'I couldn't have put it more eloquently,' said Zeb. 'However, I've noticed Victor has been cautious with what's been said.'

'And Hermione has been pretty quiet as well,' said Inger. 'We've quizzed her over our lunchtime get-togethers but she's saying nothing and is totally loyal to the VC.'

At that point the bell rang for the end of break and they all hurried away to their next lecture.

*

Later that morning, a problem arose in the science department during Sam Greenwood's practical session with a group of first years. One of them needed some batteries for a complex circuit board he was creating so Richard kindly offered to nip out at lunchtime to the local Wilkinson's store to buy some.

Just after midday, while Sam was clearing away a collection of test tubes, a disgruntled Richard reappeared clutching a brown paper bag containing four double-A batteries.

'What's wrong?' asked Sam.

Richard was furious. 'I was asked to leave the store after purchasing these.' He held up his bag of batteries.

'Whatever for?' asked Sam.

'Their display of batteries was inconsistent,' said Richard. 'I was doing them a favour.'

Sam managed to keep a straight face as Richard regaled him with the story. He had decided to realign all the Eveready batteries on the shelf so that each label faced outwards and it had begun to look like the front row of guardsmen Trooping the Colour. Then, according to Richard, a spotty-faced assistant informed him he must stop tampering with the stock. Richard had tried to explain the importance of symmetry in the presentation of products when the manager finally appeared and escorted him on to the pavement.

'So I guess you won't be going back there,' said Sam.

'Sadly, I shall have to,' said a despondent Richard. 'According to *Which* magazine they sell the most cost-effective lightbulbs.'

*

269

Over lunchtime in the drama studio, Zeb was talking to Angela Raynard, now a final-year history student. The quiet introvert had been the star of last year's *The Importance of Being Earnest* as Lady Bracknell. Zeb had quickly realized this timid young woman blossomed on stage. During rehearsals for *Twelfth Night*, Angela was bringing the part of Viola to life and Zeb was excited at the prospect.

'I want you to come to the front apron of the stage in act one, scene two,' said Zeb, 'when you drag yourself ashore and say, "What country, friends, is this?" after your vessel has capsized.' Angela was hanging on to every word. She knew Zeb had invited theatre agents to the dress rehearsal next month and, for the first time in her quiet life, she was sure what she wanted to be . . . *an actress*.

On Saturday morning Vijay gave Zeb a lift to the university. It was a beautiful day as they left Crayke village and drove into York. Beyond the hedgerows lambs were bleating and cattle grazed contently, while sunlight on the fields of green unripe barley created sinuous patterns in the breeze. Above a woodland carpet of bluebells the warmer days had broadened the leaves of an avenue of sycamores. The car windows were wound down and Zeb was enjoying the wind in her hair.

'Come on then,' she said. 'Tell me.'

Vijay stared at the road ahead. 'What?' he murmured.

'You've got something on your mind. I heard you pacing up and down in the night.'

'Sorry,' said Vijay. 'You're right. It's a call I received as I was leaving the hospital yesterday.'

'Yes?'

'It was from New York.'

'Go on.'

There was a lengthy pause. 'I've been offered a consultancy post. Very well paid. An attractive proposition.'

'Sounds good,' said Zeb.

'Except it's in New York.'

'Ah . . . I see,' said Zeb.

Neither spoke as they passed the chocolate factory and slowed as they caught up with the busy city-centre traffic.

'So that's what was on my mind,' he said. 'We could live there together of course, but I know how much your work here means to you.'

Zeb was quiet. This was unexpected. Suddenly it appeared there was a tug of love between her work and this man. 'It's a big decision,' said Zeb. 'You're working this afternoon and I'm busy with this charity event. Let's discuss it over a meal tonight.'

'I could book the Dean Court,' said Vijay.

'That would be lovely.'

As they pulled up in the university car park, Vijay took Zeb's hand. 'I love you. You know that, and I don't want our work to come between us.'

Zeb kissed him on the cheek and watched him drive away.

Then she looked up at the entrance to Eboracum. So many good times, so many memories. With her mind full of possibilities she walked into reception.

At lunchtime there was a hive of activity in the quad. On all four sides of the lawn, Charlie the caretaker and Albert had arranged lines of chairs along the cobbled pathways. Then, at one end of the lawn, five rubber PE mats had been placed on the grass. At the other end were five netball posts with a cardboard sign on each, labelled 'PE', 'DANCE', 'MUSIC', 'ENGLISH' and 'SCIENCE'. These were the departments who had entered a team.

By two o'clock, every seat was filled, with students crowding behind. The bar in the students' common room was open and most were enjoying a pint or a glass of wine. Around the quad, the windows of the upper floors were open, with staff leaning out to watch the action. The doors to the staff common room were also open and the Vice Chancellor and Victor were standing side by side watching with interest.

A few paces away, Felicity and Hermione were chatting amiably. 'Richard looks intense,' said Hermione.

'He often does,' said Felicity. 'I do hope this goes well for him.'

'I'm sure it will,' said Hermione. 'His organization is always perfect.'

Felicity smiled and then waved at Richard, but he was too engrossed to notice. The dedicated scientist, clipboard in hand, was standing like a Roman emperor on the steps that led from reception to the quad. He was checking every detail on his spreadsheet and looking at his watch as the minutes ticked by. Next to him stood Jonny Halliday, megaphone in hand.

Finally, Jonny switched it on and waved to the crowd. 'Welcome, everybody, to our "It's a Knockout" tournament. It's meant to be fun but also competitive. Five department teams are taking part, each with four members, including staff and students. Please join me in showing your appreciation for our brave competitors.'

He gestured towards the staff common room and there was a roar from the crowd as Owen strode out like a gladiator with his Physical Education team in matching black tracksuits, followed by Zeb, Inger, Tom and Sam with their teams. Huge applause greeted them as they waved and then sat down on the rubber mats directly opposite their named netball post at the far end of the lawn.

Jonny pressed on. 'All funds raised today from donations, refreshments and any bets you care to make with Benny will go towards the students' emergency fund.'

The Vice Chancellor turned to Victor and frowned. 'Bets?'

'Harmless fun,' said Victor, 'and guaranteed to swell the total.'

Benny Cohen, a maths student whose father was a bookmaker in Manchester, waved from behind his table under the archway and shouted, 'Place your bets, everybody. There's time for one last flutter. The favourites, Owen's team, are two to one and the outsiders, Inger's music team, are five to one.'

Edward looked at Victor. 'I like those odds,' he whispered and took out his wallet. 'Do me a favour and put a pound on Dr Larson.'

At that moment a group of students appeared, carrying two huge cardboard boxes. They took them out to the middle of the lawn and placed them side by side.

Jonny smiled. 'The first event involves dressing up, so thank you to the costume department for the loan.'

'Dressing up!' shouted Owen. 'No one told me about

dressing up.' He turned to Zeb on the next mat. 'Just like last year's pram race when I had to wear a skirt and a wig. This is your doing.'

Zeb grinned. 'I knew nothing about this, Action Man, so shut up and listen to the rules.'

'OK, everybody,' said Jonny. 'This is it. For our first challenge, each team will run to the middle of the lawn. Then every competitor must collect two items, one from each box, and put them on. You will continue to wear this costume for the rest of the tournament . . . so choose wisely.'

Owen groaned while the audience greeted this announcement with huge enthusiasm.

'Then,' continued Jonny, 'you must run to the netball posts, where you will be given a ball. Each team member has one shot at scoring a goal and then you run back to your mat. The first team back scores five points and the last team to return scores one point. An extra point is awarded for anyone scoring a goal.'

Tom turned to his team: Rosie, Ellie MacBride and Billy Whitelock. 'Don't hang about with the costumes. Grab anything quickly. It's unlikely anyone will score a goal in a rush so get back here as fast as you can.'

Zeb's team stood up and did some stretches. 'I don't care who wins,' she said, 'so long as we beat Owen.'

Inger looked at her team. 'We can pick up points scoring netball goals so take your time.'

Sam shrugged and smiled at his science students. 'Just have a good time,' he said laconically.

Owen stared fiercely at Rod Parfitt, his rugby scrumhalf, and the two superb female athletes who completed his team. 'We're here to win. So, fast and furious, everybody. Get ready.'

Jonny Halliday turned to Richard, who placed a neat tick on his clipboard and picked up his whistle. 'You start when you hear the sound of the whistle. On you marks, get set . . .' Richard blew his whistle and they were off.

Chaotic scenes followed as everyone grabbed a skirt or a pair of baggy shorts along with a hat or scarf. Owen emerged first wearing a tutu and a crown, closely followed by Zeb in a pair of knickerbockers and an Ebenezer Scrooge nightcap. Both missed their shot at goal and sprinted back, closely followed by their teams.

Tom, wearing a bicorne hat and gripping a miniskirt that was clearly meant for a larger person, looked like Napoleon in drag. When he reached the netball post and attempted to score a goal, the skirt fell down round his ankles midst hoots of laughter from the crowd.

Inger, in a pair of overalls and a very fetching French beret, stood alongside Alexandra Midwinter, in flared trousers and a sailor hat. Both women took careful aim and scored a goal. Sam, wearing all that was left in the boxes – namely, a frilly ballgown and a feather boa – was comfortably last but didn't seem to mind.

Scores were totted up by Richard and passed on to Jonny, who announced that Owen's team was in the lead thanks to their fast finish, with Inger's music team close behind, having scored a couple of goals. Owen beamed and raised his fist in the air just as Vijay arrived from the hospital. He walked via the internal corridors to the staff common room, where he spotted Victor and Edward.

'Welcome,' said Victor.

'How is it going?' asked Vijay.

'Dr Peacock is a fierce competitor,' said Edward.

'Yes, I've learned that.'

Edward gave a smile. 'She is such an asset to Eboracum.'

Vijay gave a slight nod of agreement. 'I'm sure she is.'

The perceptive Victor had seen his reaction and wondered what was on his mind.

More games followed, all with competitors retaining their choice of fancy dress. They included a piggy-back race around the netball posts and back again, won comfortably by Zeb's team. Then there was an egg-and-spoon race and a three-legged race. Tom, clutching his miniskirt and being considerably taller than his partner, Ellie MacBride, kept tumbling over, much to his embarrassment and Ellie's delight. The crowd were loving their antics and they cheered their favoured teams while Benny was happy to make a small fortune behind his bookmaker's table.

Finally, after Richard had totted up the scores, Jonny announced it was a tie for first place between Owen and Inger. Zeb was third, and Tom and Sam tied for last place. The decision was a shoot-out, with each team member having one opportunity to score a goal through the netball hoop.

After seven shots, including one by Owen, still wearing his crown and tutu, that ran around the hoop but fell back to the grass, the score was two all with only Alexandra Midwinter left. She picked up the ball, composed herself and repeated the shot she had performed so often as goal shooter for her netball team.

From a first-floor window, Ben Laverick adjusted his zoom lens and recorded the moment with the ball in mid-air and the confident Alexandra stretching up with the hint of a smile. Inger's team had won. The crowd cheered, Owen gave her a hug and the Vice Chancellor sent Victor to collect his winnings.

Richard presented the trophy – a small silver cup – to Inger, and everyone retired for drinks and cakes in the staff common room. Vijay stood back and watched as Zeb enjoyed the celebrations with her friends.

It was late that evening before Zeb and Vijay had finished their meal in the Dean Court Hotel. Vijay poured a final glass of white wine for Zeb and sat back to drink in the sight of this beautiful woman.

She sipped her wine and looked calmly into his eyes. 'I thought about what you said.'

'That's good,' he said quietly.

'I know how important this consultancy post must be to you. New York sounds exciting. A new chapter.'

Vijay looked tense. 'So what are you saying?'

'Simply that where you go, so do I.'

He leaned forward and held her hand. 'Zeb, I watched you today surrounded by your friends. It's obvious both how much your colleagues and students respect you and how much you love your work. I can't take that away from you.'

'Vijay, love is a two-way street. I want to be with you. We can move on together to the next stage in our lives.'

Vijay was silent for a moment. Suddenly there were tears in his eyes. 'I don't know what to say . . . Yes I do.

This is an enormous decision. You need to take more time, really think about it.'

Zeb looked at him for a long moment. 'All right, I will. But let's go home now. I feel like dancing.'

Richard and Felicity were watching the late-night news. Helen Sharman had become the first British person in space, flying with the Soyuz TM-12 mission, and the supporters of Manchester United were still celebrating after their victory over Barcelona in the European Cup final.

However, Richard had his mind elsewhere, so Felicity switched off the television. 'Well done today, Richard,' she said. 'It went perfectly. You must be so pleased.'

'Thank you ... but I've been thinking about something else.'

'About what, Richard?'

'Spreadsheets.'

'Oh, really?'

'Yes, I was reflecting on today's "It's a Knockout" event. Everybody had fun. It ran smoothly. Staff and students competed well together. But I've been thinking about something Jonny Halliday said.'

'Your best student. You've mentioned him many times. A very sensible young man who has done a good job as President of the Students' Union, by all accounts. And what was it he said?'

'Sometimes it's easier just to *tell* people. Simply set out the games, tell them how to score points and let them get on with it.'

'I agree,' said Felicity.

'But that would have made my spreadsheet redundant.'

Felicity leaned forward and held his hand. 'Richard, you are a wonderful man and a brilliant scientist. Sometimes in life, people just need freedom. Today was a case in point and your young assistant is right. All you had to do was set up the games on the lawn, explain the purpose of each challenge and blow a whistle. Your student helpers could then collate the scores and you could relax.'

'That sounds persuasive, but it's hard to let go of controlling the variables in my life.'

'I understand that, Richard. Believe me, I do. And, frustrating as it is at times, I put up with your idiosyncrasies because I love you.'

Richard looked into her eyes and understanding dawned.

'I've just realized something,' he said. 'It's important. I don't always need to rely on a file-management system involving application software.'

'Go on. What exactly is it you want to say, Richard?'

He took a deep breath. The penny had finally dropped.

'Felicity . . . I love you more than spreadsheets.'

Chapter Seventeen

When Petals Fall

Inger was sitting by her piano, collecting the music she needed for the *Twelfth Night* rehearsals. The performances were only a couple of weeks away and there was still much to do. She glanced at the vase of flowers next to her. They were fading now. Yet another bunch of roses had arrived a week ago and she still didn't know who the mystery admirer might be.

Tom was packing his satchel in the hallway and called out, 'Can I help with the exhibition?'

Inger stood up and put the sheet music in her shoulder bag. 'It's all in hand. I spoke to Ben yesterday. He's got some of his students working with him this morning. I'm out all day doing school visits and won't be back until late, maybe five thirty, so I'll meet you then and go home to change.'

'OK. I'm out in schools this morning, then I've got lectures so I'll see you later.'

It was Friday, 7 June, the day of Ben Laverick's 'Vienna'

exhibition. The music room was the perfect venue and the Vice Chancellor had shown huge support; he had ordered wine and nibbles from a local hotel for the event.

Tom and Inger walked outside to a perfect morning of golden light shimmering in the eastern sky and the buzzing of insects, both completely unaware of what the day would bring.

Victor and Pat had finished breakfast in their kitchen in Easingwold and were preparing to leave for York. Victor had worked late into the night completing his Faculty of Education report to the governors, while Pat had prepared a collection of sketches showing his scenery suggestions for *Twelfth Night*. He had agreed with Ben he would start work today creating the background images on large rolls of canvas.

'A significant date today,' said Victor thoughtfully. 'June the seventh.'

'Go on,' said Pat.

'It's the anniversary of Alan Turing's death. I always feel a little despondent on this day. He was a brilliant mathematician and logician. I wish he could have lived longer, there was so much more he could have achieved.'

'Terribly sad,' said Pat. 'A war hero who was persecuted for being gay. Will it ever change, I wonder?'

'I think it will in our lifetime,' said Victor.

'I do hope so,' said Pat. He collected his sketches and put them in his satchel. 'So . . . what's the arrangement for tonight's photography exhibition? I said I would work with some of Ben's students on scenery design until lunchtime, then return home.'

'It's a half-seven start,' said Victor. 'There's wine and nibbles but maybe we should eat before we leave. I could be home by six.'

Pat took his *Hamlyn All Colour Vegetarian Cookbook* from the shelf in the kitchen and flicked through the pages. 'Fine. I'll make my risotto with spinach and herbs.'

'Perfect,' said Victor as he collected his car keys from the hall table. 'Come on then. This makes a nice change, both travelling together into work.'

'Looking forward to it,' said Pat, 'but let me choose the radio station.'

'Lord save us,' muttered Victor.

Vijay and Zeb were already on their way into York. On the radio, Jason Donovan was singing 'Any Dream Will Do'.

'How do you feel?' he asked Zeb, who was looking preoccupied.

'There's still a lot to do, but rehearsals are going well.'

Vijay had his eyes fixed firmly on the road. 'I was actually thinking about our conversation concerning New York.'

Zeb paused. 'I've made my decision.'

Vijay gripped the wheel a little tighter. 'And . . .'

'I shall give a term's notice and leave at Christmas.'

'Are you sure?'

'Yes. I want us to be together. They'll find another Dance tutor. It will give Edward and Victor time to make an appointment in the autumn. I could be with you at Christmas.'

'My contract starts in September,' said Vijay. 'In that case I'll accept their offer. I can still fly back a couple of times.'

'What about your home?' asked Zeb.

'We could rent it.'

'And then there are your parents,' added Zeb.

Victor shook his head. 'I know. That's the difficult part.'

'I'm going to wait until after *Twelfth Night* to tell Victor and the others,' said Zeb. 'I need to pick the right moment.'

'I understand,' said Vijay as he drove into the university car park. 'I'll pick you up at five so we have time to get home again before tonight's event.'

She kissed him on the cheek. 'I love you,' she said softly.

He smiled. 'I'm a lucky man.'

She watched him drive away; then she turned and walked into reception.

At eight twenty Hermione checked her appearance in the mirror in her office and smoothed the creases in her pin-striped Jaeger business suit. Satisfied, she sat at her desk and took the cover from her IBM Selectric typewriter with its golf-ball head and smiled. She was content in her tidy, efficient and well-organized world. With her Pitman's shorthand, speedy typing and faultless filing system, she knew she was valued by the Vice Chancellor. He often said she was 'his eyes and ears'.

However, recently a few doubts had crept in. Richard had provided a staff training day and a future almost beyond comprehension had been presented. He spoke of a time when everyone was connected to the internet and typewriters like hers, while built to last, would become obsolete. She hoped those days would be far off. On a happier note, yesterday a letter had arrived from Monsieur Lavigne with a renewed invitation to Dinan in

August. She fed a sheet of notepaper into the typewriter and had typed 'Dear François' when there was a knock on the door and Victor walked in. He had a report in his hand.

'Good morning, Hermione. I have an eight thirty with Edward.'

'Good morning, Professor Grammaticus. Yes, it's in the diary.'

'Incidentally,' said Victor, 'well done once again for identifying the font on the bursar's typewriter. Remarkable detective work. I can't help wondering if that anonymous letter to the police back in September came from the same source. I don't suppose we will ever know.'

'I doubt we will. But it was a font I knew well.'

'Interesting word . . . *font*,' mused Victor.

'Really?'

'Yes. It derives from the Middle French *fonte*, something that has been melted, a casting for metal typesetting.'

'Fascinating,' said Hermione while wondering how the professor picked up all this discrete knowledge. 'I'll tell him you're here, shall I?'

'Thank you,' said Victor and headed back to the corridor.

'Good morning, Victor,' said Edward. 'I'm aware you are teaching at nine. I simply wanted to pass on an update from Elizabeth Glendenning regarding Gideon Chalk.'

'I see,' said Victor and he sat down.

'Elizabeth said the governing body, in order to avoid adverse publicity, suggested we should let sleeping dogs lie.'

Victor gave a wry smile. 'With the word *lie* being appropriate in the case.'

'Exactly,' agreed Edward. 'There is no doubt Gideon was the *criminosus.*'

Victor was familiar with the Latin for the *guilty man.* 'I concur,' he said. 'Quite frankly, I'm glad to see the back of the *mercantile miser.*'

It was Edward's turn to smile. He always relished conversations with this brilliant academic. 'So, Miss Frensham has sent off the advertisement for a new bursar to commence next term.'

'Good to hear,' said Victor.

Edward nodded. 'These are whirling days, Victor. It's hard to keep up.'

'And I have this for you to read,' said Victor. 'It's my report for the governors.'

'Excellent,' said Edward. He stood up and put it on his desk. 'I presume I shall see you at the Vienna event this evening.'

'Yes, looking forward to it.' Victor glanced at the clock. 'So, if you will excuse me, Edward, I have a lecture at nine.'

'The subject being?'

'Mathematics in the National Curriculum.'

'Ah, yes, it's gathering momentum, isn't it?'

And where will it all end? thought Victor as he headed off to the lecture block.

At morning break, Ben and Alexandra Midwinter were in the music room arranging a wide range of hessian-covered display boards into a series of alcoves. Beside them, on a table, was a huge collection of A3 black and white photographs.

'These are probably the best ones,' said Ben. 'I should like them to tell the story from arrival in Vienna right through to the concerts. The interaction with the other choirs is important and we have some good close-ups.'

Alexandra held up the first photograph. It showed the choir approaching St Stephen's Cathedral. 'This is one of my favourites,' she said. 'You can see the aniticipation in everyone's faces.'

'Can I leave you to start arranging what should go where?' said Ben. 'I want to see how Pat and my students are getting on with painting the scenery in the art room.'

She was tempted to kiss him on the cheek as he left but they had agreed to use caution when they were in the university.

Ben turned to Pat. 'I wish you could work here full time,' he said. 'These are wonderful.'

Pat smiled, wiped his paint-covered hands over his smock and stood back to assess the latest creation. It was an Italian street scene, dark, gloomy and foreboding. 'I can't stay any longer,' he said, 'but your students have got the idea. Big, bold brush stokes, nothing too detailed, simply background atmosphere. It's the actors under the spotlights the audience wants to see.'

'I appreciate your help, Pat. Maybe if you have time you could call back next week to see how we've done. The stage construction is complete; it's just the extras now.'

Pat pulled off his smock and walked over to the sink to wash his hands. 'Happy to call in again,' he said. 'I've really enjoyed this morning. You have some inspirational students and I'm looking forward to your exhibition this evening. So see you later.'

They shook hands and Ben watched him walk away, in awe at the talent of this man.

'Hello, stranger,' said Owen as Tom walked into their study. 'How did this morning go?'

'Mixed, to be honest,' said Tom as he dropped his satchel on the floor. 'I'll never get over the range of schools we visit. Most are great but some are still in the Dark Ages. One headteacher quoted "Spare the rod and spoil the child" when he was talking about discipline in his school, even though corporal punishment was banned years ago. He told me the world was changing and he wished it wasn't.'

Owen shook his head. 'Sounds like he needs to move on. So . . . where else have you been?'

'A terrific village school, a complete contrast. Got talking to one of the staff. He was inspirational, a young guy who had retrained after being a porter at Killinghall Hospital.'

'Pardon?' said Owen. 'Did you say Killinghall?'

'It's a lovely village near Harrogate.'

'Maybe not the best name for a hospital,' said Owen.

Tom smiled. 'OK, I'm starving. Let's have some lunch.'

Tom and Owen both selected a chicken salad in the refectory and sat down at a table where Richard Head was sitting alone and deep in thought.

'Hello, Richard,' said Tom. 'Shall we join you?'

'Of course,' said Richard.

'What's on you mind?' asked Owen.

'Weddings,' said Richard.

Owen looked surprised. 'What . . . yours?'

'Yes. Felicity and I have agreed on the second of November and she seemed happy with that.'

'That's wonderful news,' said Tom.

'Congratulations,' said Owen.

'And how do you feel?' asked Tom.

There was a pause. 'Generally fine, although there are things . . . little things, but nevertheless, important.'

'Such as?' asked Owen.

'Well, for example, last weekend she put horseradish sauce on my beef sandwiches.'

Owen looked puzzled. 'What's wrong with that?'

'I don't like horseradish.'

'Why don't you mention it?' said Tom.

'She might be offended. Also we had a cream tea and she put jam on top of the cream. I never do that.'

'You need to pick the right moment to discuss this with her,' said Tom. 'I'm sure she will understand.'

'Perhaps you're right,' said Richard. 'She's a very understanding woman. In fact I've often thought Felicity could have made an excellent psychotherapist.'

Too true, thought Tom and Owen simultaneously.

'Anyway, must go, I need to set up an air-pressure experiment for my second years.' He stood up and walked away.

'Go on,' said Tom. 'What are you thinking?'

Owen had turned his attention back to his chicken salad. 'I think Felicity deserves a bloody medal.'

*

At six o'clock Tom was preparing a light tea in the kitchen while Inger had a shower. The portable television on the worktop was tuned in to the news. The singer Jimmy Osmond had got married, Mount Pinatubo in the Phillippines had erupted, creating an ash column over four miles high, and it was Tom Jones's birthday.

Shortly before seven they were ready to leave. 'I'll drive, shall I?' said Tom. 'I've no doubt you will be enjoying a few glasses tonight.'

Inger smiled. She was wearing a floral summer dress and sandals. Her blonde hair hung loose over her shoulders. 'Thanks. Yes, looking forward to the evening.'

On arrival at the university, they followed a stream of colleagues and students into the music room, where Ben Laverick gave them a wave. He was chatting with the Vice Chancellor. They collected glasses of wine and Tom spotted Owen making the most of the vol-au-vents on the refreshment table.

Rosie appeared and took Inger's arm. 'This is brilliant. Let's wander round together.'

Inger smiled and set off with Rosie while Tom joined Owen in devouring the delights of the buffet.

'Excellent as always, Benjamin,' said Edward.

'Thank you,' said Ben. 'I appreciate your support.'

'We could make this an annual event, perhaps highlighting the work of each department. This has certainly been good for morale. Dr Larson and her students are clearly thrilled that their work is being recognized in this way.'

'I'm happy to help in any way I can,' said Ben.

'I see you have already begun preparations for the staging of this year's drama production.'

'Yes, it's almost completed and Pat was in this morning helping with the scenery.'

'Good that he is being involved, a very talented artist.'

'Speaking of talented artists,' said Ben, 'I intend to go to London soon. The National Gallery is opening its Sainsbury Wing to the public.'

'That's right,' said Edward. 'The Queen is doing the honours.' He looked around as the crowds gathered. 'Well, I'll leave you to it, Benjamin, and congratulations once again.' With that he retired to the Lodge and a glass of sweet sherry.

Inger and Rosie were looking at photographs of the choir performing 'Ode to Joy' when Felicity appeared. She was very excited. 'I have news,' she said. 'Richard and I have decided to set a date for our wedding.'

'That's wonderful,' said Inger.

'About time too,' said Rosie. 'When is it?'

'In the autumn,' said Felicity. 'Richard has suggested Saturday, the second of November.'

'That's ideal,' said Inger. 'It will be during the half-term week.'

Felicity smiled. 'Yes, but that's coincidental.'

'What do you mean?' asked Rosie.

'In his inimitable style, Richard mentioned this was the date of the conjunction of the Moon and Venus.'

'Really?' said Rosie. 'Why is that significant?'

'He told me my friendly visage, like the Moon, always

faced the Earth while Venus is one of the brightest stars in the sky.'

Inger grinned. 'How romantic.'

'So I'm guessing he sees himself as the bright one?'

'Exactly,' said Felicity.

Half an hour later, Inger found herself alone for a moment and she walked into an alcove of display boards where the final group of photographs had been mounted. She scanned the scenes before her and memories of the concert in Vienna flooded back. It had been a great success – such a happy time.

The last photograph was a view from the back of the audience. It showed the immensity of the cathedral and the huge numbers watching the performance.

Something caught her eye. As Ben had taken the photograph, a man on the extreme left of the back row was in the act of turning his head. He had a scar on his left cheek.

'No . . . no!' said Inger. She took a step back and put her hand to her mouth. 'My God . . . it's him.'

Her mind was racing.

How was it possible? Why was he there? Am I in danger?

There was no doubt it was Kai Pedersen.

The Norwegian engineer had caught the train back to Leeds from London and he was now sitting in his room in the Queen's Hotel. His work in London was almost complete.

He opened his Filofax, stared at the calendar and

smiled. That night back in 1986 was still vivid in his mind. It had been the time of the summer solstice and Inger had struggled beautifully. He stroked the scar on his cheek. The time for retribution was close now. On his last brief visit to York he had seen the posters advertising *Twelfth Night* and he knew Inger would be there. Eight roses . . . eventually she would understand their meaning.

He put a circle around 22 June.

Inger was quiet as Tom drove her home and he assumed she was simply tired. Back in their apartment Tom was boiling the kettle for two mugs of hot chocolate while Inger sat down at her piano. Her mind was in turmoil. She needed to speak to Tom but the time was not now. Next to her was the vase of roses. Every time it had been the same, always eight red roses.

Realization began to dawn. She felt as though she had suddenly stepped back into a world of chaos and the walls were closing in.

Inger recalled how Kai Pedersen had boasted about Norway's remarkable engineering project, Atlanterhavsveien, the Atlantic Ocean Road, with its *eight* bridges. Kai had driven her to the largest of them, the Storseisundet Bridge, when it happened.

The room was still as she stared at the vase of roses.

As she watched, petals began to fall and flutter down on to the carpet.

Chapter Eighteen

Old Sins Cast Long Shadows

'Storm's coming,' said Tom.

Inger frowned. 'When?'

'It was on the news. Sometime later tonight.'

Inger looked in the hall mirror, checked the silk scarf around her neck and smoothed the creases in her black dress. 'Let's pray it doesn't arrive during the performance.' She picked up a bottle of champagne and opened the door.

Tom collected his sound and lighting script from the kitchen table and slipped it into his satchel. As they walked out to the car, Inger stared up at the darkening sky. A sultry calm lay heavy on the land and the heat was oppressive. It was 6.30 p.m. on Saturday, 22 June, and the final performance of *Twelfth Night* was an hour away. Both yesterday's dress rehearsal and the afternoon production had been superb, and Tom and Inger were confident tonight would go equally well . . . so long as the rain held off for a few more hours.

*

Members of the audience were taking their seats in the quad and there was a murmur of excited conversation. Staff and students, wives and partners, parents and friends were all looking forward to this special event in the Eboracum calendar. Those who couldn't get seats were crowded under the archway that led to the car park.

Inger looked composed and spoke quietly to each member of her string quartet while they were tuning their instruments. Ben Laverick had checked the stage and Zeb was giving final words of encouragement to her actors. All was ready and, as Richard and Tom gradually dimmed the lights, silence descended.

At precisely seven thirty, Zeb walked to the centre of the stage with a microphone in her hand. She was wearing a black linen trouser suit and a black band in her red hair. As always she spoke in a clear, confident voice. 'Good evening, everybody, and welcome to Eboracum's annual drama festival. This year we present a production of *Twelfth Night*, one of Shakespeare's much-loved comedies. I'm sure you all know the story, full of confusions and deceptions, along with Viola and Sebastian's reunion. It is a drama of its time, with its class distinctions and approved heterosexual marriages.'

She paused and smiled at her friends and colleagues. 'Thank you to everyone who has made this possible. The stage has been constructed by our Head of Art, Ben Laverick, and his students, with the support of the wonderfully creative professional artist Patrick St John-Stevens. Musical accompaniment, as always, is provided by Dr Larson and her orchestra, while Professor Head and Dr Frith have taken charge of sound and lighting.'

She turned to face the audience. 'Last night at the dress rehearsal we had a variety of distinguished guests including theatre agents and local press and their support is appreciated. Dr Tremaine has kindly adapted the play to last two hours and there will be a fifteen-minute interval. So far the weather has been kind but you will be aware of the warnings for later this evening, so fingers crossed it will hold off until our finale.'

Then she looked down at Edward and Victor on the front row. 'Finally, without the support of our Head of Department, Professor Victor Grammaticus, and our Vice Chancellor, Canon Edward Chartridge, these special occasions in our university lives would never take place. I thank them most sincerely.'

Victor glanced at Edward. He had noticed the emotion in her voice and, for a moment, he wondered about the significance of this heartfelt message.

Zeb walked to the side of the stage. 'Once again our students have worked hard and I know you will enjoy their performance. So settle back, and' – she gestured to Inger with a smile – ' "if music be the food of love, play on".' As she left the stage she stood behind the curtain with tears in her eyes. It was the first of many endings.

Inger stood up, smiled at her string quartet, and Adam Kite began to play his violin. For a couple of hours she would immerse herself in the peace that music gave to her.

It had been a difficult couple of weeks after seeing the Vienna photograph that included Kai Pedersen. Inger had not shared her concerns with Tom because she didn't know how he would react. But it had become clear to her that the roses she received must have been sent by Kai. Inger wondered if it was a warning or simply malicious taunting. It felt as though she was being stalked by the Norwegian engineer, a nightmare in the shadows.

Kai Pedersen had arrived in York the previous day and booked into a hotel on the outer ring road. On the evening of the performance, he had driven into the city centre and entered Eboracum via the car park at the back of the university. From there he had joined the crowd under the archway to watch *Twelfth Night* from a distance. As he stood among the audience like a spectre in the night, he heard the rumble of thunder in the distance.

The performance was superbly acted and appreciated by everyone. Angela Raynard, starring as Viola, brought the play magnificently to life. Zeb watched in awe at the confidence of this otherwise shy young woman and was pleased she had given Angela this opportunity. Rosie's adapted script had been a perfect vehicle for her to display her talent. Little did Angela know it then but she was destined to become an actress on the West End stage. The drama students alongside her rose to the occasion and Malvolio's downfall and Olivia finding happiness were all woven into a drama of love, identity and deception.

Meanwhile, every line was followed with meticulous attention by the prompt, Ellie MacBride, as she sat with her script in the wings.

The standing ovation was well deserved and Zeb wondered if she would miss this part of her life. These were special nights that, for her students, would never be forgotten. Then there were speeches by the Vice Chancellor and Jonny Halliday, the President of the Students' Union, followed by the presentation of a bouquet for Zeb. After more applause, Tom and Richard quickly unplugged the sound system and carried it indoors.

Vijay was waiting for Zeb as she descended the steps at the side of the stage. 'Another triumph,' he said and squeezed her hand. 'Come on, let me get you a drink,' and they followed the crowds into the staff common room.

Amid the throng lurked Kai Pedersen, who had eyes only for Inger, watching her congratulating the string quartet as she walked with them to join the others.

As Vijay headed for the bar, Rosie and Inger ran up to Zeb and gave her a hug. 'That was brilliant,' said Rosie. 'You must be so proud.'

'I am,' said Zeb quietly. She was almost too emotional to speak. This was her personal finale and she knew she would soon have to share her decision.

'A wonderful performance,' said Rosie.

'Probably the best yet,' said Inger. 'And I've just remembered – I brought a bottle of champagne with me but it's still in the car. I'll get it.'

Tom, Owen and Sam were heading back from the bar with drinks. 'For you,' said Owen, holding out a glass of red wine for Zeb. 'Well done, Drama Queen. Bloody marvellous.'

'Just perfect,' said Tom. 'You have some outstanding talent.'

'Thanks,' said Zeb. 'And great job with the lighting.'

'I enjoyed helping. Richard has sorted the sound system – it's all safe under cover now.' There was a crash of thunder. 'Where's Inger?' asked Tom.

Rosie took her glass of orange juice from Sam and glanced back at the open door that led to the quad. 'She'll be back in a minute. Just collecting some champagne from the car.'

Tom stared into the darkness. 'I could have done that.'

Inger had left the bright lights of the staff common room, hurried round the quad and walked under the archway towards the car park. In the far distance a flash of lightning split the sky, followed a few seconds later by a rumble of thunder. Inger paused for a moment when she reached her car and glanced up nervously. It felt as though a stifling electric tension was waiting for the moment of release.

At that moment, she heard hurried footsteps behind her. Before she had a chance to turn around, a strong hand had covered her mouth and she was held in a vice-like grip. A voice she recalled so well whispered in her ear, 'You must not scream. Stay calm. I only want to talk.'

He removed his hand from her mouth, turned her round and grabbed her by the shoulders. 'Inger, I've missed you.' A fiery spike of lightning lit up his face. It was Kai Pedersen and the scar on his cheek was pure white in the eerie light.

Inger struggled but it was useless. He was too strong. 'Let go of me,' she shouted.

'I told you to be quiet,' Kai said as he pressed his hand against her mouth, more forcefully this time. 'You know you must do as you are told, Inger. I don't believe that you've forgotten that rule.' He stared at her with a malicious smile. 'It's been five years and you never explained why our relationship ended. We could have been good together.'

Inger struggled but he pushed her against the car and pressed his face to hers. The kiss was like bitter hemlock and she recoiled from his grasp. Kai smiled. He had always preferred to be feared rather than loved. 'It's time to finish what I started,' he said as he began to loosen her scarf.

'Leave me alone,' she cried. 'Why are you doing this?'

'Isn't it obvious?' he said quietly. 'I love you.'

'Impossible,' said Inger. 'If you loved me, why did you hurt me?'

'I'm sorry for that. It will never happen again.'

Inger grabbed his collar. 'You're right. It's over, Kai. It was then and it is now. You can't bully me into submission ever again.' There was a steely determination to her voice. 'Now go. I want you out of my life.'

Kai paused in surprise. This was unexpected and for a moment he hesitated.

Inger sensed this was her only chance to get free; she kicked out at Kai's ankle and bit his hand. Kai yelled in pain, stumbled backwards and released his grip. She ran round the far side of the car, looking for a means of escape. He jumped to his feet and stood blocking off her route back to the archway. She turned and ran towards the entrance to the car park. At that moment there was a simultaneous lightning flash and rumble of thunder. The storm was overhead and a torrent of rain crashed down. Ahead of her was the road and the tarmac beneath her feet became instantly slick with rainwater. But she kept running, knowing that Kai was not far behind and gaining on her.

Kai followed her without thinking. She was almost within his grasp. Inger darted into the road, and Kai didn't see the van that slewed across in front of him in an attempt to stop. Nor was he aware of the moment his life ended as he was tossed into the air and his head hit the kerb.

Inger heard the sound of the horn, the screech of brakes and the thud of impact. She leaned back against a tree as cars flashed their warning lights and came to a halt.

In the staff common room, Tom was becoming concerned. He gave his drink to Sam. 'Hold on to this,' he said. 'I'm going outside.' He walked across the grass, past the rows of chairs and stood under the archway looking out into the darkness. There was no sign of Inger and he wondered if he had missed her in the confusion as students around him sought shelter. He turned up the collar of his jacket and stepped out into the torrent of rain that was engulfing them all.

It was then that Tom saw her. Inger was staggering

back through the car park and towards the archway. She was soaked through.

'My God! What happened?' said Tom as he took off his jacket and threw it over her shoulders.

'Oh, Tom. It was him.'

'Who?'

'Kai. He was here. He followed me and I ran.'

Tom stared through the driving rain. 'Where is he? I'll kill him if he's hurt you.'

'I ran into the road. He was hit by a car.'

'Come on,' said Tom. 'Let's get you inside.'

'But he might be seriously injured, Tom. We can't just leave him.'

'Yes, we can,' Tom replied as he guided Inger towards the staff common room.

Zeb and Rosie were shocked to see Inger in such a state.

'What happened?' asked Rosie.

Inger shook her head. 'Slipped and fell.'

'You're soaked,' said Zeb.

'Let's get you to the cloakroom to dry off,' said Rosie.

Owen stared at Tom. 'You look like a drowned rat,' he said, but he could see Tom was worried.

'What happened to Inger?' asked Sam. 'Is she OK?'

'She fell,' said Tom.

'You need to get her home,' said Owen. 'Can I do anything?'

'Thanks,' said Tom. 'I'll manage.'

It seemed to take a long time before Inger reappeared from the cloakroom with Zeb and Rosie. Tom put his arms around her, thanked everyone and headed out to the car park. He helped Inger into the car and minutes later they were driving home with Inger, still in shock, shivering beside him. Tom was seething with anger but somehow he managed to hold it in check.

Back in their apartment Tom made a hot drink for Inger while she changed into her dressing gown. For a few moments she sat on the edge of the bed reflecting on the horror of the night. She recalled her father once saying, 'Old sins cast long shadows,' following a court case in Oslo when, after many years, the police had tracked down an elusive drug dealer. It seemed to Inger that it was also true of Kai Pedersen. The violence he had inflicted upon her years ago had lived long in the memory. There had been enduring consequences but now it was over ... or was it? They talked long into the night until Inger eventually fell asleep in Tom's arms.

On Sunday morning Tom and Inger were listening to the local morning news. The reporter announced there had been a fatal road accident involving a Norwegian tourist during the thunderstorm on Saturday evening, and Inger froze, shock and relief warring within her. They sat together on the sofa and Tom held her tight. 'It will be fine,' he said quietly. 'You can move on now and I'll be beside you.'

By Monday morning Inger felt a little better. There were tutorials, reports to write, students to support and trusted friends alongside her. Tom was driving on their way to Eboracum and slowed up in the busy traffic outside

York Railway Station. There was a man in a flat cap selling copies of the local newspaper behind a large poster. It read: 'Norwegian Tourist in Fatal Road Accident' and Tom hoped that the misery Inger had endured had died with him.

As they approached Eboracum, Tom peered up through the windscreen at the scudding clouds. 'It's raining again,' he grumbled. He glanced across at Inger. 'What is it?'

Inger sat back and smiled softly. She was looking at the rainbow.

Chapter Nineteen

Hymns and Pimm's

'I did wonder,' said Victor. It was Friday morning, 28 June. Zeb was in Victor's study and had told him of her wish to resign. 'It was when you thanked Edward and me on the final night of your drama festival. I sensed a hidden message there.'

'There was,' said Zeb sadly. 'I'd told Vijay earlier in the day that I wanted to be with him in New York.'

'And I understand why,' said Victor with a gentle smile. 'Love can be a fickle companion.'

Zeb walked to the window and stared out. 'Oh, Victor. I shall miss all of this. It's been my whole life.'

He walked across his study to stand beside her. It was a still and sunlit morning and, in the quad below, life went on regardless. Students were heading to the refectory for an early-morning coffee and a bacon sandwich, while Richard Head and Sam Greenwood were staring up at the sky discussing yet another miracle of the cosmos. Tom Frith and Owen Llewellyn were chatting outside the door to Cloisters while Inger Larson hurried through the archway to her music room. Rosie Tremaine and Ellie MacBride were sitting on a bench studying a manuscript and Jonny Halliday gave them a friendly wave as he walked by, clutching a huge poster advertising tomorrow's Staff v. Students cricket match. It was a scene they both knew so well.

'You've obviously given this a lot of thought.' He sighed deeply. 'I shall miss you not just as a colleague but also as a friend.'

Zeb turned, stretched up and gave him a hug. 'Thank you, Victor. We've been through so much together.'

'I know,' said Victor. 'So, it's a term's notice, which I appreciate. That gives us plenty of time to find a new Head of Drama.'

'I hope so,' said Zeb. 'Vijay's contract starts in September. He said he would fly back to England on a couple of weekends.'

'I'm sorry you will be apart.'

'I know, but we'll manage. I wanted to be fair to you.'

'Just a thought,' said Victor. 'What are your commitments today?'

'Tutorials this morning, then I'm free.'

Victor walked back to his desk and picked up the telephone. 'In that case let's see if Edward can join us for lunch and we can keep this to ourselves just for now.'

'Good morning, Vice Chancellor,' said Hermione. She put a typed list on Edward's desk.

'Excellent as always,' said Edward with a smile.

'Thank you. It's all organized for a six o'clock start,'

she said. 'The caterers will set up tomorrow at four in the Lodge garden while the cricket match is taking place and I'm expecting around sixty attendees.'

Edward scanned the list. 'A barbecue, sandwiches, strawberries and cream and, of course, the absolutely essential English summer garden party drink . . . Pimm's.'

Hermione nodded in approval. 'I knew you would want to make this a reflection of your appreciation for your colleagues.'

At that moment the telephone rang and Hermione lifted the receiver. 'Vice Chancellor's office.' She nodded. 'Good morning, Professor Grammaticus. Yes, he's here.'

At morning break, Inger and Rosie were in the staff common room enjoying a coffee. Rosie had a photo-copy of the front cover of her book, *Oscar Wilde: A Man of Importance.*

'I'm so pleased for you,' said Inger. 'It's a wonderful achievement.'

'It's all happened so quickly. My editor has been ter-rific and it's gone through the copy-editing stage. I've had a chance to check the latest draft in justified text and it looks fine. The launch is in late September in Waterstones in York.'

'We shall all be there,' said Inger. 'So . . . is there another in the pipeline?'

'Yes, but we're still discussing what it's going to be.' Rosie sipped her coffee and smiled. 'Incidentally, you do realize we're in the staff team tomorrow for the cricket match. Have you ever played before?'

'I don't even know the rules.'

Rosie nodded. 'Give me tennis any day.'

'It should be fun,' said Inger. 'Tom's really keen. Apparently he was a fast bowler for his club, whatever that means.'

'And Sam has bought a special pair of gloves.'

'Why?'

'To protect his hands when he's batting. He's taking it very seriously.'

'Oh well,' said Inger. 'At least we've got Edward's garden party to enjoy afterwards. They're always special.'

The bell went for the end of break and, as they wandered out, Rosie decided not to tell Inger that the students would probably be hurling a hard ball at her at seventy-five miles an hour.

In their study, Owen and Tom were meeting with Sam to discuss the cricket match. Owen had a handwritten list in front of him. 'OK. It's a twenty-over match and this is the team. There're six men: you two, plus Victor, Richard, Ben and me. We've also got five women: Inger, Rosie, Zeb, Hermione and Selina. Victor and Ben can open the batting and, after that, we need to mix up men and women in the order but in such a way that we definitely win. So we can stick the women in the middle somewhere or maybe at the end.'

'Don't let Zeb hear you say that,' said Sam. 'She'll have your guts for garters.'

'Also, I think it's meant to be fun,' said Tom, 'and Inger has never played before.'

'In that case she can go in near the end with you and Hermione,' said Owen.

'Don't underestimate Rosie,' said Sam. 'Stick her in at number three and me at four.'

Owen nodded. 'Fair enough. Then I'll go in at five. We probably won't need anyone else. Tom can open the bowling and I'm the wicket keeper.'

'So who's the captain?' asked Sam.

'Has to be Victor,' said Owen. 'He was telling me he's been practising Geoffrey Boycott's forward defensive shot so it looks like he's taking it seriously.'

'Fine. Sounds like we're sorted,' said Sam.

Owen grinned. 'I've seen Jonny Halliday's team and it looks pretty good, but with my batting and Tom's bowling they've no chance.'

At lunchtime Hermione joined Inger and Rosie for lunch in the refectory.

'Zeb rang to say she can't be with us,' said Inger. 'She has another engagement.'

'That's right,' said Hermione. 'She's meeting up for lunch with the Vice Chancellor and Professor Grammaticus.'

'How the other half live,' said Rosie with a wry smile.

'Congratulations on your book, Rosie,' said Hermione. 'The Vice Chancellor was waxing lyrical about it this morning. He's delighted.'

'It's something I've always wanted to do,' said Rosie, 'and Sam wants to take me out to celebrate.'

'Good idea,' said Inger with a smile. She sat back and stared out of the window at the blue sky. 'What about the summer holiday? Have you and Sam got any plans?'

'We're going to Cornwall for a week,' said Rosie. 'I'm in a chess tournament there, so it's business and pleasure.'

'And what about you, Hermione?' asked Inger.

Rosie smiled. 'Has the handsome Frenchman been in touch?'

Hermione's cheeks reddened slightly. 'Actually, yes. François wrote to me, inviting me to Dinan, and I've replied saying yes. I'm going for ten days in August to stay with him and his sister.'

'I'm so pleased for you,' said Inger. 'He's a lovely man.'

'And what about you?' asked Hermione.

'Tom and I are going to Oslo to spend a week with my family, but at the moment he's more concerned that I learn the rules of cricket before tomorrow.'

'Actually, I'm looking forward to it,' said Hermione. 'I played hockey and cricket at university.'

Inger and Rosie looked at her in surprise. There was clearly more to this lady than met the eye.

Edward, Victor and Zeb were enjoying a light lunch in the Lodge beneath the portrait of Lord Nelson on Plymouth Hoe.

'So, America,' said Edward. 'How exciting.'

'Mixed feelings,' said Zeb quietly, 'but I've promised Vijay.'

'A fine man,' said Victor.

'So don't change him,' said Edward mischievously. 'Matthew nine, seventeen: "Neither do men put old wine into new bottles."'

Victor studied the face of the cherubic Vice Chancellor. 'Meaning?'

Edward beamed. 'The bottles might break.'

'Very apt,' said Victor.

'Actually, I like him just as he is,' said Zeb with a knowing look.

'But of course,' said Edward, 'and I wish you every happiness.'

'What about an announcement?' asked Victor.

'Probably best we don't drip feed this,' said Edward. 'Let's do it formally at the end of term before the dinner dance.'

'How do you feel about that?' asked Victor.

'That's fine,' said Zeb. 'Gives me more thinking time.'

Early on Saturday morning Tom looked out of their bedroom window. A pink dawn crested the horizon and caressed the treetops around the vast fields of the Knavesmire. Honeysuckle intertwined with the hedgerows and York was bathed in sunshine. It was a good day to be alive. Inger was still asleep, and Tom walked into the hallway and stood thoughtfully for a moment. A decision made, he took an old newspaper from his satchel and set off for their small garden beyond the conservatory. He sat down on a bench next to a beautiful Peace rose, with its yellow petals and heady scent. Then he opened the newspaper to one of the inside pages and read it once again.

Suddenly Inger appeared in her dressing gown and smiled. 'Hi. You're up early. What are you reading?'

'Nothing special,' said Tom.

'Mmm,' said Inger, full of curiosity. 'It doesn't look like nothing to me, Tom Frith.' She reached for the paper and her smile quickly disappeared when she read the headline. It concerned a certain Norwegian who had been killed in a road accident.

She sat down beside Tom, suddenly sad and distressed. 'This is awful,' she said. 'I feel so guilty. If I hadn't run away, maybe he wouldn't have dashed straight into the road.' She shook her head. 'I haven't even gone to the police to say what happened.'

Tom put his arm around her shoulders. 'Inger, the article says clearly it was a tragic accident. There were plenty of witnesses who have spoken to the police. They all said a man ran blindly into the road and the horrendous weather meant there was no chance for the driver to stop. There's no mention of anyone else involved.' He looked into her eyes. 'You don't need to go to the police.'

'I just feel dreadful about it,' Inger said. She was close to tears.

Tom held her close. 'This man caused you so much pain and he was trying to hurt you . . . again.'

'Maybe if I hadn't struggled it wouldn't have happened.'

'We both know that isn't true, Inger. Don't let him win.'

'What do you mean?' she asked.

'Think of his actions . . . going to Vienna . . . coming to York . . . the roses. He wanted to get back into your life to control you again. It's time for you to take back control.' Tom paused as Inger began to sob. 'Inger, this man was evil but it's over. He can't hurt you now, or anyone else.' Tom pointed to the newspaper. 'Let others handle this. It's time for you to focus on the future . . . our future.'

There was a long silence while Inger found the words. 'You're right, Tom. But the only way I can deal with this is to never mention him ever again.'

'That's fine,' said Tom. 'We can do that.'

'Thank you. For everything,' she said as she rested her head on his shoulder.

They walked back into the kitchen. Tom put the newspaper into the bin and they settled down with a hot drink. Tom turned on the radio. George Michael was singing 'Praying For Time'.

By two o'clock on Saturday afternoon the university cricket field was teeming with staff and students. A refreshment tent had been erected next to the pavilion, onlookers were settling into their deckchairs and a group of Owen's PE students were rolling out the giant scoreboard with its tin plate numbers. Charlie Cox, the Eboracum caretaker, had mowed the pitch to rival Lords' Cricket Ground and was admiring his work. Peter Perkins and Frank Bottomley, in their white coats, had volunteered to be the umpires and were standing beside him.

'Perfect,' murmured Perkins.

'Never better,' agreed Frank.

Charlie nodded. 'It'll do.' Effusive praise had never been a part of this dour Yorkshireman's vocabulary.

Outside the pavilion, the Vice Chancellor, who regarded himself as a cricket aficionado, was dressed in his old Oxford University sweater, cream trousers and striped cap. Next to him stood the two captains, Victor Grammaticus and Jonny Halliday, both in their cricketing whites. While Jonny's attire had never seen a washing machine, Victor's was immaculate, with neat creases in his shirt and trousers. Edward tossed a coin, Jonny called heads and elected to bat first.

The staff team walked out to raucous cheers. They were clearly a mixed bunch. All the men were in their cricket whites except for Richard in a yellow shirt and baggy green shorts. Inger wore her blue jogging suit and stood close to Rosie, who was dressed in a white blouse, skirt and long white socks. Zeb was in her favourite leotard and Fame legwarmers and Selina, in a khaki shirt and shorts, looked ready for a stint in the garden. It was Hermione who really caught the eye. In her immaculate cricket outfit and university sweater, she strode out as if she was about to play for England.

Tom opened the bowling with his fierce pace, and wickets fell quickly with Owen leaping around behind the stumps and taking catches. A determined Jonny Halliday came to the rescue with a careful thirty-two runs, along with Ellie MacBride, who crashed Victor's slow right arm spin for three sixes over the boundary rope. A score of 103 runs was on the scoreboard when Sam bowled the final ball and Owen nodded in satisfaction.

The two teams gathered in the refreshment tent, where Mavis Shuttlebottom was serving tea from a giant pot and the trestle tables were covered in plates of cucumber sandwiches, boiled eggs and slices of Dundee fruit cake.

As Tom collected his cup of tea Mavis pointed to a plate of her rock-hard flapjack. 'Your favourite, Dr Frith,' she said with a look that brooked no argument. 'Take two,' she said. 'I made it specially for you.'

'Thank you,' said Tom through gritted teeth as he picked up two of the dense slabs. He sat down next to Sam and the supremely confident Owen.

'We've got Victor opening the batting,' said Owen, 'and I've warned Jonny to go easy on him. Then Sam and I will knock off the runs.'

Fifteen minutes later a bell rang and Victor and Ben walked out in the sunshine to a tumultuous welcome from the crowd. Much to Ben's amusement, Alexandra Midwinter opened the bowling with Jonny Halliday and the wicket-keeper, Ellie MacBride, was soon in action.

Rosie and Sam were sitting outside the pavilion with their pads on, waiting their turn. 'You'll be fine,' said Sam. 'It's a simple game. Just keep your eye on the ball.'

Rosie grinned. 'Never underestimate a determined woman.'

Owen came to sit beside them. 'Too slow,' he muttered. 'Victor's doing his bloody Boycott impression.' The Head of Faculty was a study in concentration but sadly didn't score any runs. Finally he was clean bowled by Alexandra Midwinter and Rosie walked out to the wicket. She cracked the first three balls to the boundary and was caught off the fourth. 'That's more like it,' said Owen as Sam walked out to take her place.

As Sam passed Rosie she gave him a determined look. 'OK, Einstein,' she said. 'Beat that.'

A slightly unnerved Sam swung his bat at the first ball he faced and missed it completely. The clatter of his stumps echoed round the ground and he slumped off disconsolately back to the pavilion. 'As you were saying,' said Rosie. 'Just keep your eye on the ball.'

It was Owen's turn to come to the rescue as wickets began to tumble around him. Richard was bowled first ball. Zeb was clearly leg before wicket; the appeal 'Howzat!' was raised but Peter Perkins shook his head. 'Not out!' he called and Zeb blew him a kiss, but the reprieve was short-lived – soon she was bowled too.

Owen held out as his partners fell. Inger was caught immediately and looked relieved, Selina struck a mighty six on to the pavilion roof and was then clean bowled.

Tom walked out to the wicket when the scoreboard read 82 runs for 8 wickets. Owen approached him. The Welshman looked determined. 'Tom, you're a brilliant bowler but we all know your batting is useless. You look like a bloody giraffe holding a stick of candy floss. So block this ball and leave the rest to me.'

Somehow Tom and Owen survived until the penultimate ball of the nineteenth over when an over-confident Owen was caught on the boundary. 'Bollocks,' he muttered as he walked off. The score was 90 for 9 and Hermione stood up and strode out to the middle. She had been disappointed when she saw she had been put down on the team sheet as number eleven. It was clear to her that Owen did not consider a mere secretary could hold a cricket bat, never mind use it. With a glint in her eyes she walked out to join Tom.

There was one ball left in the over and she calmly drove it out to a space in the field and jogged through for a single run. Jonny Halliday had saved the final over for himself and he was confident the Vice Chancellor's diminutive personal assistant would not survive his electric pace.

However, Hermione, with a straight bat and perfect timing, struck the first two balls for four. With the score on 98 for 9 and only five runs to win, Jonny hurled down a fierce bouncer that was meant to sail over Hermione's head. She leaned back and hit the ball into the air with all her might and perfect timing. It flew like a rocket over the boundary and the heads of the crowd and into the refreshment tent, where it landed on Mavis Shuttlebottom's plate of flapjacks. The plate smashed into countless pieces but, remarkably, the flapjacks survived unscathed.

A roar went up from the crowd. The match was won and Hermione raised her bat to the heavens. Tom ran forward to give her a hug. 'You did it,' he cried. 'You're brilliant,' and they walked off together, unaware that their last wicket stand would become the stuff of legend.

There was resounding applause as Edward announced that Hermione was the player of the match. He presented a small trophy to Owen, who held it aloft and then passed it to Hermione. 'Well done,' he said. 'Sorry I put you in last.'

'How about putting me first on next year's list?' said a jubilant Hermione.

'Definitely,' said Owen who, late in life, was gradually coming to realize that women were definitely not the weaker sex.

At six o'clock Tom and Inger followed a group of colleagues towards the beautiful garden at the rear of the Lodge where the scent of old-fashioned roses filled the air. A walkway of metal arches had been constructed, where Victorian roses scrambled for space and light amongst the honeysuckle and clematis. Tom and Inger held hands as the sounds of summer lifted their spirits. A light breeze caressed Inger's summer dress and Tom sensed the whisper of silk against her skin.

Edward, in a cream suit and a yellow cravat, was standing next to a table covered with a snowy white cloth. On it was a huge pitcher of Pimm's being served by a young waitress in a black uniform. Chopped fruit including strawberries and orange floated on the surface surrounded by wheels of cucumber and cubes of ice.

'Welcome,' said Edward, 'and please do have a refreshing drink.'

The waitress filled two large goblets and served them with a garnish of fresh mint.

'Thank you,' said Inger. She held up her glass. 'This really is the taste of summer.'

'Quite so,' said Edward. 'First produced in 1823 by James Pimm and now a traditional summer cocktail.'

'I didn't know that,' said Tom. 'Thank you for the invitation.'

'Always important,' said Edward quietly. 'Staff morale is vital in a university such as this. So enjoy your evening. Incidentally, your bowling today was quite magnificent.'

Tom gave a sheepish smile and they walked away to join the others at the refreshment table. Tom was happy to see Inger relax as if a huge weight had left her shoulders. Conversations ebbed and flowed in the balmy air of this perfect summer evening.

Inger had been speaking with Rosie and Zeb and she caught up with Tom under the welcome shade of a cherry tree. 'Tom, I've had a thought.'

He smiled. 'Go on.'

'Zeb and Rosie said they would attend chapel in the

morning and Edward was thrilled. Perhaps we should go along as well.'

Tom squeezed her hand, 'Yes, let's do it.'

On Sunday morning, beneath a cerulean-blue sky, sunlight turned the stones of the chapel amber and bronze. Wisteria clung to the ancient walls like a lover's embrace while bright-winged butterflies hovered above the buddleia bushes with their lace wings. When they walked in, Edward was standing by the altar checking his service book. Refracted light from the stained-glass windows touched the pews with a golden hue and lit up the choir stalls.

This was where Edward found peace. In his church he was always soothed by the calming polyphonic chants of the choir and the few moments of stillness in a hectic university life. 'Proverbs thirty,' he murmured to himself as he studied his Bible reading . . . "Every word of God is pure, he is a shield to them that trust him."'

He spotted Tom, Inger, Rosie and Zeb on the back pew and walked to greet them. 'So pleased you could join us,' he said with a gentle smile. He looked at Zeb. 'Elizabeth, this really is a wonderful surprise . . . welcome.'

'Always good to find a little peace in this busy world,' said Zeb.

Edward nodded in understanding. 'Very true.'

Later in the service Edward stood in the pulpit and delivered his sermon. He had chosen the theme of farewells, but only Zeb knew why. The final-year students thought it referred to them.

Edward smiled down at the congregation. 'Saying goodbye is often hard, but it is simply a part of life. The Bible contains verses that help us understand and cope with farewells. We are offered comfort and hope through the scriptures. For example Corinthians two, chapter thirteen, verse eleven says, "Finally, brethren, farewell. Become complete. Be of good comfort, be of one mind, live in peace; and the God of love and peace will be with you." '

When everyone stood for the final hymn and sang 'Lord of all hopefulness', Tom looked around him. It had been a weekend of hymns and Pimm's and he was content. Inger had found peace in her life once again, and as her sweet voice rang out it lifted his spirits.

Chapter Twenty

Different Dilemmas

'I've made a decision,' said Zeb, 'and I wanted to share it with you before the meeting.'

It was Friday, 12 July, the last day of term, and Zeb, Tom, Owen and Rosie had gathered in Inger's study. 'Victor will be making an announcement and it concerns me,' she said. 'There's no easy way to say this . . . but I'll be leaving at the end of next term. Vijay has been offered a consultant post in New York and I'm going with him.'

There was a stunned silence.

Rosie was the first to react. Her green eyes were soft with sorrow. She gave Zeb a hug. 'I'm so pleased for you,' she said. 'He's a wonderful man.'

'Thanks, that means a lot,' said Zeb, but there were tears running down her cheeks. 'I've been putting off telling you all until I was absolutely certain.'

Inger gave a sad smile. 'Oh, Zeb. This is the last thing I expected when you rang. I shall miss you so much.'

'Vijay is a lucky man,' said Tom, trying to lighten the mood. 'A new life in New York. Exciting times ahead.'

Owen was sitting with his head bowed and Zeb walked over to him and ruffled his hair. 'I'm sorry, Welshman. No offence, everyone . . . but it's Owen I shall miss the most.'

'It's a shock,' murmured Owen. 'It never occurred to me that you would leave.' He looked up at her and shook his head. 'I'll miss you, Dancing Queen.'

Zeb stretched out her arms. 'Come here, you lovely man,' and they held each other for a long time.

Then there was an awkward moment as everyone looked around. Tom glanced at his wristwatch. 'The meeting's at ten. Maybe we should go down.'

'Let's talk more over lunch,' said Zeb. 'Refectory at twelve. Lots to share.'

It was a sombre group of friends that stepped down the metal stairway to the quad and into the staff common room. Victor saw them enter and knew immediately that Zeb had shared her news. She took her place beside him and he leaned over and squeezed her hand. Dapper as always in his crisp white shirt, royal blue waistcoat and red bow tie, he stood up to address the faculty. 'Good morning, everyone, and thank you for your attendance.'

He scanned all the familiar faces and noticed Owen was staring down at his trainers, Rosie was dabbing away a tear and Inger was as still as a statue, her mind elsewhere. Victor knew Zeb's decision would hit everyone hard. He pressed on. 'I wanted to commend all your efforts during this past year. There have been many highlights, including a successful field week, the concert in Vienna, another triumph of a drama festival plus a strong likelihood of a record number of first-class honours degrees.'

There was a ripple of applause and many smiles. Victor knew he had their attention. 'Now, the autumn term will be very significant for one of our colleagues. I have a piece of news concerning our Deputy Head of Faculty.' He looked across at Zeb, who was picking at the threads on the sleeve of her summer frock. 'We all know of Zeb's talent and the prodigious body of work that she has shared with us over the years here in Eboracum. When I look around this room I know that everyone has received her support at some time. Her energy is remarkable and her loyalty to our faculty is unsurpassed.'

There were rustles and murmurs in the room as colleagues wondered what was coming next. 'Zeb's partner, the surgeon Vijay Kapoor, has been offered a prestigious consultancy post in New York. His work there commences in September and Zeb intends to join him at Christmas. This means Zeb will be with us for one more term and a new Head of Drama will be in place in January 1992.' He turned to Zeb and smiled. 'We wish you all the luck in the world.' Again there was spontaneous applause but it was clear to him that this was not the moment for Zeb to respond. She was leaning on the table and had lowered her head to conceal her tears.

He turned back to face everyone. 'So, very best wishes to you all for the summer vacation. This evening we have our dinner dance in the Assembly Rooms. It begins at seven thirty and I know this will be a fitting conclusion to our academic year.' He glanced down at the paper in front of him. 'Looking ahead, the next faculty meeting will be at ten o'clock on Friday, the sixth of September, with Freshers' Week commencing Monday the ninth. Our full lecture programme will begin the following week. So, thank you all and the meeting is now closed.' Conversations broke out everywhere and Zeb was immediately surrounded by well-wishers and colleagues.

It wasn't until midday that Zeb found a relatively quiet corner of the refectory, where she was joined by Inger and Rosie. Tom and Owen arrived a few minutes later and at first they all began to eat their lunch in quiet contemplation.

Eventually Zeb broke the silence. 'It still seems unreal but it's taken time for me to realize that I want to spend the rest of my life with Vijay. So there it is.'

The floodgates opened. Everyone spoke at once and Zeb smiled. She was among her trusted friends.

After lunch there was a big surprise for Owen when he walked into the quad. Maddy Defoe, a Year Two student, was waving to him. Next to her was a young man in a wheelchair. It was Chris Scully.

Owen's star rugby player had suffered spinal injuries after his daredevil leap from the Ouse Bridge a year ago. Since then he had gone through a long process of rehabilitation down in Hampshire. Owen had visited him regularly and encouraged him to take up wheelchair rugby. In his T-shirt, Chris's upper body strength was clear for all to see. This was a very powerful young man.

Owen ran over to them. 'What a wonderful surprise. Great to see you, Chris. You should have told me you were coming.'

Chris looked up at Maddy and squeezed her hand. 'Thank Maddy. It was an impulse thing. She came down to visit my parents and we thought it would be good to catch up with you at the end of term. We're here for a couple of days.'

Maddy blushed slightly. Like Chris, she had been in a serious accident, when she and her brother, Josh, were the victims of a hit-and-run. It had left her with a limp, whereas Josh was confined to a wheelchair. He was now training with the England wheelchair rugby team, and he and Chris had become great friends.

Owen was clearly moved by this unexpected reunion. 'I'm thrilled you're here.'

Chris could see the impact he was having on the tough Welshman. 'I hear we're unbeaten this year,' he said.

'Yes,' said Owen. 'We have a great team.' He looked down wistfully at Chris, knowing it would have been even better with him in the side.

Chris seemed to understand and smiled up at Owen. 'Maddy has arranged for me to meet up with some of the lads and their girlfriends in the Cross Keys pub tonight. Can you call in? It would be great to catch up and find out what's been going on.'

'Sounds good,' said Owen, 'and I'd love to, but it's the staff dinner dance. So, it will have to be early if that's OK.'

'That's fine,' said Chris. He looked around the quad, timeless in the summer sunshine. 'This place doesn't change, does it?'

'Guess it never will,' said Owen wistfully. 'Students come and go and the staff just get older.'

'What are you doing now?' asked Maddy. She too

sensed Owen's sadness. 'We could go to the students' common room and show you how the other half live.'

Owen smiled. 'Come on then.'

'And you can tell me about every game and your brilliant tactics,' said Chris.

Owen grinned. 'Cheeky sod!'

The three of them set off under the shadow of the archway for an unexpected conversation and an afternoon Owen would never forget.

At one thirty Tom set out to keep his annual promise to his Year Three students. He walked past the Minster towards High Petergate and into the Guy Fawkes Inn, a medieval meeting place and the birthplace of the notorious plotter. This group of students had arrived at Eboracum with Tom back in 1988 and there was a special bond between them. He enjoyed catching up with their news and, on this occasion, it was a time of celebration. Following the voting, Ellie MacBride had been elected as the President of the Students' Union for her final academic year at Eboracum. They were all raising their glasses to her when he approached the bar and ordered a jug of beer and another of lemonade. Ellie saw him and hurried over. 'Thanks for coming,' she said with a smile. 'Another year.'

'Well done,' said Tom. 'I heard the news earlier today.' He leaned on the bar and smiled at Ellie in her summer dress, her black hair caressing her tanned shoulders. 'You've come a long way, Ellie. I'm pleased for you. It's well deserved.'

Ellie's eyes never wavered as she looked up at Tom. 'It's thanks to you and Rosie,' she said quietly. She touched his arm gently. 'You've always believed in me, Tom. That counted for a lot.'

Tom was silent for a moment. He had never really fully understood this woman with her changing moods and vibrant zest for life. 'So what's in store for you in the summer?' he asked.

She smiled, recognizing the brief moment of intimacy had passed. 'The market stall once again. That always pleases my mum and dad.' Then she paused. 'Also . . . Jonny has asked me to go to Florence with him. It sounds wonderful. The Duomo, Michaelangelo's David, the list is endless. Just not sure. He's a lovely man . . .' There was a silence and Ellie sighed and looked thoughtful.

Tom leaned closer. 'Ellie . . . Florence is a remarkable city. I'm sure you would enjoy it.'

She sighed and shook her head. 'He's just got a teaching job in London. Seems pleased. Says it's a great school. Not sure a long-distance relationship would survive.'

'It will if you want it,' said Tom. 'And you might move down to London . . . in time.'

'Maybe.' She smiled.

He paid for the drinks, picked up the jugs and walked over to join the rest of the group. They were discussing what they would do in the summer vacation. Poppy Hartness had secured a holiday job at Lightwater Valley after the news of the imminent opening of Europe's longest rollercoaster. The conversation was lively and relaxed and the list of casual employment included a holiday camp kitchen porter, a slipper-bath cleaner, driving a pop wagon and even painting garden gnomes. An hour later Tom walked slowly back to Eboracum, reflecting on Ellie

MacBride's complex journey through life. The interlude in the pub had distracted him from the news of Zeb's eventual departure, but when he arrived back in the quad it began to weigh heavily on his mind again – until he had an idea.

Inger was in her music room in conversation with Adam Kite. She was trying to convince him to enter the Young Musicians' Festival in Leeds Town Hall.

'Do you really think I'm good enough?' he asked. Even at the end of his first year he was still wearing his old school blazer. He took no interest in his appearance and fashion was a mystery to him; his life revolved around music and countless hours of violin practice.

'Adam,' said Inger with finality. 'I wouldn't suggest it if I had any doubts of your ability. This could be a great opportunity for you.'

'If you say so,' he said. He was still a very shy young man and had found difficulty in making friends. 'I really love music. It's a sort of companion for me.'

'I understand,' said Inger. 'I really do.' She looked with compassion at her most talented student and sensed he was destined for a great future. It was essential for her to lead him gently on those first steps.

'What are you doing during the holiday?' she asked.

'I'm working in York. I've got a job in Banks music shop on Lendal.'

Inger knew the shop well. It was in the city centre, a short walk from Bettys Tea Rooms. 'In that case, I'll call in during one of your lunch breaks and we can discuss how to develop your music even further.'

He stared down at the hard calluses on the fingers of his hand. 'Thank you. I should like that.'

'Do you like scones?' asked Inger suddenly.

'Yes, I do,' replied Adam, looking puzzled.

'I'll treat you to something similar but even better: a Fat Rascal, it's a Bettys speciality.'

Adam held his violin tightly and smiled.

In the Lodge, Edward and Victor were chatting with Frank Bottomley while Hermione had just served a tray of tea. She placed a plate of homemade ginger biscuits in front of the bursar. 'Your favourite,' she said with a warm smile.

'You remembered,' said Frank with a grin. 'Thank you.'

'Always a pleasure,' she said and walked back to her office.

Frank picked up a biscuit and crunched into it. Crumbs scattered over his creased suit. 'You've got a good one there,' he said.

'I agree,' said Edward. 'She's remarkable.'

'Have you noticed?' said Frank. 'She's got Mona Lisa eyes. Doesn't miss a thing.'

'Yes,' said Victor. 'You're right. A very observant lady.'

Edward watched the crumbs scatter down Frank's waistcoat and on to his Axminster carpet. 'Thank you for all your help, Frank,' he said. 'Your work since the departure of Mr Chalk has been most appreciated. I was hoping you could stay on in September to assist the newly appointed bursar for a week or two. The appointment will be made next month. So it's just a transition phase to make sure everything runs smoothly.'

'Of course,' said Frank. 'Anything to help.'

'Perhaps when you've finished your biscuits you could see Miss Frensham on your way out and complete the paperwork.'

'Of course,' said Frank as he reached for another biscuit.

Frank had enjoyed his second cup of tea and a final biscuit. Like Hansel and Gretel in the fairy tale by the Brothers Grimm, he left a trail of crumbs behind him as he left.

'He's a good man,' said Victor as he noticed the discomfort of the fastidious Vice Chancellor for whom tidiness was next to godliness.

Edward nodded. 'I suppose old seeds bring new growth.'

'Very true,' said Victor.

Edward stood up and stared out of the window. In the distance, tourists were walking along the city walls from Robin Hood's Tower to Monk Bar. 'So . . . what are we going to do about a new Head of Drama?'

Victor sighed. 'I'll give it due attention.'

'I thought you might,' responded Edward with a wry smile.

At two thirty in the science lab, Richard was tidying his store cupboard when Felicity walked in. 'Hello,' he said. 'You're early.'

'We finished at twelve so I drove straight here.'

'That's wonderful,' said Richard. 'Perhaps you would like to help. I've almost finished.'

'Of course. What can I do?'

'The pipettes need to go back on the bottom shelf.'

Felicity began to stack the glass tubes. 'I've bought a new dress for this evening,' she said with enthusiasm.

Richard frowned. 'The pipettes need to be in order of size, tallest on the right.'

'I should have guessed,' said Felicity.

It was late afternoon when Tom and Owen met up in their study. 'Just had a great meeting with Chris Scully,' said Owen. 'His girlfriend, Maddy Defoe, has worked wonders. He's really positive.'

'Good to hear,' said Tom. 'It sounds as though Maddy is a perfect influence for him.'

'She loves him, that's for sure,' said Owen. 'It's written all over her face when she looks at him.'

'Does he feel the same?' asked Tom.

'Yes. I think he does.' Owen smiled.

'That's great ... for them both,' said Tom as he sat down at his desk. 'There's something I want to talk to you about. Just an idea.'

Owen sat down opposite him. 'Go on.'

'Have you considered applying for the Deputy Head of Faculty post now that Zeb will be leaving?'

Owen shook his head. 'Qualifications, Tom. Think about it. I haven't got a doctorate like you. That brings status.'

'I don't think that counts,' said Tom. 'You're well respected and you know what the job involves.'

'Not sure. I've never really thought about promotion. I just love my job.'

'Victor would need someone like you,' said Tom, 'and you have a lot of experience here in Eboracum.'

'What about you?' asked Owen. 'I could say the same. All that extra work you put in for teaching-practice placements . . . and you're a bloody good tutor.'

'No, it's not for me,' said Tom. 'I'm still a newcomer.' He could see Owen was considering the proposal. 'Just go to Victor and ask his advice. I think he would be delighted to have you on the shortlist.'

'OK, Englishman,' said Owen. 'Point taken. Thanks for the suggestion. I'll talk it over with Sue first.'

'Do that,' said Tom, 'and I'll see you both tonight.'

'I'll be in my red suit,' said Owen. 'You won't miss me.'

'Thanks for the warning,' said Tom.

At five thirty Tom and Inger were driving home. On the radio Bryan Adams was about to become the UK number one with '(Everything I Do) I Do It For You' and Inger turned up the volume.

By six o'clock Inger was getting changed for the dinner dance while Tom was in the kitchen drinking tea and watching the news on the portable television. Luciano Pavarotti was coming to London at the end of the month and would be singing to an expected audience of one hundred thousand in Hyde Park. Meanwhile, the Labour MP Terry Fields had received a sixty-day prison sentence for refusing to pay the poll tax. *Brave man,* thought Tom.

When their taxi arrived, Tom realized once again how lucky he was to have Inger by his side; she looked stunning in a beautiful black evening dress. Her long blonde hair hung over her bare shoulders and she clutched a silk shawl for the late-night journey home. Minutes later they stepped on to the pavement outside the Assembly Rooms and walked through the soaring colonnade beneath the portico of stone. They gave their tickets to the doorman and headed first for the cloakrooms and thence the ballroom. Above their heads the chandeliers were sparkling with light; the disc jockey was playing soft music. Owen and Sue were on the far side of the dance floor and waved a greeting.

Victor and Pat were sitting at the head of a long table with Richard and Felicity and they were joined by Rosie and Sam. Then Vijay arrived with a round of drinks and Zeb, who, in a fabulous red dress, gave everyone a hug. When she got to Owen she squeezed his hand. 'Owen,' she said, 'my tough Welshman with a heart of gold. You're my hero.'

'Hero?'

'Too bloody right,' she said with a grin. 'Not all heroes wear tights,' and she kissed his stubbly cheek and skipped away.

Later, after an excellent sea bass meal, couples began to take to the dance floor, with Peter Perkins and his wife Pauline leading the way. Hermione was sitting at a table chatting with Zeb. 'Inger tells me Monsieur François Lavigne is a charming man.'

Hermione smiled. 'Yes, he is. I'm looking forward to meeting him again. His sister wrote me a letter and enclosed a photograph of their home in Dinan. It looks beautiful.'

'I hope it works out for you,' said Zeb.

'Your New York announcement was a surprise,' said Hermione, 'but I'm so pleased for you. Edward and

Victor have asked me to prepare an advertisement for the *Times Educational Supplement*. So there will be interviews next term.'

'And I shall do my best to support,' said Zeb. She looked across the room where Victor and Pat were sipping red wine at the bar. 'It's a shame they can't dance together,' she said.

Hermione gave a mischievous smile. 'Why don't we ask them?'

'Good idea,' said Zeb, jumping up. 'You ask Victor and I'll ask Pat.'

Victor and Pat looked surprised when Hermione and Zeb suddenly appeared beside them. 'Professor Grammaticus,' announced Hermione. 'Would you care to join me in the next dance?'

Pat grinned. 'Go on,' he said. 'You know you're good,' and Victor and Hermione stepped on to the dance floor.

Then a determined Zeb took Pat's hand and tugged him from his seat. 'Come on, you beautiful man. Let's dance.' A waltz had been announced and she led him into the middle of the floor. Moments later they were twirling with precise steps. Zeb looked up at the handsome face of this talented man. 'I'm afraid I'm not Victor,' she said, 'but the day will come when you will dance together on this floor and I want to be here to see it.'

Pat nodded. 'My life has always been tempestuous. Maybe one day.' He glanced across at Victor, who gave him an encouraging wave. 'It's strange, isn't it?' he said. 'You just know, don't you?'

Zeb knew he was talking about the unspoken feelings of love. 'Yes, Pat, you really do.'

'Victor thinks the world of you . . . You must come back to see us.'

'I was considering that,' she said, 'and I've discussed it with Vijay. He wants you and Victor to fly out with me to New York during the October half-term. He could organize everything: hotel, flights, restaurants.'

'You're an angel,' he said. Suddenly the music changed. 'It's a quickstep. Come on, let's strut some stuff, as they say.'

'But can you keep up?' asked Zeb with a smile.

'Always,' said Pat and he held her close as they swept around the floor at dazzling speed. When the music stopped Pat took her hand and smiled. 'Zeb, Victor says this often to me. The dying of the light will come for us all one day. You have one life. Make the most of every day. This is your time. Believe it.'

'I do,' she said. 'I really do.'

Tom and Inger had taken a break from the dancing and they were enjoying a drink. Rosie and Sam were on the dance floor. 'So, how's Rosie these days?' asked Tom. 'She seems content with Sam.'

Inger stared at her friend, holding on to Sam and dancing as the lights dimmed. 'I think she's fine now,' she said, 'and Sam is being sensible. There's no rush, and Rosie was badly hurt last year by that cheating solicitor.'

'She's a great colleague. The students love her.'

Inger smiled. 'And the publication of her book will give her huge confidence.'

'I agree,' said Tom. 'She's a determined woman and I

have sympathy for her opponents at her next chess tournament in Cornwall. She's a winning machine.'

The last dance was announced and Tom stood up. 'Come on. It's the last waltz.' Inger smiled as they walked on to the dance floor.

At the end of the evening, heartfelt goodbyes were exchanged as everyone set off for home. When Tom and Inger's taxi pulled up outside their apartment on the Knavesmire they stepped out and, hand in hand, walked up the path beneath an ethereal sky and a sprinkling of stars in the vast firmament.

They were both tired and soon they were relaxing in bed and reflecting on a special day. 'Sometimes a fresh start is a good idea,' said Inger suddenly.

'What do you mean?' asked Tom.

'Just thinking about Zeb and her decision.'

'It will be good for her,' said Tom. 'Another adventure.'

Inger looked intently at Tom. 'Do you still keep in touch with that headteacher in New Zealand?'

Tom nodded. 'The one who wanted us both to teach in his school? Yes, from time to time.'

Inger turned to face him and smiled. 'In that case, why don't we book a holiday there and call in on him?'

Tom grinned as peace descended on them like a comfort blanket. The conversation had clearly ended – Inger had fallen asleep in his arms.

And in that moment Tom Frith understood their own adventure was about to begin.

About the Author

Jack Sheffield grew up in the tough environment of Gipton Estate, in north-east Leeds. After a job as a 'pitch boy', repairing roofs, he became a Corona Pop Man before going to St John's College, York, and training to be a teacher. In the late seventies and eighties, he was a headteacher of two schools in North Yorkshire before becoming Senior Lecturer in Primary Education at the University of Leeds. It was at this time he began to record his many amusing stories of village life as portrayed in the Teacher series comprising: *Teacher, Teacher!*, *Mister Teacher*, *Dear Teacher*, *Village Teacher*, *Please Sir!*, *Educating Jack*, *School's Out!*, *Silent Night*, *Star Teacher*, *Happiest Days*, *Starting Over*, *Changing Times*, *Back to School*, *School Days* and *Last Day of School*.

University Secrets is the third novel in the University series and follows on from *University Tales* and *University Challenges*.

In 2017 Jack was awarded the honorary title of Cultural Fellow of York St John University.

He lives with his wife in Hampshire.

Visit his website at www.jacksheffield.com.